P9-CFF-840

"Did you happen to get a look at your new neighbor?"

Jenna clamped her lips tight before the demand for a description could emerge. The new neighbor she had seen was a little girl. Married men were off-limits. So were single guys with kids. It wasn't that she had anything against children, per se. They were great at a distance. It was just that the idea of being responsible for another person, especially a little one, was… overwhelming.

She had enough problems with a dog.

"Admit it, you really want to know. Tall, sandy-blond hair, nice shoulders and a to-die-for butt."

Jenna groaned. "All I saw was a little kid."

Jenna leaned on the railing, sipping her drink and staring next door. A to-die-for butt? On an off-limits dad?

That really wasn't playing fair.

Dear Reader,

When I wrote *The Mommy Plan*, and met Rachel's brother Sloan and his teenage daughter, Brook, with her pierced eyebrow, I just knew they had a story of their own to tell. I also felt he deserved a happy ever after for himself and his kids.

It took a while to coax the story from him, and you'll understand why when you read it, but here it is. I had a good time seeing Rachel, James and Molly again, and hope you'll also enjoy catching up with them and seeing how they're doing.

I'm dedicating this story to a very special person—Linda, my husband's birth mother. Years ago she had the courage and strength to let him go so that he could have a better life than she could provide at the time. She also had the courage and love to let him back into her life, proving that you can never have too many people who love you. If she hadn't let him go, odds are we would never have met and married. If she hadn't let him back in, my husband (and the rest of us) would have missed out on knowing so many wonderful people.

A birth mother who gives up a child out of love is definitely a hero in my book. As are the adoptive parents who make the child their own.

I love hearing from readers, so please let me hear from you! Your letters and e-mails just make my day! Visit my Web site at www.susangable.com, e-mail me at Susan@susangable.com or send me a letter at P.O. Box 9313, Erie, PA 16505.

Susan Gable

THE PREGNANCY TEST
Susan Gable

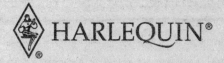

HARLEQUIN®

TORONTO • NEW YORK • LONDON
AMSTERDAM • PARIS • SYDNEY • HAMBURG
STOCKHOLM • ATHENS • TOKYO • MILAN • MADRID
PRAGUE • WARSAW • BUDAPEST • AUCKLAND

If you purchased this book without a cover you should be aware that this book is stolen property. It was reported as "unsold and destroyed" to the publisher, and neither the author nor the publisher has received any payment for this "stripped book."

ISBN 0-373-71285-5

THE PREGNANCY TEST

Copyright © 2005 by Susan Guadagno.

All rights reserved. Except for use in any review, the reproduction or utilization of this work in whole or in part in any form by any electronic, mechanical or other means, now known or hereafter invented, including xerography, photocopying and recording, or in any information storage or retrieval system, is forbidden without the written permission of the publisher, Harlequin Enterprises Limited, 225 Duncan Mill Road, Don Mills, Ontario, Canada M3B 3K9.

All characters in this book have no existence outside the imagination of the author and have no relation whatsoever to anyone bearing the same name or names. They are not even distantly inspired by any individual known or unknown to the author, and all incidents are pure invention.

This edition published by arrangement with Harlequin Books S.A.

® and TM are trademarks of the publisher. Trademarks indicated with ® are registered in the United States Patent and Trademark Office, the Canadian Trade Marks Office and in other countries.

www.eHarlequin.com

Printed in U.S.A.

Books by Susan Gable

HARLEQUIN SUPERROMANCE

Don't miss any of our special offers. Write to us at the
following address for information on our newest releases.

Harlequin Reader Service
U.S.: 3010 Walden Ave., P.O. Box 1325, Buffalo, NY 14269
Canadian: P.O. Box 609, Fort Erie, Ont. L2A 5X3

To Linda, who had the love and courage to let him go,
as well as the love and courage to welcome him back
with open arms and an open heart.

And in memory of eHarlequin's beloved Sir Jamey, who
touched our hearts with his gentle spirit and sense of humor.

Special thanks to:

Jen Widholm, from Realityworks.com, for helping me out
with information on the Baby Think It Over® program and
the infant simulators—what a great idea!

Sus, for the encouragement and ability to spot a missing
word at 100 paces.

Holly, for administering a kick in the pants
when I needed one. I love your car. Really!

Jen, always there, always with the right thing to say.
Best friends are true treasures, and you're a
one-of-a-kind gem!

CHAPTER ONE

"ERIE SUCKS."

Sloan Thompson gritted his teeth as he shut off the pickup, then turned to face his daughter in the passenger seat. Slowly counting to ten, he forced himself to relax his grip on the steering wheel. The move had been tough on all of them. "Lucky for you, then, our house is actually in Millcreek, huh?"

"The mailing address is Erie." Brook folded her arms and leaned her forehead against the window. "I don't see why we couldn't just stay in Texas."

He had a long list of reasons, and ninety percent of them came back to the sullen teenager next to him. She needed a new start. New friends. Friends more appropriate than the crowd she'd run with in Fort Worth.

"Well, I like it." Ashley released her seat belt and leaned in to the front, wrapping her arms around Sloan's neck. "It's closer to Granddad and Aunt Rae. And I can't wait for snow!"

He chuckled, grateful for the six-year-old's enthusiasm. At least she cooperated. If only she could stay six until her twenty-first birthday, then magically fast-forward to adulthood, skipping over adolescent hell. "I'm glad you like it, Peach, but let's not rush the snow, huh? Besides, I don't think August is prime snow time, even this far north."

A huge green-and-yellow truck rumbled to a stop in front of the house. "Okay. Operation Moving Day will now commence."

"Whoopee." Brook toyed with her seat belt, but left it fastened.

"Look, Granddad's here! I can't wait to have all my stuff again." Ashley slammed the door and ran toward her grandfather.

After living with his father for the five weeks since he'd started his new job as chief engineer at an Erie TV station, Sloan knew exactly what Ashley meant. He couldn't wait to have all his stuff back, either. And while he appreciated his dad taking them in while he searched for a house, he needed their own space again. "Brook, I want this day to go smoothly. Make that happen and maybe I'll set up your computer tonight."

She turned to him, her pierced eyebrow arching in a way that made the little silver ball move.

God, how he hated that thing. But it had been one of his many compromises, an attempt to ease the friction between them.

"I'm perfectly capable of doing it myself. Besides, it doesn't matter. The DSL isn't hooked up, is it?"

"Not yet."

"So I still won't be able to talk to my friends."

Sloan sighed, then reached for the cell phone attached to his belt and held it aloft. "Thirty minutes tonight, but only if everything's done to my satisfaction. And you keep your attitude in check today."

"Okay." She slid from the truck.

Pretty pathetic that he was reduced to bribing her with phone time. But it beat listening to her grumble the whole day.

By midmorning, all the furniture was in place. His sister, Rachel, paced the screened front porch, directing traffic while jiggling her fussy ten-month-old son in her arms. "Those boxes go in the third-floor attic for now," she instructed one of the movers. Frequent relocations while growing up in a military family had made both Sloan and Rachel experts on unpacking and setting up a household.

Sloan lifted a white rag from Rae's shoulder and wiped at Jamey's mouth, where drool oozed around the small fist the teething baby chewed on. "Your momma's bossy, do you know that?"

"I learned from a pro. My big brother."

"Nah, we both learned from the old man."

"I heard that," their father hollered from the living room, where he was involved in arranging Sloan's electronic equipment.

Rachel smiled. "Busted."

Sloan shrugged. "Nothing new about that. He won't ever need a hearing aid." The light in his sister's eyes warmed him. For the longest time he'd thought he'd never see her smile again, but his new brother-in-law, James, and James's daughter, Molly, had put the spark back in Rae's life. Still, the baby had sort of surprised Sloan. After all the effort it had taken for her to recover from losing her son, he hadn't expected her to risk motherhood again. It was quite a testament to James and Molly that they'd taught Rachel to risk so much for love.

Feet thundered down the stairs inside the house, and Sloan turned to find Molly and his younger daughter in the foyer. "We got Ashley's bed all made, Mom. What's next?"

"Good job. Now start unloading the boxes, and put everything away. Don't just dump it onto the floor. *Away.*"

"Okay. Come on, Ashley. Bet we can have it done before my dad and Brook get her room together!" Molly grabbed Ashley by the hand, dragging the smaller girl back upstairs.

Another pair of movers climbed the porch steps, arms loaded. Rachel studied the symbols on the sides of the boxes. "Take those down to the basement, please." She shifted the baby onto her other shoulder. "Wonder if James is getting anywhere with Brook?"

"I doubt it. Brook's not stupid. I'm sure she suspects we've 'planted' him with her on purpose." He ran his hand through his hair, raking back the annoying piece that fell across his forehead.

"Hey." His sister placed her hand on his elbow. "Remember, you're not alone anymore. We're just over an hour away now, not twenty. Dad's only twenty-five minutes from you. We want to help."

"I know." That was what had brought him north in the first place, to be near them again. But he wasn't sure if, even with the support of his family, he could reclaim his daughter and get her back on the right track. "And I need that help. I love her, Rae, but damn, sometimes she makes it so hard."

"Parenthood's not for sissies, is it?"

Sloan shook his head.

"Good thing you're not a sissy then." Rachel grinned, and for the first time in a few years, he felt optimistic. Maybe Brook wasn't lost to him after all.

BROOK SMOOTHED the blue-and-purple comforter, then flopped down on the bed, watching her aunt's husband connect the stereo speakers. Real subtle of them to assign the shrink as her work partner.

At least so far he hadn't said much of anything to her, besides the necessary stuff, like where did she want this or that. Come to think of it, even though she'd met him several times at family reunions and holidays, she'd never spent much time around him.

No question her lame-o dad thought she could use counseling. Like she needed some other adult asking stupid questions and not really listening to the answers.

A moving guy—the cute young one with the tight gray T-shirt and great muscles—stepped into the room, biceps bulging as he gripped a garment box. "Here's another one of yours." He smiled at her and set it next to the closet.

"Thanks." Brook stretched, knowing full well what it did to the tank top she wore—not that she was stacked or anything, but still, she wasn't bad—and then bit back a grin when the guy's eyes widened.

"Uh, sure."

"More boxes?" Uncle James prompted him. "That need to be brought in? From the truck out front?"

"Oh, right." Moving Guy flashed her another quick smile, then turned and headed out.

Uncle James caught him in the doorway. "Have you noticed her father? Her grandfather? Both former military men. Both very protective of their family. Especially the females. Especially the ones who are still minors."

"M-minors?"

"She's fifteen. Jailbait for you. So keep your eyeballs to yourself or one of the Thompson men is likely to knock them right out of your head."

The guy's tanned face lost some of its color. He gave her one more quick glance, then disappeared down the hallway.

Brook climbed from the bed, grabbing a blade off her dresser to cut the tape on the garment box. "Jeez, you're as bad as he is."

"*He* being your father, I assume."

"Who else?" Brook plucked some clothes from the bar in the box and hung them in the closet.

"There's nothing wrong with your father wanting to protect you."

"There's nothing wrong with me wanting to breathe, either."

"Yes, I saw what your 'breathing' did to that guy. Playing with fire like that is likely to get you burned." He reached for another cable and disappeared behind the stereo again.

"Yeah, well, it's cold here in the north and maybe I just want to be warm."

The furniture muffled his response. "Warm and burned are two different things."

"Whatever." Brook fingered the fringe on her favorite short skirt before putting it away. "I think it's pretty sad that they sent you up here to analyze me."

He straightened and looked at her. "I'm thinking it would probably take more than a day to analyze you, Brook. You seem like a rather complex person to me. Besides, I'm not allowed to treat family. It's unethical."

"Yeah, right. You can't stop yourself, from what Aunt Rae's said."

His face colored a bit. "Well, official and unofficial are also two different things. I'd always be happy to talk to you, Brook, or offer you some advice."

"And then spill your guts to my father. No thanks."

"If you want to talk to me confidentially, that's not a problem."

Brook tipped the box over and dumped several pairs of sandals and mules onto the floor. She knelt in the closet doorway. "I'm fine."

He chuckled, making her glance up in surprise. "That's what your Aunt Rachel always says. Usually she doesn't mean it."

"Well, I do." She turned her back on him and kept positioning her shoes. Who was she kidding? Her father had totally messed up her life, taken her away from the only home she'd ever known, her friends, her boyfriend, Brian.

And according to her sources, Brian, that slimeball,

was already sniffing around Heather Blake. Which explained why he hadn't been taking her phone calls or answering her IM's the few chances she'd had to use a computer after they'd left Texas.

Yeah, her life was just great.

"THE DOG STILL HATES ME." Jenna Quinn watched the little brown-and-white Cavalier King Charles spaniel jump onto the couch and snuggle up to Margo. The remainder of the pink slush oozed from the smoothie machine on her kitchen island, so Jenna flipped off the tap.

"She doesn't hate you. You just haven't bonded yet."

"Okay, she doesn't hate me. But she doesn't like me much, either. I wish I knew what was wrong with her."

"She misses your grandmother, same as you do." Margo scratched the dog's ears.

"Yeah, well." Jenna didn't want to talk about that. Despite eight months' grieving time, she missed the carefree, vivacious woman who'd taught her so much about life. And from whom she'd inherited, among other things, a pet she hadn't been prepared for.

"Your first mistake was trying to un-paper-train her. I don't think that scored points with her. And you have to admit, a paper-trained dog is much easier—you don't have to take her out, especially in the winter. For another thing, stop calling her 'the dog.' Try using her name." Margo glanced down at the animal on her lap. "Right, Princess?"

"Thank you, Dr. Dolittle. Here." She pressed the cold glass into her friend's hand, then collapsed into the recliner. She surveyed what was now the living room of her loft apartment. The tall, three-section oak entertainment center divided the space, concealing her bedroom on the other side. "Drink up. That's to say thanks for helping move the furniture. This place really needed an overhaul."

Margo raised her glass in salute. "No problem. And you're right. I mean, really, you'd had that arrangement for what, three whole months?" She laughed before sipping her frosty daiquiri.

"Yeah, well, I have to change what I can these days." Ever since sinking her savings and her inheritance from her grandmother into buying—well, mortgaging—the building and opening her own casual jewelry store downstairs, Jenna had been grounded.

No, not grounded. That made it sound like she was being punished. Okay, sometimes that was how she felt. She searched for a better way to phrase it. Putting down roots, maybe. Trying her best to change her wanderlust ways.

Moving the furniture around helped preserve what was left of her sanity.

"So, now, tell me. How was your date last night?"

Jenna groaned. "I'm giving up men."

Margo snorted, then choked. Her face turned the color of the drink she set on the coffee table. She coughed and spluttered, waving a hand as Jenna moved forward to the edge of the seat. The dog, long-plumed tail swishing through the air, licked her cheek.

"I'm okay." Margo cleared her throat to prove it, then

gently moved the spaniel aside. "It's just the idea of you giving up men is so, so…ludicrous! Hon, you draw men like you draw breath. It's a force of nature. Unstoppable. And you'd probably die if you tried."

"Thanks. You make me sound like a first-class slut."

Margo giggled. "No, you're not! I never said that. You'd only be a slut if you slept with them all, which you don't. You just…" She shrugged. "Experience them? Date them? Smile at them? Like I said, you can't help yourself. It's out of your control."

"That's so reassuring. I can't control it, and I'd die if I tried."

"Need I mention I'd probably die, too? I mean, how can I live vicariously through you if you give up men?" Margo sighed, settling back against the cushions, drink in hand once again. Princess laid her head on Margo's lap.

"Get one of your own and live it up for yourself. I've been telling you that for years."

"I'm trying. It's just that, well, the guys I meet through work are either body-worshipping egomaniacs, or they think dating me is a great way to get free massages. 'Hey, sweetie, could you just rub my shoulder?'" she mimicked in a low voice. "Either that or they think certified massage therapist means hooker."

Jenna laughed. Margo's complaints hadn't changed a bit since she'd left the day spa and rented space downstairs from Jenna-the-new-landlord, opening her own naturopathic shop combined with a massage-therapy office. "Someday the right guy is just going to walk into your life. Trust me."

"Perfect. And in the meantime, you share your love life with me. So tell me, what put you off Mr. Last Night?"

"For one thing, he got annoyed when I bowled a better game than he did."

"Oops. Hate that competitive guy thing."

"Yep."

"What else?"

Jenna wrinkled her nose. "He smoked. I had to come home and shower to get the smell off me. When am I going to remember to ask first?"

"Strike two. Yuck. I don't have to ask if you even bothered to kiss him good-night. Blech. Might as well suck on an ashtray. What was strike three?"

"Strike three was three years old." Jenna pressed her thumb and pinky together, then held up the remaining fingers. "I got to meet her because Joe was running late, so he picked me up before dropping her off at the baby-sitter's. And while she was a sweet little thing, her daddy kept looking at me all night like he was measuring me for an apron." She shuddered. "On our first date."

Margo burst into laughter again. "Oh, girl, he didn't know you very well, did he?"

Jenna narrowed her eyes. "Gee, thanks. With a friend like you…"

"Just being honest. If a best friend isn't honest with you, who will be?" Margo retrieved a black notebook from the end table. She traced the pink script lettering on the front. *Take-Out Menus.* "Here. Use some of your fantastic non-apron-related skills and get us some dinner. You owe me more than a drink for my furniture-moving services." She gestured toward her empty glass. "I'll take another one of those, too."

After some debate over which type of food they were in the mood for, Jenna ordered Chinese. Egg rolls, beef and broccoli and Szechwan chicken complemented the second batch of strawberry daiquiris. With a favorite movie popped into the DVD player, their girls' night in was well underway.

When the end credits rolled, they cleaned up. "You want to do a final drink on the deck?" Jenna asked. "It's a beautiful night."

"Nah. I've had my limit, and it's been a while, so I'm gonna go now. But thanks." Margo picked up her purse.

"Okay. Since I don't have to drive, I'll finish off that little bit of daiquiri I stuck in the freezer. Wait a minute and I'll walk out with you."

They stepped through the sliding glass doors that led from the dining area out to the deck. A sticky August breeze stirred the branches of the oak just over the fence behind her building. Jenna set her glass on the railing, then lifted her face toward the sky. Clouds blocked the stars. She inhaled deeply, catching the distinctive scent of approaching showers. "Guess I'd better drink fast."

Margo headed for the stairs, pausing at the top. "By the way…" She pointed at the glow in the upper window of the house behind Jenna's building. "Did you happen to get a look at your new neighbor? Very cute."

Jenna clamped her lips tight before the demand for a better description could emerge. Besides, the new neighbor she had seen was a little girl. Married men were off-limits. Nor did she want to date a single guy with kids. Hence no more Joe. It wasn't that she had anything against children, per se. They were great at a distance. It was just the idea of being responsible for another person, especially a little one, was…overwhelming.

She had enough problems with a dog.

"Admit it, you really want to know. Tall, sandy-blond hair, nice shoulders and a to-die-for butt. Great-looking guy."

Jenna groaned. "Oh, that is so not fair. I saw a little kid. Damn."

Margo chuckled and shrugged. "Sorry. Hey, I'm not averse to kids. Maybe I'll have to investigate the new neighbor and his hot buns a little closer." She started down. "Night, hon. Catch you on Monday."

Jenna leaned on the railing, sipping her drink and staring over the fence. A to-die-for butt? On an off-limits dad?

That really wasn't playing fair.

CHAPTER TWO

FAMILY FUN NIGHT generally wasn't much fun anymore, Sloan thought wryly as he accepted the pizza boxes from the delivery guy. Maybe he should take two aspirin first. Maybe that would make Brook's sullenness more bearable.

God knows he'd tried everything he could think of to make her happier, so maybe the fault was in him. Why couldn't he find the right way to reach her? To connect with her?

Leaving the door open to allow the early-September breeze to blow through the screen, he turned and hollered up the stairs. "Girls! Dinner's here!"

"Be right down, Daddy!" Ashley called back.

He carted the pies through the living room and plonked them on the dining-room table. Paper plates and napkins graced each place, and Ashley's "Friday Folder" from school was set carefully next to his seat. Second week of school down, and already the child's responsible nature was a breath of fresh air for him.

"Did you get me some mushroom?" the six-year-old asked as she trotted in.

"Yeah, Peach, I got you some mushroom." He grimaced in distaste and she giggled. "Where's your sister?"

Ashley shrugged. "I think she left as soon as you got home from work."

"Without asking me?" While dismayed, he wasn't exactly surprised. Brook's behavior hadn't improved much in the three weeks they'd been in the new house. In fact, she resented the move so much she'd barely spoken to him, except for curt remarks and requests for him to get the DSL up and running so she could IM with her old friends.

The friends he'd been glad to leave behind.

"Any ideas where she went?"

Ashley pointed out the side window. "Sometimes she goes to that jewelry store in the building behind the fence." She flipped open a box, then stopped to stare at him. "Does this mean we have to wait for her to get home to eat?"

"Family Fun Night has been a tradition for a long time. One Friday night every other week is not too much to ask for her to behave in a civilized manner and participate in this family."

Ashley closed the lid with a resigned sigh, then offered him a wide smile. "Okay." She held out her hand. "Then let's go find her."

He scooped her into his arms for an impromptu bear hug, then spun her around before setting back on her feet.

The child giggled. "Hey. What was that for?"

"Just 'cause I felt like it."

Hand in hand, they went out the front door and onto

the walk. Their little side street didn't have much traffic, in stark comparison to the sound of cars whizzing by on Twelfth Street. Passing the brown wooden fence on the far side of their driveway, they left the sidewalk to cut through the parking lot on the side of the commercial building. In front, a green-with-white pinstriped awning shaded the storefront walkway.

The window of the first store displayed a beachlike scene. Colorful towels set off the jewelry: necklaces and earrings with golden sand dollars and seashells. *Element-ry* read the sign on the door. *Fun Jewelry Inspired by Nature.*

Yeah, this place was right up Brook's alley.

As Sloan pushed open the door, a chime rang. He ushered Ashley inside. In the middle of the room, a tree reached to the ceiling. More jewelry, this time gold-covered leaves, dangled from the branches. The burble of a fountain competed with soft classical music accompanied by sounds of a gentle rain. Ashley let go of his hand and raced over to the water.

A thud echoed from a doorway at the side of the room, and he heard muttering. "Stupid computer." Another thud. "Technology. Great if it works."

A moment later a woman appeared in the doorway, her cheeks flushed, her hands smoothing back her shoulder-length red hair. "Hello." She flashed him a broad smile, one that chased the flustered expression from her face. "I'm Jenna Quinn, the owner. How can I help you? Is there something in particular you're looking for?"

He nodded. "Yes, ma'am. My daughter."

"Your daughter?" She stepped closer. The blue-and-white Hawaiian-type pants she wore tied at the ankles gaped open as she moved, exposing slender calves. Her white blouse had billowy sleeves and a lace-up neckline that was only partially laced, revealing smooth skin with a light smattering of freckles and a very feminine shape.

He forced his glance upward, face warming. What in the hell was he doing staring at those…laces? The store owner's green eyes widened and she tilted her head slightly, and he realized she was waiting for him to answer her. He cleared his throat. "Yes, my daughter. She's about yo high—" he indicated his chin level with his hand "—short, um…" He turned toward the fountain in the far corner of the shop. "Peach, what color is your sister's hair right now?"

"It's regular today, Daddy." Ashley leaned over the rim of the fountain's base and gestured at him. "Come and see the fish!"

"In a minute, hon. Okay, so Brook has brownish-blond hair. She's fifteen. Pierced eyebrow."

"Oh, Brook! Yes, I know her. So you're my new neighbor." Her cheeks flushed again as she extended her hand.

His fingers closed around hers. "Yes. I'm Sloan Thompson, and that's my other daughter, Ashley. Nice to meet you."

"Likewise. Brook's a sweet kid."

"Sweet? Are you sure we're talking about the same girl?"

Tiny lines appeared over the bridge of her nose.

"Never mind." He released her hand. "Have you seen her today?"

"No. But I know a lot of kids like to hang out over by Lakewood Park. Maybe she's there?"

"Where's that? Is that the little park a few blocks from here?"

She nodded. "Go down to Tenth Street, turn right, and head over a couple blocks. It's right across from the church. Can't miss it."

"Thanks."

"Da-ad!" Ashley called with the impatience only a six-year-old could muster. "Come see the fish!"

Jenna laughed, a smile lingering again on her mouth. "Da-ad, you're taking too long."

"Story of my life."

"Come on, I'll introduce you to Moby and the gang."

"Moby?" He followed as she led him across the shop. The usual glass cases one expected in a jewelry store lined the sides of the room, but they had been decorated in unusual ways. One, filled with a thin layer of sand and beach towels, mimicked the front window display, and another contained a variety of real—well, probably not real, but silk—flowers surrounding golden imitations. A set of four-leaf-clover earrings in another case caught his eye. They looked familiar but he couldn't figure out where he'd seen them recently.

"The big guy there, that's Moby," Jenna said, pointing to a koi that was twice as big as the other three fish in the plastic "pond" at the base of the fountain.

"Do the other ones have names?" Ashley asked.

"Actually, no. I haven't gotten that far yet. Can't decide what to call them. If you have any good ideas, let me know, okay?"

His daughter's face glowed with the honor of being asked to do something as important as name someone's overgrown goldfish.

"Would you like to feed them?"

"Sure."

Jenna reached behind the fake-rock formation and brought out a plastic bag filled with little pellets. Opening the zipper seal, she held it toward Ashley. "Take a handful, and then step back."

"Step back?" His daughter's eyes got huge. "How come?"

Jenna laughed. "You'll see."

The fish were already swimming near the surface, bulgy eyes on the bag in the store owner's hands. When Ashley tossed the feed in, the water roiled, splashing all over as they rushed to scarf down the pellets. His little girl giggled and clapped her hands. Jenna beamed at her.

"That's cool! Dad, look at them!" She turned to him. "Can we have fish like these?"

"No, we cannot. Where would we put such a big fountain in the house?"

"The basement?" she offered.

"I don't think so, Peach. I imagine it gets pretty cold in the basement in the winter around here."

"Tell you what," Jenna interjected. "You can come over here and feed Moby and the gang anytime you like. Okay?"

"Okay."

"That's very nice, but I don't want my daughters making pests of themselves." Not in a shop where the owner wore such…strange clothes, and all sorts of bangles—an earring that climbed the outer part of her ear, clanging bracelets on her wrists. "Well, we have pizza that's going to be cold before we get to it. Let's go and find Brook." Taking Ashley's hand, he headed for the front door. "Nice to meet you, Miss Quinn."

"Oh, please, not Miss. That's just one step away from ma'am."

"My daddy raised me to be polite. He whupped my butt more than once for referring to a lady too familiarly." Had he assumed wrong? There was no wedding ring on her hand, and she certainly wore plenty of other stuff. "Mrs.?"

She laughed, tossing her head. Her hair—he was certain other women would kill for hair that red, and shiny—bounced like she was in some kind of shampoo commercial. "No, definitely not. Just call me Jenna. I don't think that would be too familiar. After all, we are neighbors. I live upstairs. Besides," she dropped her voice, "I promise not to tell your daddy."

He grinned. "Okay, Jenna. Like I said, nice to meet you." The chime sounded again as he opened the front door and followed Ashley out.

Jenna tried not to stare at his butt in the well-worn jeans, but hell…Margo had been right. It was a to-die-for butt, tight in all the right places, with the nicest curve. And the broad shoulders. She smiled to herself. What she'd enjoyed the most about her new neighbor had been the faint but adorable little twang in his voice. Brook had mentioned they'd come from Texas. The kids had even stronger hints of the South in their voices. But *his* voice…too damn cute. She'd love to have that little twang whispering words of passion in her ear. The man was hot, just like the state he came from.

Too bad he was off-limits.

With a soft sigh, she headed back to the office and the paperwork. Sinking into the chair behind her desk, she eyed the computer. "If I turn you back on, are you going to behave yourself? No more freezing up? I'd hate to have to whack you again. We're friends, you and me." She booted up the tower and prayed it was true.

SLOAN AND ASHLEY WANDERED down Tenth Street, passing numerous other people out for a walk in the early evening air. A pack of kids on inline skates blew past, then a man walking a huge English sheepdog, followed by a few people on bikes. Apparently this section of Tenth was fitness central. It made sense, given the light traffic and the even pitch of the road.

As they came to the corner across from a large brick church, Sloan saw the park—and Brook. Leaning against a picnic table surrounded by other kids, she faced away from him, watching a game of basketball taking place on the asphalt court. A puff of smoke billowed up from the group, and Sloan's chest tightened.

"Brook," Ashley hollered before Sloan could tell her they were going to sneak up on her sister and "surprise" her. "Hey, Brook!"

His older daughter turned around, and guilt filled her face. One of the boys jumped off the table and quickly ground something beneath his foot.

Okay, so she was surprised anyway. Still, he would have liked a closer look at what her new friends were smoking.

Please, Brook, do the right thing. You've got a second chance here to get your life on track. Sloan plastered a false smile on his face and went to collect his kid. She met him halfway, casting a final glance over her shoulder at the other teens.

"Dinner is waiting on you, kiddo."

She shrugged, raising the thin straps of the barely-there tank top she wore. "Didn't realize what time it was. Sorry."

"You *do* own a watch. You do know it's Family Fun Night. You left without asking or even having the courtesy to let me know where you were going."

"Do we have to do this here?" Brook tucked her short, bobbed hair behind her ear. Sunlight glinted off a small gold four-leaf clover.

So that's where he'd seen them before. *Oh, hell.*

"Where did you get those earrings?"

"These?" Brook fingered one. "From that store by our house."

"And you paid for them how?" Sloan had seen the price tag, and while not expensive by any means, they still cost more than a few weeks of her allowance. And saving had never been Brook's strong point.

"Jenna gave them to me. I did a favor for her."

"Right." Just like the pharmacy back in Fort Worth had given Brook the lipstick, eye shadow and nail polish. That had been one of the most humiliating moments of his life, when he'd been called to retrieve his daughter, who'd been caught shoplifting. Luckily he'd been able to talk the manager out of pressing charges, giving Brook another chance.

Ashley tugged on Sloan's hand. "Daddy? Can I play on the swings?"

"Not now, Peach. Another time. We've got things to do." First on the list was figuring out if Brook had stolen the earrings or not. So much for Family Fun Night.

"You don't believe me, do you?" Brook folded her arms across her chest. "You think I'm lying."

"Wouldn't be the first time," he muttered.

"Why don't you go and ask Jenna herself? She'll tell you. She gave them to me."

"Maybe I'll just do that."

They walked home in silence, and even the warmth of Ashley's little hand in his couldn't lighten Sloan's mood. Already Brook was screwing up. When they reached the house, he nudged Ashley up the sidewalk. "You girls go on inside. Brook, warm up the pizza. I'll be back in a few minutes."

"Where you going, Daddy?"

"Just next door. I won't be long."

Hurt flared in Brook's eyes and her mouth tightened. "Go ahead. You'll see I'm telling the truth." She turned and stomped up the stairs, letting the porch door slam shut.

"Should I still pick a DVD for later?" Ashley looked up at him.

"Yeah, Peach. Even if your sister doesn't want to watch, you and I will have our own Family Fun Night."

"Okay." With a quick smile, she turned and skipped up the remainder of the sidewalk, entering the house with far less drama than her sibling.

Sloan strode back to the jewelry store. A Closed sign hung in the middle of the door. Damn. But the woman had said she lived upstairs. Surely there was another entrance?

He walked the length of the building's front. The place next to Jenna's store was a natural remedies and therapeutic massage office. The one on the far end was empty with a red-lettered For Rent sign in the window. But he found nothing that looked like an entrance to apartments on the upper story.

He peered around the corner. Nothing on that side of the building but some gravel and a few stray blades of grass poking up between the stones.

He retraced his steps along the front sidewalk, and turned down the side that offered more parking. At the far end of the building there was a metal door in the wall, with a doorbell and intercom box alongside. Sloan pressed the button. If that didn't work, he could always climb the set of stairs that led up to a deck behind the building.

"Hey, that was fast," Jenna's tinny voice declared from the box on the wall. "Bring it up."

A buzz and click announced the unlocking of the metal door. Sloan opened it, finding himself in a stairwell. A door to his left went into the shops. He climbed the stairs. On the landing at the top he found an oak coat tree and another door, which flew open.

"Oh," Jenna said.

"Not who you expected?"

"Unless you're hiding some Mexican takeout, no, you're not who I was expecting."

"You should really look before you open your door."

"Probably." Her voice was laced with humor, causing a tightening in his stomach—one he hadn't felt in a long time. It wasn't that he'd consciously avoided women, just that there'd been little opportunity to pursue a relationship since his wife's death.

"But maybe I like to live a little on the wild side," she continued.

That he could believe. "There's wild, and then there's dangerous."

"Thanks, Dad." She winked. "You wanna come in or are you going to stand on my landing all night?"

"I just wanted to ask you something." He entered her apartment and moved aside so she could shut the door behind him. The loft occupied the entire top floor of the building. To his left, a set of sliding glass doors led onto the deck he'd noticed from downstairs. A kitchen area butted against the outer wall to his right, with white cabinets and glass doors revealing turquoise and yellow dishes within. A butcher-block island boasted several tall stools with pink cushions. In the living area, another woman lounged on a sectional sofa, scratching the head of a small brown-and-white dog.

Bright colors seemed to be the standard here—a rainbow-colored decoration that reminded him of a DNA helix hung from the ten-foot ceiling near the living area.

"Margo, this is Sloan Thompson, my new neighbor. Sloan, this is Margo Weber, my good friend. She runs Natural Health, next to my place downstairs."

Margo waved. "Hi, there. Welcome to Erie. It's nice to meet you." She gave Jenna a look he couldn't quite decipher.

"Likewise, ma'am." He inclined his head.

Jenna sputtered. "You gotta stop that ma'am stuff, Tex. Makes us feel old."

"Sorry, sugar. Old is not what comes to mind for either of you. Sweet young things is more accurate."

"That's better." Jenna waggled her fingers at him while Margo snorted. "What can I do for you? Can I get you a drink?" She gestured toward the island. "Tonight the house special is margaritas, to go with the Mexican food that you weren't delivering."

"No thanks, nothing. I just need to ask you a question." He inclined his head toward the sliding glass doors. "Perhaps we could step outside a moment? No offense, ma'—Margo—" he glanced at her friend "—but I'd prefer to speak to Jenna in private."

"Oh, you two go right ahead." Margo waved. "I'm fine." She hid her amused expression behind the green, frosted glass in her other hand.

Jenna glared at Margo, silently threatening to put an end to their Friday night ritual if Margo couldn't keep her big mouth shut. As Jenna escorted Sloan to the deck, she thought she heard Margo chanting, "Flirting, little kid, flirting, little kid."

Okay, so discretion wasn't Margo's strongest suit.

Jenna sighed. She wasn't flirting, and she was well aware that hunky Mr. Texas had a little kid.

The sliding glass door trundled shut behind them. "What can I do for you? I know every food place that delivers to the neighborhood, the best bowling alley, and fun spots. I can give you directions to just about anywhere. What do you need?"

"I need to know if you gave my daughter a pair of four-leaf-clover earrings."

"Hmm? Earrings? Yes, I gave them to her. Why?"

His features softened, his blue eyes taking on a look of relief.

"That was very nice of you, but not necessary. I'm trying to teach my daughters the value of hard work. I'd appreciate it if you didn't give Brook gifts in the future."

"Hey, now, just a minute. It wasn't exactly a gift. Brook ran an errand for me. She also tamed the computer from hell, even if the taming didn't last. I gave her the earrings to say thank-you."

"Oh." His mouth pinched tight and his eyebrows drew down. "Guess that's different, then." He turned in the direction of his house, and Jenna could feel him drifting, thinking about his family.

"She really is a sweet kid."

He didn't move. "Wish she'd try a little of that sweetness out at home. I've gotta get back. Thanks." Obviously distracted, he headed for the outside stairs and started down without a single glance her way.

Jenna returned inside. Margo gave her a smug, smart-ass look. "I knew you couldn't resist him. Did he ask you out?"

"No, Miss Know-It-All. And I didn't flirt with him, either."

"Did so. All those smiles. What were they?"

"What do you want me to do? Scowl at him? Besides, he's not my type. The man has not one but two, count 'em, two kids." But he was definitely cute. A widower, poor guy. Brook had mentioned losing her mom. Jenna's heart went out to him—to all of them. She could see he and Brook weren't operating on the same wavelength. In fact, he reminded her a lot of her own parents: logical, structured, kind of intense. And Brook reminded her of herself, more of a free spirit, interested in things her father wouldn't consider important at all. Maybe it was Brook she should be feeling sorry for. Jenna knew how overbearing parents could suck the life and joy out of a more zestful soul.

"Don't tell me you're actually losing your touch? And admit it, I was right about his butt."

"Margo, just give it a rest," she snapped. "Yes, he's got a great ass. So what? Grow up." Damn. Two minutes with the man, and she was actually channeling her parents.

"Grow up? This from the fun-loving, female Peter Pan?"

"Sorry, Margo. That was out of line."

"Yes, it was. But I forgive you."

The buzzer rang, announcing, she assumed again, the arrival of dinner. But Jenna didn't feel much like eating now.

SLOAN LINGERED in the hallway. After watching the movie with his younger daughter, he'd sent her off to bed and then lost himself briefly in video games, where virtual violence—crashing cars, shooting aliens, blowing things up—had relieved some of the tension coiled inside him. Enough so that he felt calm enough to go talk to Brook again. Hopefully, this time he would get it right.

He peered into Ashley's room first. Curled on her side, she slept. How he longed for the blissful sleep of childhood.

Outside Brook's door, he could hear the muted sound of music spilling from her headphones, and the clackity-clack of her keyboard as she IMed her friends, no doubt expounding on what a shithead her father was.

And that was exactly how he felt. He rapped on the door, though he doubted she could hear him over the music. After a few moments, he stuck his head inside. "Brook? We need to talk."

With an exaggerated sigh, she removed the earphones, letting the pounding beat spill out even louder. "What do you want?"

"Turn that off for a minute, please. I want to talk to you."

"Why bother? You don't listen when I talk to you."

"I'm sorry about the earrings thing, Brook. It's just like I've told you before. Once a trust is broken, it's very hard to rebuild it."

"Yeah, whatever."

"No, not whatever. It's going to take time for me to

trust you again. Running off without permission, without letting me know where you're going, isn't going to help. Picking the wrong kinds of friends isn't going to help."

"You don't know a damn thing about those kids I was with, and yet you're judging them."

"I know I saw them smoking. That's not the right kind of crowd, Brook."

"It was just a cigarette, not weed." Her jaw set and her pink-frosted eyelids shuttered halfway, giving her a sullen, pouting look.

"I don't care if it was just a lit Q-tip, it's still an indication that things aren't right. You have a chance to start over, do the right thing."

Brook glanced at a picture on her dresser. "If Mom were here, she'd—"

"Don't. Don't you dare invoke your mother. There is no way in hell she would have approved of you shoplifting or smoking cigarettes, weed or not. And since it was weed I caught you with—"

"You're never going to let me live down my mistakes, are you?" she yelled. "Just like you couldn't let Mom live down her mistake. You come across all holier-than-thou, like you never messed up in your life!"

Sloan had a hard time forcing speech past the tightness in his throat. When he finally spoke, his voice was soft. "I messed up with your mother."

"I'll say. Maybe if you'd been a little more understanding, she'd still—"

"Quit while you're ahead, Brook. You think you know what happened between your mother and me, but you don't. So I suggest you just stop right now before we both regret it." His eyelid twitched, and he pressed a finger against it. He would not lose his temper like he'd done that night with Beth. He would not yell. He would do the right thing. "Shut down the computer and go to bed."

"But—"

"No *buts*. Do what I say." He wheeled around and fled from the second story as quickly as he could, eager to put some distance between them. So much for his apology. He stormed out the front door and plopped himself down on the top step.

The quiet of the night was broken by the sounds of intermittent traffic on Twelfth Street. He covered his face with his hands and sucked in a deep breath.

His wife had died because he'd lost his temper and said things he shouldn't have, no matter how justified he'd been. His anger had driven her out into a night far different from this one.

He wouldn't make the same mistake with Brook.

CHAPTER THREE

SHE WASN'T SPYING on him. Not exactly. It wasn't as if she had binoculars or anything. Still, she really didn't need them. Even in the dim light from the streetlamps and the moon, from her deck she had a clear view of the man slumped on the front step of his house. He looked like he'd lost his last friend.

Which meant he needed one. Checking on him would be the good-neighbor thing to do.

Being a good neighbor couldn't get her into any trouble, right?

Jenna slipped back into the loft and retrieved a purple leash from a hook by the door. "Princess? You wanna go for a walk?"

The dog lifted her head from a pillow on the sofa, stared at her for a moment, then sighed, plopping her snout back across the cushion.

"Oh, brother. Look, this suffering-martyr routine has to stop. I'm not that bad. I feed you, make sure you have water, attempt to play with you. I've mollycoddled you long enough. Tough-love time." Jenna strode across the living area and snapped the leash onto the dog's matching purple harness. "Gram wouldn't have wanted either one of us to just mope around. Let's go." She tugged gently, but the dog didn't budge. "Okay, then, have it your way." She scooped the dog under one arm and headed outside.

At the bottom of the stairs she set the spaniel down. Princess shook herself, offered Jenna a glance over her shoulder, hoisted her snout in the air—Gram had sure named her right—then trotted toward the sidewalk.

"That's more like it." Resisting the urge to hum or do some other inane thing to look casual, Jenna followed the dog the short distance to Sloan's house. "Well, hey, there," she called out.

He raised his head. "Hey yourself."

Princess scurried down the cement path that led to his steps, pulling Jenna along. *Way to go, dog.*

Princess nudged his hands with her nose, tail wagging her entire butt.

"Traitor, you don't wag for me," Jenna murmured as Sloan patted the dog. "Nice night for a walk."

"Mmm. I suppose."

"Everything okay?"

"Sure."

"So, this glum look is your normal one?"

The corner of his mouth twitched. "Yeah."

"Bummer. That's a terrible way to go through life. Did you make that face one day and it got stuck, just like your mom always warned you?"

He chuckled. "I guess. You know, I think Mom did warn me about that." He laughed again. "I haven't thought about that in years. Thanks."

Being a good neighbor gave Jenna the warm fuzzies in a way flirting never had. "You're welcome." She rocked on her feet, toying with the end of the leash in her hands, trying to think of something else to say. Prying would just make her seem nosy. But still… "Something my gram used to tell my parents occurs to me."

"Oh?"

"Yeah. She'd say, 'Fifteen—'or whatever age I was at the time'—isn't fatal. For the child, or the parent.'"

"Easy for your grandma to say. She wasn't raising Brook."

"I'm sure it's even harder because you're alone. Being a single parent has to be the toughest job on the planet. It's got to be hard on Brook, too, being at this age and having no woman to talk to, confide in."

"That's one of the reasons we moved. I was actually hoping to get a job in Pittsburgh to be close to my sister, but this is what came up." Realizing he'd spilled too much, Sloan gave the dog's soft head a final tousle, then wiped his hands along his jeans. He glanced up at Jenna, narrowing his eyes. What in the world had possessed her to stop and chitchat? "I don't want to keep you from your walk."

"Huh? Oh, yeah. Our walk. Well, actually, there was something I wanted to discuss with you."

"Besides my parenting skills?"

"Well, it sort of relates. Remember earlier you said you were trying to teach your daughters the value of hard work?"

"Yes."

"Well, the holiday season is coming up, and I really could use some more help at the shop. If it's okay with you, I'd like to offer Brook a part-time job."

He rose to his feet. Being an extra step higher made him tower over her. He found himself staring down at the freckles on the luscious cleavage exposed by the lace-up blouse. With a start, he forced his eyes to hers. "I don't know about that." He didn't know if he wanted either of his kids around her. She seemed kind of…out there. On the wild side. More honestly, he didn't know if *he* wanted to be around her. A tempting distraction like her was the last thing he needed right now, what with Brook and all.

Not to mention he didn't need a woman like her doing the tempting. When he got involved again, it would be with a dependable, sedate woman. Not a flighty redhead. One burn had been enough.

"Please? She's great with my temperamental computer. Damn thing keeps freezing on me."

"Really? Glad to hear she takes after me in something."

"You're good with computers, too?"

"Chief engineer at a television station definitely requires strong computer skills these days."

"Great. Then I know who to come to when I feel like throwing the thing out the window. But honestly, I need the part-time help. I think it would be perfect for Brook. She seems to like jewelry."

Maybe, despite his misgivings about Jenna, a job *would* help teach Brook responsibility. And he wouldn't have to worry about transporting her, either, since the job was next door. "I'll think about it."

BROOK FINISHED wiping the last countertop and headed for the office to return the paper towels and Windex. Not exactly the thrill-a-minute job she'd envisioned when Jenna had approached her two weeks ago, but still, it sure beat staying home, baby-sitting Ashley every day. After finally agreeing Brook could take the position, Dad had enrolled her kid sister in an after-school program at the elementary school, leaving Brook with free afternoons when she didn't have to work.

Life was looking up.

She found Jenna bent over the worktable in the office, a pair of tiny pliers in her hand as she strung a beach-glass necklace.

"Okay, that's done. Now what?" After stuffing in the cleaning supplies, Brook slammed the door of the storage cabinet.

The doorbell chimed, and Jenna looked up at her. "Now you go and help that customer."

"If you actually want to sell something, you might want to do it yourself." It was a good thing Jenna wasn't paying her on commission. A great salesperson Brook wasn't.

"Nah. You can do it. Just smile and be yourself."

"Whatever." Brook squared her shoulders as she went back out onto the floor. "Hello. Welcome to Element-ry. Can I help you find something?"

When the guy checking out the stuff in the beach case turned, Brook did her best not to stare. Tall. Dark hair. Wide shoulders encased in a Millcreek High team jacket, despite the fact that Jenna kept insisting the weather was unseasonably warm for the end of September in Erie.

Then he smiled at her, flashing a set of teeth that screamed time-spent-at-the-orthodontist.

And Brook's stomach got all squishy.

"I'm looking for something for my mom. For her birthday." He stepped in her direction, bringing with him a soft scent of cologne. "Hey, don't I know you? Where do you go to school?"

"M-Millcreek High." Great, she was stammering like an idiot.

His smile got bigger and he nodded. "That's what I thought. I'm a senior there. I think I've seen you around."

He'd noticed *her?* Wow. "Um…" She cleared her throat. "What does your mom like? Does she like the beach? Flowers? Is she into fall and leaves?"

The boy shrugged. "Beats me. I just want something pretty, something different to give her."

"What about some of the beach-glass pieces we have? They're made from little pieces of glass that wash up onto the lakeshore. Years in the water polish them smooth." She directed him to the proper case, hoping he wouldn't notice her hands trembling when she pulled out some earrings to show him.

It seemed to take forever. He made her show him some of the gold pieces, then they went back to the beach glass. While she helped him, the door chimed again. Brook spared a quick glance to see two girls she knew from school come in with a girl she didn't recognize. Then she returned her attention to the boy and the drop earrings with green glass he'd selected. "Would you like me to wrap these for you?"

"Really? That'd be great." His simple thanks made her heart pound. "I'm horrible at wrapping."

"No problem." Using floral paper, Brook made quick work of the task, sticking a gold bow on the top. She fumbled a few times with the register but got everything squared away, then slipped the gift and his receipt into a bag. Their fingers brushed as he took it from her, and she resisted the temptation to sigh. "I hope your mom likes it. Come again."

"If you're working here, I think I will." He turned and sauntered from the store, causing a ripple of whispers from the group of girls lingering near the fountain. They stared at him as he left, then quickly swarmed Brook, all of them chattering at once.

"Ohmigod! Do you know who that was?"

Brook shook her head.

"That's Dylan Burch. He's a major track star at school," said Kelly, who was in Brook's English class.

"And so hot! Did you get a load of those green eyes?" asked Lana, from History.

"I wasn't looking at his eyes," said the girl Brook didn't know. The others snickered.

"What did he want? Did he ask you out?" Lana asked.

"No." Brook's face warmed. "He bought something for his mom's birthday." Kelly and Lana crowded closer, wanting all the details. The other girl wandered around the store, peering into the cases, ending up back at the tree. Brook showed Lana and Kelly a seashell necklace Kelly wanted to buy with her baby-sitting money. Eventually, Brook made her second sale of the afternoon, and the group left.

"Hey. Sounded busy out there. How did it go?" Jenna asked when Brook headed into the office.

"Good. I made two sales."

Jenna smiled at her. "See, I told you. Just be yourself."

"Met a really hot guy, too."

"Oh yeah?" Jenna knotted the strand of fishing line that made the base of the necklace she was working on. "Hot guys are definitely something I can appreciate. Tell me about him."

Brook launched into a description of Dylan Burch, playing it cool while trying to make Jenna understand just how incredible he was.

"Sounds yummy." Jenna laid the completed necklace aside. "Think he'll stop back?"

"He said he might."

"That would be great."

"I had a boyfriend in Texas," Brook confessed. Jenna arched her eyebrows. "But he was a moron. I was only gone like a week and he started chasing after another girl."

"Guys will do that. But don't sweat it. You're young. There will be plenty of guys in your life."

"You think so?"

"Absolutely. Look at you. You're adorable, with that short, sassy haircut, those bright blue eyes. I guarantee that the boy you left behind will only be the first moronic guy in your life." Jenna laughed.

It was cool to have a woman to talk guys with. And clothes. And jewelry.

Twenty minutes later, as they were getting ready to close, her dad came into the store, Ashley on his heels. Her kid sister immediately ran over to the fountain, calling out, "Hey, Moby! Hey, Goldie!" She pulled the bag of food from the spot in the back, tossed a handful into the water and giggled as the fish splashed.

"Oh, hey, look out, I think it's a tidal wave!" Jenna called, laughing as well.

"You ready, Brook? Have you decided what you want to do tonight? It's your turn to pick."

Brook started to roll her eyes, but Jenna poked her in the back. "Don't do that. Be glad he wants to spend time with you," she whispered. "Some parents don't give a damn about their kids."

"I decided I want to go bowling." Brook glanced over her shoulder at her boss and new friend. "And I want Jenna to come, too."

GETTING STOOD UP by Margo for a girl's night in had never been better, Jenna decided, checking out Sloan's...form...as he stood on the lane, about to bowl. And since her friend had gone off to Pittsburgh for the weekend to a massage-therapist conference or something, Jenna didn't even have to put up with a million questions, or insinuations that she was flirting or that this was a date.

Not with two kids, it wasn't. It was just another good-neighbor thing to do.

Although watching Sloan move was leading to some thoughts that probably didn't qualify as "neighborly." Those could only lead to trouble. She shouldn't have agreed to join them.

But Brook had wanted her to come. And Jenna liked making those kinds of wishes—the kind her parents never had time for when she was growing up—come true.

Music blasted, and black lights, glow-in-the-dark patterns on the rugs, and disco balls reflecting sparkles gave the alley a cosmic appearance. When they'd arrived at Greengarden Lanes, Ashley had loved it, Brook had tried to play it cool, and Sloan's eyeballs had nearly popped out of his head. Apparently he'd never participated in disco bowling back in Texas.

She chuckled as he came off the lane, shaking his head over the easy pickup he'd missed.

"I don't know how anyone's supposed to bowl accurately with these crazy lights. What are you laughing at?" he asked.

"Who, me? Nothing." She rose from the bench and retrieved her ball from the return. "Let me show you how it's done, Tex."

She found her mark on the smooth floor, took her strides, then let the ball go, arm following through. She froze in place, waiting, watching. The ball struck just to the side of the headpin, sending nine of them down easily. The final one rocked back and forth. "Come on, come on!"

It toppled over.

"Yes!" She tightened her hand into a fist and jerked it downward. "Yes!" She did a happy dance, all wiggles and shakes, then turned to face her companions. "And that, my dear Tex, is how it's done."

A slow smile spread across his mouth, and he nodded. "So I see. Is the dancing part mandatory, or optional?"

"Well, since it's your first time and all, we'll make it optional tonight. Unless you get a turkey. Then it's mandatory." Besides, as far as she was concerned, three strikes in a row—a turkey—should make anyone dance a little bit.

Brook brushed past them on her way to the alley. "She's killing you, Dad."

"Yes, she is."

But he didn't look annoyed by it. In fact, he seemed totally okay with it. Imagine that. A man not threatened by a woman whupping his butt at a sport. "Maybe you should join Ashley on the lane with the bumpers up," Jenna quipped.

"Maybe I should."

Frame by frame, the evening rushed by. "I'm getting some pizza. Anybody else?" Jenna asked, heading for the upper level.

"I'll come. I could use something to drink," Brook said.

Sloan watched them climb the steps and move toward the crowded table that offered all-you-could-eat-or-drink pizza and pop. Jenna wore a pair of floral-print jeans that showed off a delightful set of legs, and a green top that she'd cinched with a wide brown leather belt.

Her easy laughter made everyone, male and female, notice her. Friendly, outgoing—what wasn't to like?

The way his older daughter also noticed her? Brook watched her every move, from the shake of her head to the smile, and especially the way men came on to her.

Maybe letting her take the job hadn't been the right thing to do. Brook had enough raging teenage hormones to deal with. She didn't need lessons from a woman who seemed to attract men without any effort at all.

Including himself, if he wanted to be completely honest, which he didn't. There was just something about the woman…

But his wife had attracted at least one man more than she'd needed. And that had left him slightly wary.

"Daddy, watch me!" Ashley staggered up to the line and heaved the ball onto the floor. It rolled slowly toward the pins, bouncing off one bumper, then the other, eventually knocking over three pins. She spun around and did a dance that mimicked Jenna's earlier tail-shaking victory celebration.

Maybe she was already affecting both daughters. He swallowed a sigh. "Great job, Peach."

Closing in on the end of the second game, Sloan found himself with two strikes in a row. The girls were cheering him on, and Jenna gave him a thumbs-up. "Go for it."

When all the pins toppled over again, a round of gobbling erupted behind him to honor his turkey. He turned to find Jenna and Ashley's gobbles turning to giggles while Brook eyed the pair with disdain. He started to leave the lane when Jenna held up her hand. "Uh-uh. You owe us a mandatory dance."

Ashley giggled again and covered her mouth.

"This ought to be good," Brook murmured. "Maybe I'll just die of embarrassment now."

"I think the moment has passed," Sloan said, coming off the wooden floor.

"That's the problem with not seizing the moment," Jenna replied. "It's gone too quickly. Guess he doesn't dance, huh?" she asked Brook.

"I dance. I just don't think wiggling my butt on a bowling lane constitutes dancing."

"Coward," Jenna whispered as she passed him on her way up. The smile and wink she offered took the sting from the word.

By the time they'd reached the middle of the third game, he'd more than adapted to the weird lights and was leading Jenna by seventeen points. Ashley had quit, sprawling on the bench. Brook had wandered off to the other end of the bowling alley when she'd recognized several kids from school. Sloan wrapped up the tenth frame with a strike and a spare, breaking 200.

Jenna left the frame open. Still, she came off the lane with a bounce in her step. "You're a quick study. Great game."

"Thanks." He sat on the bench next to Ashley and unlaced his bowling shoes. "I think that's it for the night. Somebody's tired."

"I'm not tired," Ashley said, opening her eyes.

Jenna laughed. "No, not much."

"I'm going to go round up Brook. Will you help Ashley take care of her shoes?" he asked Jenna.

She looked at him kind of funny, then nodded.

He dropped his shoes on the rental counter as he went by, then headed in the direction Brook had gone. He found her with a mixed group of about seven teens. He crooked his finger at her. She climbed the steps to the upper level. "What?"

"Come on. We're ready to go."

"Can I stay a bit longer? One of the guys will drive me home."

Sloan shook his head. "Absolutely not. Do you know these guys well? How old are they? How long have they had their licenses?"

"Da-ad, please, I'm not—"

"Brook, I said no. Now let's go."

"You don't even consider what I want. It's just always no," she muttered, folding her arms across her chest.

"Not true," he said. "I let you take the job, didn't I?"

"Whoopee." She stared at him for a minute, then took off in the direction of their lanes.

On the ride home, Brook's pouting filled the extended-cab pickup with tension. She hadn't even tried to slip into the front seat, where she'd sat on the way to the lanes. That suited Sloan just fine. Let her sulk in the back. He busted his ass to make her happy, to compromise with her, but the moment something didn't go her way, she got moody. Loving his kid shouldn't have been a chore, but sometimes she made it feel that way.

"I had a lot of fun tonight," Jenna said, breaking the quiet. "Thanks for letting me tag along."

"Well, thanks for showing us your favorite bowling alley."

Silence returned until they got close to home. Then Sloan said, "I'll drop you off first, Jenna."

She snorted. "Please, don't be ridiculous. Just pull into your driveway and I'll walk home. It's not like it's that far, and besides, the weather's nice. If it were cold or snowing, I'd take you up on the door-to-door service."

"You sure?"

"Absolutely. Besides, after those three slices of pizza tonight, I could use any extra exercise I can get."

He pulled the truck up to the door of the detached garage and shut it off, opting to leave it outside. As she slid out, Jenna repeated her thanks.

"Hold up a minute, Jenna." Sloan held the door for Ashley. "Peach, inside and into your pajamas. I'll be up to tuck you in as soon as I get back from walking Jenna home."

"Okay, Daddy. But I'm not tire—" Ashley's protest got lost in a yawn, and Sloan rumpled her hair.

"Of course you're not tired. Do it anyway."

Ashley headed for the back door, which Brook let slam just in front of her. Sloan shook his head. That girl was going to turn all his hair gray long before his time.

"Did you say 'walk me home'?" Jenna asked, emerging from behind the truck. "You're joking, right?"

"No, sugar, I'm not. A gentleman sees a lady home.

Think how I'd feel if you were mugged or something between here and your apartment."

"The odds of that happening—"

"Aren't worth risking it. These northern men must have it all wrong if they don't know how to properly treat a woman." He bent his elbow, offering it to her.

She tutted, shaking her head, but accepted it. "Okay, Tex. If it makes you happy, you can walk me home."

"Thank you. That's considerate of you."

"Does it?"

"Does what?"

"Does walking me home make you happy?"

Actually, he rather liked it, the warmth of her body alongside his, her arm threaded through his. But he wasn't sure if he liked liking it. "I suppose."

"Ooh, be still my heart." She chuckled. "I think you've got the manners thing down, Tex, but your sweet talk needs a little work."

The walk, even at a leisurely stroll, took all of two minutes, if that. Before he knew it, they stood at the metal door to her building, a bright security light beaming down on them. She unlocked the door, stepped over the threshold and turned to face him. "So tell me, what does make you happy?"

He shrugged, more than a little surprised at the question. "Doing the right thing. Being a good chief engineer, keeping the station running well—"

She groaned.

"Doing a good job with my kids, which I'm not so sure of with Brook, um—"

"Brook *is* a good kid. Cut her and yourself a little slack. But that's not what I'm talking about. Do you ever do anything that just makes you feel happy?"

"Like what?"

"Like, watch the sun set. Dance in the rain—or at the bowling alley. Make a snow angel." She paused. "Okay, I suppose making snow angels isn't something you could do very often in Texas. Did you ever just watch the clouds go by and look for shapes in them?"

He raised his eyebrows at her. "Do I look like a girly-boy to you?"

"Absolutely not." She swept her gaze over him and he felt it every bit as strongly as if she'd actually run her hands along his body. When she lifted her eyes back to his face, something flickered there, something that raised the temperature in the little alcove. "No," she said, her voice slightly raspy, "you don't look like a girly-boy to me. You seem to be one hundred percent prime male."

He swallowed hard as she pressed her lips together, looking up at him. *Wooiiee.* He hadn't felt a rush like this in a very long time.

Kiss her.

He wanted to. Desperately. And as if she could read his mind, she took a step closer to him. She brought with her a spicy, exotic scent, something tropical he couldn't quite place. She looked up at him, lips slightly parted.

Damn, how he wanted to just pull her into his arms and lay one on her.

But he wasn't a man who let his wants rule his life. Duty first, that was how he'd been raised. Do the right thing.

His duty was to the two girls in the house next door.

"I, uh, I should get going. I need to make sure Ashley's gone to bed."

Disappointment drained the light from her eyes, and part of him wanted to put it back. But he couldn't.

She nodded. "Sure. Thanks again. I really did have fun tonight."

He waited until she'd closed the door and he heard her footsteps on the steps inside the stairwell. "So did I, Jenna. So did I."

But fun wasn't always part of a father's job description.

CHAPTER FOUR

"THAT PENSIVE, sort of bemused expression on your face just screams man-problems."

Jenna dropped the earring and jumped in her chair, barely maintaining her grip on a little pair of needle-nose pliers. "Jeez, Margo, how many times do I have to tell you, don't sneak up on me like that?" The office had a back door to Margo's shop, and more than once Jenna had sworn she was going to install a bell on it like the one she had on Element-ry's front door.

"Uh-huh." Margo brushed the pieces of red beach glass aside and perched on the edge of the desk. "I don't hear you denying it. So what gives? Tell me all about your weekend. And the man who's making you look like that."

"There's no man." Surely a special place existed in hell for a woman who lied so blatantly to her best girl-friend—a front-row seat, so to speak. She hadn't been able to get Sloan and Friday night's near-miss kiss out of her mind. For a moment there, a spark had flamed to life in his blue eyes, and she'd been certain he'd felt the same pull she did. But then it had gone out, and she hadn't been sure if she'd imagined the whole thing.

"Right. Which is why you've been mopey all day."

"There's no man!" Might as well move her reserved seat directly in front of the brimstone fire. Better for roasting marshmallows.

"Then maybe it's time you get one again, girl, because you're getting cranky. You need some fun. When's the last time you went on a date?"

"Umm…" The bowling didn't count. Not with kids with them. Holy crow, she'd fallen into a rut. She couldn't even remember.

The front door chimed and they both looked toward the office entrance. Brook appeared in the opening, a dreamy expression on her face.

"You're not scheduled to work tonight, Brook," Jenna said. Her other part-timer, Nicole, was in. "What's up?"

"I just had to tell somebody. Guess who drove me home from school?"

"Pssst." Margo poked Jenna in the side. "See that look on her face? You had the same one," she whispered. "Guess a guy."

Jenna narrowed her eyes at her friend. "I did not." She turned her attention back to Brook, who bounced on her feet. "Who?"

"Come on, guess!"

"Uh…some cute guy?"

"Yes!" Brook squealed. "Dylan Burch! The track star who bought a pair of earrings for his mom's birthday a week ago? Remember?"

"I remember. See, I told you there'd be another guy in your life."

"See, *I* told *you* it was a guy." Margo folded her arms and nodded. "I know these things."

"And he asked me out! Saturday night there's a dance at school, and he asked me!"

"That's great, Brook."

The front door opened again. "Hello?" called a small voice.

Brook turned around and groaned. "Ashley. What are you doing home from school? Why aren't you at the aftercare program?"

The little girl pushed aside her older sister and came into the office. "Dad has to work late tonight. To make up for being home this afternoon while they poured the new driveway." Ashley sidled up to Jenna. "Can I feed the fish?"

"Sure. You know where the food is."

"Yea!" She darted back into the shop.

"Damn, I forgot Dad was working late tonight. Ugh. That means I'm stuck with the pest."

"New driveway? Is that why your dad asked if he could park on the side of my building for the next few days?"

"I guess," Brook said.

Margo poked Jenna in the ribs again. "When did he ask that?"

"This afternoon."

"Uh-huh. See, I know these things." Margo pursed her lips. "Men."

Jenna straightened in her chair. "Wait a minute, did your sister say they *poured* a new driveway? As in cement?"

Brook shrugged. "I guess. Why?"

Jenna laughed, yanking open the top drawer of the desk and rummaging inside. "'Cause we're going to have some fun and commemorate your new house, that's why."

HIS NEW BOSS HAD SCORED bonus points with Sloan, telling him to forget about making up the time he'd taken off in the afternoon and just go home to his family. Sloan pulled the truck into a space near Jenna's back door and tried not to think about her. About the near kiss.

Too late.

He toyed with the idea of going into her shop to thank her again for letting him use her parking lot while the new driveway set, but that probably wouldn't be smart. The more time he spent in her company, the more he found himself drawn to her. And that wasn't a good thing.

He climbed from the truck. Best he got home and made sure Brook hadn't reduced Ashley to tears over some stupid thing—or almost as bad, ignored her little sister completely.

The leaves were starting to change color. Reds, oranges, brilliant golds. Maybe he was going to enjoy the change in seasons again. Then again, someone—namely him—was going to have to rake the leaves up when they fell. The breeze flapped the yellow tape strung across the end of the driveway. Sloan trudged up the front steps and into the house.

Silence greeted him. "Girls?"

Nothing. Not one blessed sound. The hair on his

arms stood at attention. A rush of adrenaline pumped into his body. Where the hell could they be?

He reconned the living room and kitchen. No signs of after-school snacks or anything, but a pair of backpacks on the floor near the fridge offered some reassurance. Opening the door to the back porch, he finally heard them. Shrill laughter filled the backyard. Relief flooded him, and he yanked open the screen door—then stopped in his tracks.

Four female forms knelt in the grass by the garage, alongside the edge of the new driveway. He clenched his teeth.

They were messing with his new driveway.

Ashley glanced up at him. "Daddy! I'm a movie star!" She jumped up and raced toward him, throwing herself into his arms. He caught her reflexively.

"Please don't tell me that means what I think it means."

Brook rose, scowling. She turned to Jenna, who placed something in the formerly smooth concrete. "See, I told you he'd be mad."

"He's not mad." Jenna climbed to her feet, then offered a hand to Margo. "Are you?"

"I did tell the girls they weren't to write in the cement." And he hadn't wanted stray leaves, or stray cat paw prints, or anything else in there, either.

"Well, there you go. We didn't write in it. Not yet, anyway. We just put their handprints in it, and a brand-new penny to commemorate your new house. Besides, this isn't vandalism, it's art." She crooked a finger at him. "I think you should put your handprint in there, too."

Brook snorted. "That'll be the day."

"Yeah, Daddy, do it! We're all a family and this is our new house. You have to put your hand in there, too." Ashley cupped his face with her damp, clammy and slightly abrasive palms. "Please?"

He sighed. Her little face looked so excited. Besides, he needed to prove his older daughter wrong. First it had been "my dad doesn't dance" and now it was this. Not to mention Jenna's faith—albeit somewhat misplaced— that he wouldn't be mad about the whole thing, although he couldn't understand why what she thought mattered to him.

"All right. For you, Peach."

He set Ashley down and strode over to examine their handiwork. He laid his palm against the cool concrete, pressing in to make a firm indentation. Ashley clapped.

"There, that wasn't so bad, was it?" Jenna offered him a paper towel as he clambered to his feet.

"I wanted nice smooth concrete," he muttered. "It's a guy thing."

"Smooth is overrated. This is much more interesting. I'll make it up to you," Jenna said, her approving smile making him feel as though he would run through the cement in his combat boots if it made her happy.

If it made her smile at him like that.

"You will? How?" he asked.

"Um...I'll take you to dinner," she announced.

"Dinner? You and me? You mean, like a date?" *A date?* Did he have cement in his head, or what?

The brightness in her eyes faded a notch, and the wind-kissed roses in her cheeks deepened a shade. "A date? Well, I wouldn't call it a date, exactly, um…"

Brook stomped her foot. When Sloan glanced at his older daughter, she scowled at him, then flipped her hair and stormed onto the porch. Apparently, she didn't think her father should be dating.

And that irked him.

"Why not?" he replied, loudly enough for his voice to carry to his sulking teen. "I'd love a date with you."

Margo chuckled, then coughed, covering her mouth.

Ashley looked up at Sloan with round eyes. "A date?" Without waiting for an answer, she scurried toward the door.

"What's the rush, Peach?" Sloan called after her.

"I gotta call Molly."

"For what?"

"Never mind!" The screen door banged shut, followed by the inner door to the kitchen.

"I really am sorry about the driveway—" Jenna started.

"Don't be. I haven't heard Ashley so excited in a long time. Not to mention this is a wonderful way to commemorate our new home. I never would have thought of it." He turned to face Jenna. "And I managed to get myself a date with the girl next door. I think I can stand handprints in my driveway for that."

Her green eyes widened, then she glanced away. Not what he had expected from the flirtatious woman.

"Told you," Margo muttered. "I know these things."

A CREAK IN THE HALLWAY was followed by the sound of his bedsprings squeaking. Sloan turned from the computer, expecting to find Ashley had crawled onto his bed. He tried to hide his shock when he discovered Brook sprawled across the navy-blue comforter instead. She never sought him out anymore.

"Hey. Something on your mind, Snickerdoodle?"

"God, Dad. Don't call me that. Do I look like an infant to you?" She sat up, folding her legs beneath her. The pink long johns she wore as sleepwear reminded him of a set of flannel pj's she'd had when she was about seven. Back when she'd loved him calling her Snickerdoodle, after her favorite cookie. Before their lives had gone to hell on a highway with Beth's car accident.

"You cannot go out with Jenna."

"Really? Why not?"

"Because. She is so not your type. You'll end up annoying her, and then she'll get mad and break up with you and then she'll hate me, too. And she's *my* friend, not yours."

"Not my type, huh?" Actually, she'd hit that nail squarely on the head. "Why not?"

Brook stared at the ceiling for a moment. "She's fun and happy and impulsive. You…you're…not."

"Impulsive leads to trouble. But I'm fun."

"Yeah, right, Dad. You're about as much fun as a… hot tub full of old geezers. No, wait, your idea of fun is wiring a bunch of equipment and figuring out why it doesn't work. Snore city. Face it, you're a dud, Dad."

"Gee, thanks. Maybe I should apply for my rocking chair now." Still, she had a point. His life, since losing Beth, had consisted of work and family. There had been a couple of disastrous blind dates and setups by well-meaning friends, but overall, fun hadn't been in his vocabulary. He'd been far too busy raising his girls. "Jenna must see something in me if she wants to go out with me."

"Puhleeze. She probably meant she'd take us all out for dinner and you just misunderstood. Then she was too embarrassed to correct you."

Sloan thought about that night in her stairwell. True, he was out of practice, but a grown man didn't mistake that look in a woman's eyes. The parted lips. The…aw, hell, this wasn't something he needed to be thinking about with his daughter in the same room.

"I don't think so, Brook. But, hey, don't get the wrong impression. I'm not saying this is going to be anything serious. Just that maybe it's time. Both you and Ashley are older now."

"So, you're still going out with her?"

He nodded.

"Well, great, that sucks. If you ruin this for me, I'll…"

"What?"

"I'll never speak to you again!"

I should be so lucky. Guilt flooded him, and he retracted the errant thought. He'd been trying to improve his relationship with Brook. Alienating her completely was the last thing he wanted.

Brook launched herself from the bed, pausing in the doorway. "Oh yeah, and if you expect me to baby-sit the brat while you're out messing up my friendship with Jenna, you'd better not plan on going out this Saturday. Because *I* have a date that night." She vanished into the hallway.

He shot from his chair and made it to her room in a flash, putting his palm flat against her bedroom door just as she went to shut it. "Not so fast, young lady." He entered as she threw herself onto the bed with a loud huff. "You don't just drop a bomb like that and then take off. That remark needs some explanation. Who is this boy? Where are you going? How are you getting there?"

Brook rolled onto her back, draping her arm across her eyes. "He's just a boy from school, Dad. We're going to a dance at school, so yes, there will be chaperones."

"That's good. What's his name?"

"What difference does it make? It's not like you know him."

"I don't know him *yet*," he corrected. "But I will by the time you leave this house on Saturday."

She moaned her displeasure.

Tough. It was his job to protect her and make sure she made wise decisions. Her track record for doing the right thing wasn't the best. "I mean it, Brook. This boy arrives here to pick you up, and he submits to—"

"The standard grilling and shakedown, with a side order of intimidation and threats. I know, I know."

"Okay. As long as we're on the same wavelength here."

"Whatever. Just as long as you remember, I'll babysit on Friday, but Saturday is my night." She rolled over, facing the wall.

"Fine." Pretty damn bad when you were coordinating dating schedules with your teenager. Even worse… what if she was right about him and Jenna being a bad combination?

Sloan returned to his own bedroom. The navy curtains stirred lightly, the cracked window letting in a refreshing bit of night air. Music came from Jenna's apartment, muted, moody blues. He could just see the light outside her deck door.

She was a puzzle. The bohemian clothing, the quick smile, the flirtatious nature.

Not the serious, out-to-catch-a-husband type. Not the psycho-possessive or overly needy character. Nope. She'd understand casual dating. Jenna Quinn, the perfect kind of woman to ease him back into the dating pool.

SEATED ON the bathroom floor next to the oversize whirlpool tub, Jenna dug through the plastic container of nail polish, searching for the right color to go with the turquoise, raspberry and silver broomstick skirt she planned to wear that night for her dinner with Sloan. When the phone rang, she rose and awkwardly hobbled—toe spreaders made it so hard to be graceful—to the counter to grab the portable. She sank back to the floor, phone propped between her ear and shoulder. "Hello?"

"Hello, Jenna. I hope I'm not interrupting anything important." Mallory Quinn's cool, even voice made it clear that she really didn't expect something important to take precedence over this phone call.

"Mother. What a surprise to hear from you." Jenna uncapped a bottle of pink polish and began to dab her big toe. "Actually, I'm in the midst of preparing for a very important meeting I have tonight."

"Business?" The catch of surprise in her mother's voice irked Jenna.

Pleasure, Jenna almost responded. But her mother wouldn't even have the decency to be shocked by that answer, and Jenna didn't feel like hearing any of the stock lectures, like *"When Are You Going to Grow Up and Settle Down?",* or her other personal favorite, *"Stop Wasting Your Brains and Get a Real Job."* "Actually, yes, it is business. I don't want to talk about it, though. Don't want to jinx it, you know?"

"Superstition is not what leads to business success, Jenna. You should know that by now. Goodness knows you've tried enough different approaches."

"What was it you called for, Mother?" Jenna recapped the polish, tossed it into the container and pulled out a bottle of blue, moving on to the next toe.

"I realize Thanksgiving is over a month away, and that you tend to wait until the last minute to decide things, but I wanted to see if you've made plans already."

Jenna's stomach clenched. Thanksgiving—in fact, all the holidays—had been Gram's domain. "I—I hadn't given it much thought."

"Wonderful. We'll be having dinner at one o'clock, here at the house. Your father and I do hope you'll be here."

"You're doing Thanksgiving? But Meg's off on the holidays. Are you cooking?" The one thing she'd admit

to having in common with her mother was the fact that they both did takeout far better than anything else. Fortunately for her parents, they could afford a live-in housekeeper who was an excellent cook.

"Don't be ridiculous. I'm having it catered by Dominique."

"That's a relief," Jenna muttered, changing colors again.

"What did you say?"

"I said, oh, that thief. Honestly, with the prices Dominique charges, we could feed the entire homeless population of Erie for less."

"You will be here, right? It will mean a lot to your father."

"Yes, Mother. I'll be there." For her father, who'd adored Gram as much as Jenna had, she'd go.

"Wonderful. Dinner at one. Drinks at noon. Dress to impress, darling." Her mother made a kissy-kiss sound into the phone. "Talk soon!" With that, she hung up.

Dress to impress? Jenna stifled a groan as she clicked off the phone and set it on the edge of the tub. She looked down at her foot and smiled as she realized what she'd done. Four toes, four different colors.

Just like Gram had always done for her when she was little. "Why have just one color when you can have ten?" she'd always said.

The smile drained away as Jenna pressed her lips together, a hollow ache building in her chest. Blinking back the moisture gathering in her eyes, she proceeded to finish her toes, each one another shade. When she was done, she just sat, letting them dry—and missing Gram.

She heard the door to her apartment slam and hastily ran the sleeve of her robe over her eyes. Margo bounded into the room, then pulled up short. "Hey. I came to critique your preparations for tonight. What's going on, Glum Chum?"

"My mother called to invite me for Thanksgiving."

"Oh, well, that explains it. Your mother's cooking would make anyone cry."

"That's not it. It's just…"

"You always went to your gram's for the holidays. I know. The next few months are going to be tough.…" Margo snapped her fingers. "I know what you need."

The beauty of a best friend, Jenna thought, was that you didn't have to explain what made you happy or sad. A best friend just knew those things. Out in the kitchen, Jenna heard Margo opening and closing cupboard doors, muttering as she rummaged through them. She pushed herself to her feet and walked into the main room on her heels. "What are you looking for?"

"This." Margo waved a bottle with a yellow flower on the front. "I thought I remembered seeing it in there."

She rattled the jar of Saint-John's-wort. "Did you take *any* of this when I gave it to you last year? Look, you don't like being mopey, and I don't like you being mopey, either. Please just trust me on this. Take this at least until after New Year's. Get through the holidays and the anniversary of your gram's death. Then you can go back to ignoring my advice."

"It will help?"

Margo nodded.

"It will make my mother easier to tolerate?"

Margo laughed. "Now you're pushing your luck. It's an herb, not a miracle."

"Okay." Jenna reached for the capsule her friend held out. "Now, about that critique of tonight's preparations…"

SLOAN HELD the steak-house door for Jenna, then followed her inside, catching a whiff of freshly grilled beef that set his stomach growling. Country music droned in the background, and jean-and-T-shirt-clad wait staff hustled through the maze of tables and booths. He followed Jenna to the hostess station, where she requested a nonsmoking table with a questioning look at him. He nodded, then they stepped aside to wait.

Jenna's wrinkly skirt swished around her calves. A slender silver band encircled one ankle, and her toes, exposed in a pair of brown leather sandals, each boasted a different shade of nail polish.

"What?" she asked. "Did I step in something?"

He shook his head. "Sandals in October might work in Texas, but it seems a little…off for here."

She put her hands on her hips in mock indignation. "Hey, it was sixty today. A rare occurrence for Erie in October, so we take advantage of it when we can. No silly fashion rules."

"You strike me as someone who makes her own rules, anyway." Like the multihued toes.

"You say that like it's a bad thing."

"As the father of a teenage daughter, I'm all about rules."

The hostess motioned them forward, leading them through the packed tables to a booth on the side. Old black-and-white photographs of cowboys graced the walls, along with saddles, deer antlers and a stuffed jackalope—a jackrabbit with antlers stuck on it.

"Nice place." He slid into the red bench seat, accepting the menu.

Jenna smiled at him. "I thought that maybe if you were homesick for Texas, this would make you feel better. I think this place has the best steak in Erie."

"That was right thoughtful of you, ma'am," he drawled in an exaggeration of the twang he'd become more aware of since moving north. Her soft laughter rewarded his effort, and a surge of warmth rushed through him.

This dating stuff wasn't half-bad.

After ordering drinks, they looked over the menu. Sloan stole a few long peeks at her while she was engrossed in selecting her meal. She wore very little makeup from what he could tell, just a hint of blush and some shiny, light pink lipstick. She looked up and smiled at him. "See anything you like?"

The double entendre wasn't lost on him, but he pretended not to get it. "I'm thinking about the T-bone."

"Good choice." Was that a hint of disappointment in her voice?

His cell phone, clipped to his belt, buzzed, and Sloan set down his menu, then retrieved the intruder, checking out the caller ID. "Damn. I'm sorry. It's the station. I have to take this."

When he flipped it open, the frantic voice of one of the master control operators greeted him with the announcement they were currently off air. "Just one second," he said, then covered the speaker with his finger.

He turned his attention back to his dinner companion. "I'm sorry. I'm going to step outside and deal with this. Could you order for me? T-bone, medium, loaded baked potato and Caesar salad."

She nodded. "No problem."

He slipped from the booth, phone already back to his ear as he barked clipped questions and quick commands. If he couldn't troubleshoot and get things fixed this way, he'd be forced to do more than just step away for a call.

In the foyer, he leaned against the wall. After about ten minutes, when the master control operator told him the station was back on air, he replied, "Good job. If it happens again, you know how to find me." *But don't,* he wanted to add.

Heading back to the table, he found his date bantering with the waiter, whose deep laughter irritated him, as did the way he darted off at Sloan's approach. "I'm really sorry about that," he said to Jenna as he slid back into his seat. "But when the station is off air, it's money lost every minute."

"No problem." She waved her hand in dismissal of his apology. "How'd you end up as an engineer at a TV station? Where'd you go to college?"

"No college." He slugged back a belt of his beer, letting the remainder of his tension slip away. "School of Uncle Sam. I did a four-year enlistment in the army right after high school, ended up in communications at Fort Hood in Texas. After, I got a job at a station in Fort Worth and worked my way up."

"Self-made. I admire that in a man."

His chest swelled. "Thanks. What about you?"

"To my parents' everlasting dismay, I had so many different majors in college, it took me five and half years to complete my undergrad degree. Worse, I didn't follow in their footsteps and go to law school." She paused, lifting her margarita. "Luckily, Gram was always in my corner. She told them not everyone was cut out to be a lawyer."

"How do they feel about your business?"

"They're reserving judgment, like the prudent lawyers they are. In other words, the jury is still out on their daughter's ability to be a success in this world."

"Ouch. That seems kind of harsh."

She shrugged. "I know they love me and they've always wanted the best for me. It's just that our ideas of what's 'the best for me' are very different. They've never really accepted me for who I am. They've been waiting forever for me to grow up."

She seemed plenty grown-up to Sloan.

"Okay, here you go," the waiter announced, approaching their table with a dish in his hands. "Enjoy."

Sloan stared at the concoction in the middle of the table. Two large chunks of chocolate cake, several scoops of ice cream, all of it topped with chocolate syrup and whipped cream. He glanced across the table at Jenna, whose spoon hesitated. "What?" she asked.

"I know I wasn't away from the table that long. What's this?"

She grinned. "Dessert. This thing is so sinful you can't say enough Hail Marys to make up for it."

"Oo-kay. But why is it here *now?* Before all the other food?"

"Life's short, Sloan. Eat dessert first." She dug her spoon into the creation. Chocolate dripped from it as she raised it. "That was Gram's philosophy. Truth is, if we eat all the other stuff first, I won't have room for dessert. I'd rather take home the other stuff and enjoy this." She slid her spoon into her mouth, closing her eyes. "Mmm."

The blatant joy she took in the dessert, along with the little moan and heartfelt sigh, shot straight to his groin. What would it be like to make love to a woman who took such an obvious interest in pleasure?

"Aren't you going to have some?"

"Uh…"

"Oh, come on. Live a little. Eat dessert first for once." She winked at him.

Oh, hellfire. Here he'd thought she'd be a safe easing-back-into-dating partner and all he wanted was to put that pleased expression back on her face in a far more intimate way.

Not exactly what he'd had in mind.

She still stared at him, spoon poised over the bowl. She scooped up another bit, combining all the ingredients. She leaned across the table, offering it to him. "Open up, Tex."

He barely tasted it. He was too busy focusing on the playful spark in her eyes and controlling the unexpected attraction racing through him.

"So, how is it?"

He nodded. "Best dessert I've had in a long time." He didn't mention it was the only dessert he'd had in a long time. Or that he really couldn't taste it with her watching him that way.

Somehow they made it through the huge dish. As the waiter removed the empty bowl, Sloan sighed with relief. Surely the rest of the meal wouldn't be quite such a torment. Surely Jenna wouldn't take the same amount of pleasure in a steak or salad.

Wrong. The woman delighted in the beef. The waiter beamed when she expressed her joy.

"You would love Texas barbecue," Sloan told her after the fawning kid had once again removed himself to take care of another table.

"Don't you like your steak?"

"Oh, it's fine. Not bad for a bunch of Yanks."

"Oh, right. Everything's better in Texas. Or so I've heard."

"Better and bigger."

"Oh?" She arched one eyebrow at him. "I've heard that, too. But I'm not sure if I believe it. You up to proving it, Tex?"

He damned near choked on the bit of steak in his mouth. Coughing into his napkin, he waved off her concern when she moved toward his side of the table. "I'm okay." His eyes watered.

"You sure?"

He nodded. "Wrong pipe, is all." He cleared his throat again, then reached for his water glass.

"Sorry. Sometimes I forget people don't always appreciate my slightly warped sense of humor."

"Was it just a joke?"

A sly smile tugged at her lips. "Do you want it to be?"

He lifted one shoulder. "Honestly, I'm not sure." His libido argued with him, and he silently commanded it to shut the hell up. "You do know you're my first date in about three years, right?"

"Really? No, I didn't. But I have to confess, I find that surprising."

"Why?"

"Good-looking guy like you? I can't believe you've been on the shelf that long."

He straightened his spine, sitting taller. She thought he was good-looking. Amazing how hearing that made him feel he could take on the world. "Thanks. About a year after…my wife died, I suffered through a few disastrous blind dates. You know, setups by well-meaning friends?"

"Oh, jeez. I know just what you mean. The last time I let a friend set me up, the guy ended up being a total jerk. He was looking for someone who would take care of him. You know, do all the laundry, have dinner on the table when he got home from work, fetch him a beer while he watched the game." She narrowed her eyes. "That's not what you're looking for, is it?"

He laughed. "Hell, no. I do my own laundry, have a teenager who helps sometimes with the dinner thing, and am perfectly capable of fetching my own beers. Although, might I remind you it was *you* who invited *me* on this date. Maybe I should be asking you what you're looking for."

"Not unless you want to choke on your steak again." She chuckled, a warm, gentle sound that reached him on so many levels. "Just teasing. I believe I owed you for encouraging the kids to use your cement as a canvas."

"Yes. I believe you did." He hoped she could tell he was teasing, too. This kind of bantering was foreign to him. "But I think I'd stick my hand in it again for this."

They lingered over the rest of the meal, making small talk, exchanging unimportant stories of their pasts. Typical first-date kind of stuff. A shot of annoyance when the waiter invited Jenna to "come again soon" surprised Sloan. After all, she'd done little to encourage the younger man's blatant interest in her, unless you counted being overly kind and too damn pretty as flirting.

His own response aggravated the hell out of him. It wasn't as if he had a claim to her or anything. As he followed her through the crowd of people waiting for a table, she stopped, tilting her head. She turned to him. "I love this song," she said, as her shoulders dipped in time to the music.

The impulse to hold her close and show her how a good ol' boy from Texas two-stepped with a lovely lady warred with his normal self-restraint. A number of people grinned as Jenna turned the waiting area into an impromptu dance floor. One woman gave her a long, examining stare, then shook her head. Jenna seemed oblivious to both sets of looks.

"Come on, let's go," he muttered, taking her hand. "It's way too crowded in here now."

Warning alarms clanged in his head. This sparkling woman could make him lose his rationality. She wasn't the safe, couple-of-casual-dates partner he'd expected. She made him want to dance—something he hadn't done in a long, long time.

As he helped her into the truck, those multihued toes caught his attention once more.

If he had an ounce of sense, he'd drive her home, drop her off with a cheek-peck good-night kiss, and forget about dating her. Or dancing with her. Or doing anything else with her.

He'd put her back into the next-door-neighbor, daughter's-boss, and friend category.

Then she leaned over and clicked on his radio, setting it to the same station the restaurant had had on. She closed her eyes and began to sing along in a slightly off-key warble. Picking up enthusiasm as the song moved into the chorus, she grew louder.

Eyes closed, head bopping in time to the rhythm, totally unabashed at her less-than-stellar performance, she belted out the ending.

Damn it, she was too cute for his own good.

How could danger come in such an appealing package?

CHAPTER FIVE

THE STREETLIGHT on the corner flickered to life as Sloan pulled the truck into a spot near her door. Jenna smiled at him. "I'm glad we had dinner. I had a great time."

And she had. Even though she didn't officially date guys with kids, this had been the best non-date she'd had in ages. And the chemistry between them…well, it wasn't the kind that came along every day.

"I did, too. Thanks for dinner." He leaned a little closer to her, and she could smell his spicy cologne.

She reached out, stroked her fingers over his silky-smooth cheek. His eyes widened, then he backed away, reaching for the door. "Let me help you out."

His gentlemanly manners took some getting used to, but she found she liked them. "You're going to come in for a little bit, right?" Jenna asked him after he'd ushered her to her door.

He said nothing, and she could see the hesitation in his eyes. The man was spooked. She'd imagined the same terror in her own eyes at some good-nights—the ones she wanted to ditch and never hear from again.

Yikes. Was that what he wanted to do with her? She definitely wanted a little more from him. Nothing serious. Another non-date or two. He was good company. And she sure wouldn't complain if he wanted to drop his boots under her bed. She hadn't had a pair of boots under her bed in far too long.

"Come on, Tex. I promise not to bite."

He offered her a nervous half-smile. "I told you I'm out of practice at this. Maybe I shouldn't push my luck."

She grabbed the collar points of his long-sleeved shirt. "And maybe you should." Tilting her head back, she looked into his eyes. "I at least expect a good-night kiss. What do you say, Tex? Eat dessert first."

For a moment, the cool night air stilled, then a gust rustled the leaves in the tree in his yard, just over the fence behind her building. She watched as his feelings played out across his face. Then he said, "If I kiss you good-night now, then that means our date is over. I thought you asked me to come in for a while?"

"I did."

"I accept."

"Good." With a smile, she let go of his shirt, then turned to the door, digging her keys from the bottom of her purse. Entering the stairwell with him just behind, she started up the stairs, only to be stopped when he grabbed her wrist. She paused to look over her shoulder at him.

"Jenna, I just want to be clear. I'm not…not—"

"Not what? Not interested in women? You really are gay, even though you have two daughters and denied homosexual status the other night?"

He chuckled. "No. I just…" He blew out a quick

breath. "I just don't want you to expect anything from me. I'm really *not* looking for a woman to do my laundry and fetch me a beer."

She swiveled around. Since she was one stair above him, now they were eye level. She cupped his face in her hands. "Good. Because I don't want that, either. You've got kids, and I don't do kids. I offered you dessert, Tex, not steak and potatoes."

She leaned forward and brushed her lips across his mouth, just a hint, a friendly howdy kind of kiss. Then she smiled at him, took his hand and led him upstairs.

Princess bounded off the sofa. Ignoring Jenna's outstretched fingers, she sniffed the bottom of Sloan's khakis, then jumped up, front paws on his pants.

"Nice to see you, too," Jenna greeted the spaniel.

"Hey, pup." Sloan crouched down to scratch the dog's ears.

"Can I get you something to drink?"

"Sure. What are my choices?"

He settled on a bottled beer. Jenna poured a chilled raspberry wine cooler into a long-stemmed glass for herself while he explored her stereo and CD collection. "Give us some music, Tex."

"You've got a very eclectic collection here."

"That surprises you? I'm a woman of many moods."

"Now *that* doesn't surprise me. Seems to me most women have many moods. And you…"

She crossed the living area, drinks in hand. "I what?"

He lifted one shoulder as he placed several discs into the player. His fingers flashed over buttons whose functions had always eluded her. "You strike me…I don't know, as a very complex woman."

"Me? Complex?" She shook her head. "I'm as simple as they come. There's my philosophy." She pointed to a carved sign that hung over the sliding doors to the deck.

"'Live Well, Love Much, Laugh Often,' huh?"

"Yep."

"What about dance in the rain and make snow angels?"

"Oh, yeah."

"And eat dessert first?" His eyes darkened, and he took both drinks from her, setting them on the coffee table.

"Definitely."

"I dance," he said, taking her hand. "But I'm probably a little rusty at that, too. May I?"

With very little awkwardness, she found herself ensconced in his arms. After a few false starts where she nearly trampled his toes, he two-stepped her around the edges of the living-room rug.

"Well, what do you know? You do dance, Tex. We're going to have to go bowling again."

He grinned. "Two-stepping is not the same as wiggling your butt on a bowling alley in front of a group of strangers."

"One step at a time. One step at a time."

"You think?"

"If you give me a chance, I think I can show you that life is never more complicated than wiggling your butt on a bowling lane."

"If you say so."

The music slowed to a romantic ballad. Jenna

dropped her head to his shoulder, snuggled into him. The warm scent of spicy cologne mixed with Sloan's own musky smell. Her fingers caressed the nape of his neck. He tightened his arm around her waist, nuzzled her hair.

"Mmm." She sighed. "Nice."

"Mmm-hmm." His agreement rumbled through his chest beneath her cheek. "Very nice."

The music eventually changed again, but they continued to shift back and forth. Jenna lifted her head. As though he knew just what she wanted, he bent his neck, taking her mouth with his.

Tentative at first, brushing her lips with feathery kisses, he grew bolder, taking her bottom lip between his. Impatient when he went back to surface exploration, she cupped the back of his neck and flirted with his mouth with the tip of her tongue.

"Easy," he breathed. "No rush. One step at a time."

He resumed his leisurely kisses, stroking her face, her jawline, the curve of her ear with his fingertips. By the time he deepened things, letting his tongue coax and caress, her knees trembled, desire curled in the pit of her belly—and lower—and she'd decided she definitely wanted his boots under her bed.

Wow-eee, the man could kiss!

"Whew," he whispered, easing back. "Maybe I'm rustier than I thought."

"Rusty? You call that rusty? Then I'm in big trouble once you've had some practice."

"Really?"

"Yes, really."

His blue eyes twinkled at her reassurance. "I—I should go."

"Go? Now? You've got to be kidding me. You haven't had your drink. We haven't…had dessert." Oh, God. Maybe he didn't really feel the same attraction. But after that kiss-fest, she'd thought…

Sloan watched the flush of desire fade from her face. Bewilderment, mingled with embarrassment, replaced it.

"Oh, hey, it's not that I don't want dessert." He wrapped his arms around her, pulling her against him, making sure she could feel just how their slow-dance kissing had aroused him. "I definitely *want* dessert. Want you." He bent down and gave her another lingering lip lock to erase any further doubts she might have. Then he rested his forehead against hers.

"So why were you leaving?"

"Two reasons. First of all, I have to face a teenager when I get home. I know it's probably hard to understand—because, after all, I'm the grown-up so I can sort of do what I want—but that's the point. *I'm* the grown-up. I need to set a good example. I've always told Brook to do the right thing…not to have sex, to wait, take things slow. I can't very well jump into your bed on our first date, can I?"

"I wouldn't complain. Or tell."

He laughed. "Then there's reason number two."

"Which is?"

"There's really something to be said for anticipation. Heightens the experience."

"OHMIGOD, he actually said that?" Margo leaned on the kitchen island.

Jenna nodded as she slid the dish of chicken cordon bleu—the one edible thing she could cook—from the oven. "He did. Then he kissed me once more, turning me into a total puddle of frustrated mush, and then went home. I cannot tell you the amount of self-control it took for me not to head into the bedroom the second the door shut, grab my trusty battery-operated companion and finish what he'd started."

"You mean you didn't?"

"No. I figured that defeated the whole purpose." Jenna spooned the entrée onto teal-edged plates, then added several spears of asparagus and portions of wild rice. "Make yourself useful and pour the wine."

"I can't. I'm in shock. Since when does a carefully selected man, when granted access, turn down a trip to your bed?"

"Apparently, since yesterday." Jenna uncorked the bottle. "Aren't you supposed to be making me feel better about this? Isn't that in the best-friend handbook somewhere?"

"Um…he didn't say *no,* only *not now.* Does that help?"

"Tons." Pouring the wine, Jenna grimaced. "One really sad thing is that I think he might be right. After what he did to me last night with a few kisses, the other sad thing is that I'd wait forever for him to decide he's ready. I am so pa-the-tic!"

"No, I'm pathetic for wanting every last detail."

Margo took the plates over to the table. "Sex by proxy. Now that gives a whole new meaning to pathetic. Although…" She let the word dangle while she sat down and Jenna joined her.

"Although what?"

"I did meet a guy at the conference last weekend."

"What? And you didn't tell me?"

"All we did was talk. He lives in Morgantown."

"West Virginia?"

"Yeah, about three hours from here. He called me today. I don't know if anything will happen."

Jenna stared out the window as Margo continued to talk. Over in Sloan's house, lights shone in the upstairs bedrooms. He hadn't called. And she'd resisted the temptation to pump Brook for information today while they'd worked at Element-ry.

"Jenna? Are you listening?"

"Huh? Of course." She stroked the stem of her wine-glass, toying with a bead of condensation. "We're talking about men. I wonder what Sloan's doing?"

"Hellooo? I know it's generally about you, Princess Jenna, but can we focus on me and *my* man situation for just a few minutes?"

Jenna's face warmed. "I'm sorry, Margo. Sure. Tell me more about him." She struggled to keep her attention on her best friend's face and story, and ignore the pull of the lights next door.

SLOAN GRUNTED, shoving himself off the living-room floor, then eased back down again. His arms trembled, but he continued with the push-ups. He should have called her. Or sent flowers. Something. But he didn't want to appear overeager. Or give her the wrong idea.

Although he wasn't quite sure which idea was the wrong one. He'd enjoyed their dinner and conversation, her company. But that kind of thing smacked of friendship. Companions. A relationship—something he wasn't ready for.

On the other hand, there was the idea of…dessert…with her. Mind-blowing. He forced his thoughts from her smooth skin, her tempting lips, her sensual, fun-loving nature. The last thing he needed tonight was to greet Brook's date with a tent in his shorts. Totally wrong message to send a hormonal teenager.

With renewed vigor, he fired off a few more push-ups, then flopped onto his back, working crunches. By the time the doorbell rang, he answered it in perfect intimidation form: dripping with sweat, muscle T glued to his torso, biceps twitching. He gave the kid on the porch a long, slow appraisal. The varsity jacket didn't bode well. He knew jocks and their mindset.

The boy's face went a shade paler under the intense scrutiny and his eyes darted over Sloan, seeming to take in the dripping sweat, the muscles. He cleared his throat, then stuck out his hand. "Mr. Thompson? I'm Dylan Burch. I'm here to pick up Brook."

Sloan had to give him credit. At least he had some manners and guts. With a firm grip—not too hard, but enough to let Junior know who he was dealing with— Sloan pumped his hand a few times, then gestured into the house. "Come on in. Brook should be down in a few minutes, and that gives us a little time to get to know one another."

"Uh, sure." Dylan glanced around the living room.

"Have a seat."

The interrogation got off to an easy start, with the usual questions: what grade he was in—senior, another point lost—how long he'd been driving, stuff like that. When Sloan heard footsteps overhead, he flexed his biceps and rubbed his knuckles in what he hoped was an apparent absentminded fashion. "You have her home by eleven-thirty, not a second later. Don't even think about taking a drink while you have my daughter with you, and you keep your hands to yourself, or I break them. Clear?"

Dylan shot off the couch as Brook descended the stairs. "Y-yes sir, Mr. Thompson."

Brook wore a clingy light blue dress that showed several more inches of thigh than necessary. The instinct to send her back upstairs to change only grew stronger when he noticed Dylan's stare. "You remember what I just told you, boy," Sloan growled. "And you—curfew is eleven-thirty, not one minute after unless you want to be grounded for the rest of the month."

"Okay, Dad, chill." Brook slipped into a white sweater, then picked up her purse. "You ready, Dylan?"

The boy nodded.

"Hold up one second." Sloan retrieved his cell phone from the end table. He held it out to his daughter. "Take this. You call me if you need a ride for any reason." He narrowed his eyes and glared at the kid, who looked down at his feet.

"Okay, Dad, if aliens abduct us, you'll be the first to know."

Sloan held the door for them. "Have fun." Once it had closed behind them, he exhaled. "But not too much."

The house phone rang before he could resume his calisthenics. Of course, the portable wasn't on the base—probably buried in Brook's room somewhere—forcing him to race into the kitchen and grab the wall-mounted unit. "Hello?"

"Hey," his sister said, "what's up?"

"Oh, not much. I just sent Brook off on a first date with a new guy."

Rachel groaned. "Please tell me you weren't cleaning your gun when he picked her up."

Sloan laughed. "Who do you take me for—Dad? Nah, I'm not like that." Hell, no, he was much subtler than the old man.

"Speaking of dates, I hear through the grapevine that my big brother had a first date of his own last night."

Sloan spluttered for a moment. "How the hell did you hear that?" Then he remembered his younger daughter's rush to phone her cousin. "Ashley?"

Rae laughed. "Seems your daughter and Molly have become buddies of a sort. Don't worry, I've already told Molly she is not to instruct Ashley on matchmaking the way Cherish egged Molly on when James and I were dating. These older girls can be such an influence on the younger ones."

"Sounds like my daughter and I need to have a little chat."

"So, tell me about your date."

"You're nosy, you know that?"

"Absolutely. Now tell me."

"Don't go making something out of nothing. We went out to dinner…end of story."

"Hmm…sounds like there's more to it than that. More than you want me to know."

"Go with that instinct and butt out, huh?"

"Ooo, Sloan's got a girlfriend."

Despite himself, Sloan laughed. "Twerp. Man, you always were a pain in the neck when it came to my love life. I was glad to enlist and ship out just so I could have some peace about it."

"So, you're actually admitting you have a love life again?"

"Bye, Rae. I'll see you next weekend for Ashley's birthday party. Nice talking to you." With a broad grin, he replaced the phone in the cradle. Damn, it felt good knowing his sister was close again. And happy again.

He headed up the stairs, calling, "Ashley? We need to talk, Peach." After striding down the hallway, he paused in the doorway of her room. She sat on the floor in front of the pink dollhouse he'd gotten her for last year's birthday. She had a girl doll in one hand, a male in the other, and as he watched, she pressed the two together, making a sharp smooching sound. "I love you," she said in a high quivery voice. "Now we can get married and live happily ever after."

No more fairy tales for her. He cleared his throat.

She tossed the dolls into the house so their heads crashed into the wall, then looked up at him. "Daddy. I didn't hear you come in."

"That's 'cause I'm not in yet." He crossed her room and sat on the edge of her twin bed. "What's going on?"

"Nothing."

"I hear you talked to Molly."

Her face pinkened. "It's okay now, right? It's not long distance anymore 'cause we live in the same state, right?"

The intricacies of long-distance phone plans eluded even him. "Peach, you can call Aunt Rachel's house whenever you want. I'm glad you get along with your cousin. I just want to know why you needed to talk to her."

Ashley smoothed back her hair, then tossed her head in a startling imitation of Brook. "Oh, you know, girl stuff."

Sloan struggled to keep a straight face. "Girl stuff, huh?"

"Uh-huh. Sorry, Daddy, but you wouldn't get it."

For a moment, Sloan reflected on all the "girl stuff" he'd managed to survive as the single father to two daughters—dolls and tea parties, nail polish and dress up, Brook's first bra and period. Damnation, those last two had shaved a few years off his lifespan and added a couple of gray hairs to his chest, of all places. Their sex talks—make that their abstinence talks—had added more gray. And to think, he could look forward to doing all that again with Ashley. He stifled a sigh.

"Peach, if there's ever anything you need to talk about, you know you can ask me, right? For a dad, I know a lot about girl stuff."

She nodded. "And I have Aunt Rae. And Jenna."

"Jenna? Sweetheart, I think you're getting the wrong idea about Jenna."

"I heard Brook on the phone with Kelly last night while you were gone and she said Jenna was so cool because she knew all about girl stuff that you don't get, like guys and kissing and clothes."

"Oh, really? Hey, I'm a guy and I wear clothes."

Ashley giggled.

Kissing didn't need to be discussed. Although based on Jenna's reaction last night, he thought he knew a good bit about kissing. Not that either of his daughters needed to know that. "What else did your sister have to say?"

"That she hoped you didn't blow it with Jenna and make her hate Brook or fire her. Then Kelly said something, and Brook started making gagging noises and said, 'Oh, that's just too gross to even think about!'"

While Sloan contemplated what that might mean, Ashley jumped up and came over to him, settling on his knee. "Daddy, what's knocking boots?"

BROOK SHIVERED, then pulled her knit sweater tighter around her as they left the school. Dylan's hand moved from the small of her back.

He unzipped his varsity jacket. "Here, put this on. I could have told you that little sweater wouldn't be enough tonight, but you looked so hot in it, I didn't want you bundling up in a heavy coat."

Warmth surged through her that had nothing to do with his jacket, now wrapped around her shoulders. His aftershave drifted around her, and she inhaled deeply. "Thanks. It wasn't this cold last night."

"Erie weather. The only predictable thing about it is it's unpredictable." Dylan guided her through the parking lot to his car. She waited for him to open the door for her, but he went right to the driver's side and climbed in. With a mental shake—this wasn't Texas, after all, and manners were different here—she eased herself into the bucket seat, straightening her skirt along her thighs. She caught Dylan watching, and offered him a smile. "I had a good time tonight."

"Me, too."

"You know, if you're fixin' to kiss me good-night, you should probably do it now. My dad will be watching when we get to my house."

Dylan let the keys swing in the ignition, and he turned to face her. "Do you want me to kiss you good-night?"

"Well, yes. But, um, only if you want to."

He grinned. "I want to. But you know, your father threatened to break my hands if I touched you."

"Then I guess you'll have to keep your *hands* to yourself." Brook shifted closer to him. In the glow of the parking-lot light, she couldn't make out the emotion on his face. Had she freaked him out? She wanted him to like her.

He closed his fingers on the collar of his jacket and

drew her closer still. "Okay, I'm not touching you. I'm touching my jacket." Then he lowered his head toward her.

Brook closed her eyes, her heart pounding.

As kisses went, it was pretty good—not too sloppy, not too hard. He seemed willing to take his time. A little while later, his tongue probed her lips, and she widened her mouth to let him in. Wanting to impress him, she used a few of the kissing tricks Brian had taught her, like skimming the insides of his teeth with the tip of her tongue, and tickling the roof of his mouth.

With a groan, he pulled away. "Damn. You are one hot Texas tamale, you know that?" He started the car. "I'd better get you home. Wouldn't do to break your curfew on our first date. I want your dad to like me."

Hot Texas tamale. Brook bit back a huge grin. She liked that. "Does that mean there's going to be a second date?"

"Oh, hell yeah, baby. Second and more."

Score! Finally, a new boyfriend. Let Brian keep little Miss Heather. Dylan Burch, senior and star athlete, made Brian look like a Little Leaguer. She'd hit the big time now.

CHAPTER SIX

STILL SMILING politely at the junior partner from her mother's firm, Jenna watched out of the corner of her eye as her father slipped from the living room. The Thanksgiving feast her mother had organized was vastly different than the ones they'd had in the past, when Gram was in charge. Lawyers, lawyers everywhere, and not a safe haven in sight. So where was her father escaping to?

The fringe from her sleeve swayed as Jenna raised her glass of champagne. "Mr. Dumont, please excuse me." He nodded, and Jenna left the room, following the hallway across the house. The door to her father's study clicked shut just as she rounded the corner. She rapped once on it, then went in. "Dad?"

The burgundy leather chair behind his desk creaked as he lowered himself into it. "Jenna. Looks like you caught me sneaking off. Be a dear and pour me a glass of brandy, will you?"

"Sure." She lifted the heavy crystal decanter from the mahogany bar on the side of the room. "You couldn't take it anymore either, huh?"

"The social graces are all part of the game, my dear. And we all do what needs to be done."

Jenna set the glass on the blotter in front of him, plopped into the wing chair in front of the desk. "Doesn't mean we have to enjoy it though, right?"

"Indeed." He swigged back a belt of the brandy.

"Don't those people have families? And, if so, then why are they here?"

"They're playing the game, too."

"Great." Jenna lifted her champagne flute. "To the players. May they have some fun at some point in their pathetic lives."

"Jenna," her father chided. "That's not nice." He lifted his snifter. "I'd prefer to propose a toast to those not here to share this day with us."

"To Gram," Jenna agreed. "Who is rolling in her grave at Mother's hijacking of the family holiday for work-related politics."

"To Mom."

They both took a drink. Silence settled into the book-case-lined room. "If this isn't what you wanted to do for the holiday, Dad, why'd you let Mother do it?"

Her father swirled the amber liquid in the bottom of the glass. "Because for years your mother compromised and did what I wanted on the holidays. This year I didn't see any harm in letting her plan it how she wanted. That's what marriage is all about, Jenna. Compromise."

"Huh. That must be why I'm not married. I'm no good at compromise, especially when it means I have to have a holiday with a bunch of nonfamily members. A snore-fest of PC chitchat. For crying out loud, Dad, we didn't even have a turkey, we had individual capons. Ugh."

Dad smiled. "I thought they were quite tasty myself."

"Thanksgiving is turkey. And family."

"Well, here we are. Family. Hiding out in my office. And if your mother catches us…"

"There will be hell to pay." Jenna smiled back at him. "But, as always, she'll get over it." She eyed her father as he finished his brandy. "Dad? Gram once told me that you wanted to be a prosecutor when you started law school. Instead, here you are, with a very successful practice built by defending white-collar criminals. That's quite a difference. So, I just want to know why."

He raised his hand, gestured around the room. "Look around you, Jenna. You don't live this kind of life on a prosecutor's salary. I wanted to give my family everything I could."

"Wanted to give Mother everything, you mean. I certainly don't need—never needed—all these trappings."

"Again, dear, sometimes in life we make compromises, even with ourselves."

"Have you ever considered the cost of those compromises, Dad?"

He shook his head. "I've never asked myself that."

"Well, maybe you should."

He pushed back from the desk. As he passed her, he pressed a quick kiss to the top of her head. "A good defense lawyer learns immediately that some questions are better left unasked. Don't stay here much longer, or your mother will come looking for you." The tread of his shoes against the hardwood floor stopped at the doorway. "I think the idea of just the three of us, alone at a table, terrifies your mother. That's why she invited twenty-five other people to share the holiday with us."

"Oh, nice parting shot, Dad," she called after him. Now she had guilt for not enjoying her mother's version of Thanksgiving. Her mother, terrified? Of her? The concept baffled Jenna. Her mother swam with sharks on a daily basis and feared nothing—except, maybe, letting her hair down.

Jenna made her way back to the gathering in the living and dining rooms, making small talk, earning approving looks from both parental units. But after about another forty-five minutes, she knew she had to cut and run or end up doing something outrageous that would scandalize her mother, like tap-dancing on the parquet floor in the foyer, or gathering a group around the baby grand and plinking out "Heart and Soul" with two fingers.

After collecting her purse and coat, and taking her leave from her parents—a process delayed by her mother wanting her to talk to Judge Andrews—Jenna settled into the seat of her car with relief. She exchanged her heels for driving mocs, and let the engine warm for a few minutes while she checked her cell phone for messages. The usual happy-holiday wishes from friends could wait until later to be returned. But one surprised her. Sloan.

She wasn't sure how to define their relationship. They'd mainly been very casual in their contact since their "date," with a few stolen moments of some very hot necking. Very frustrating necking when he kept backing off. She wished the man would either just give in to the impulse and take her to bed, or cut bait. Still, she hadn't expected to hear from him today.

She tucked her phone earpiece into position and dialed his cell before pulling from her parents' circular driveway.

"Happy Thanksgiving," he answered.

In the background, Jenna heard shrieks of laughter.

"Girls, don't run in the house. Something could break, and it might be one of you," Sloan said.

"Sounds like your holiday is a lot more exciting than mine's been."

"I wondered what you were doing today. We're at my sister's house, down near Cranberry."

"Hey, I'll be driving by there in a little bit. I spent the day with my parents in Pittsburgh."

"Then you should stop by."

"Holidays are for family, Tex."

"Around here we say the more, the merrier."

"I suppose that's true only if you invite more merry people." Not staid guests.

"Merry is the perfect word for you. So, you'll stop?"

After a few more protests, she caved. Why not? She scribbled his explicit directions on the back of an old bank envelope in her purse. Without a hitch, she found her way unerringly from Route 79 to the white Victorian house with cars spilling out of the short driveway. She parked down the street, then put her black heels back on, eyeing the mocs with longing.

Sloan answered the door. "Come on in."

"I feel horrible, showing up empty-handed. That's a cardinal sin, but no stores were open."

"Forget it. We've got more than enough food to feed a platoon. Come and meet everyone."

As Sloan led her from the foyer, Jenna waved to Brook. The teen was perched on the upper level of the staircase, a cell phone plastered to her ear. She returned the wave with a big grin, pointing at the phone. "Tell Dylan I said hi," Jenna called up. The girl's smile widened. Sloan groaned in front of Jenna but stopped before entering the dining room.

"Everyone, meet Jenna, my neighbor from Erie. Jenna, meet everyone."

"Oh, so you're Jenna," said a woman carrying a pumpkin pie into the room. "The woman who finally convinced my brother to get off his butt and go out. Well done."

"Put a sock in it, squirt," Sloan said. "That's my baby sister, Rachel," he told Jenna.

"I never would have guessed," Jenna replied. Actually, that wasn't true—the siblings had the same bright blue eyes. Everyone laughed.

He led her through the house, introducing her to others in the kitchen, and some men in the family room watching a football game. Although the group consisted of a mixture of family and friends, the warmth and the camaraderie were exactly what she'd missed at her parents'. "Do you think your sister would mind if I kicked off my shoes?" she asked Sloan when they'd completed their rounds.

He shook his head. "Make yourself at home."

She smiled. "Sounds good to me."

Several hours and two slices of pie later, she'd played Twister with the younger girls, refereed an arm-wrestling contest between Sloan's father and a family friend named Jerry, and helped her team achieve victory in the charades tournament played in the breakfast nook. So it was with some reluctance that she announced her departure. Rachel pressed her to take some leftover pie with her.

Sloan held her coat as she slid back into her shoes. "I'll walk you out."

"I'd be disappointed if you didn't, Tex." She winked at him. Outside on the top step, he reached for her hand, and she entwined her fingers with his, enjoying the warmth. They walked down the sidewalk in silence, the glow from the streetlights illuminating the path. At her car, she set her bags on the hood and turned to face him. "I had fun. Thanks."

"Anytime."

She stared at him for a few moments. "Tex? What exactly are we doing here?"

"Saying good-night?"

"You know what I mean." She reached up, brushed back the errant lock of hair from his forehead.

"For the life of me, Jenna, I honestly don't know."

JENNA SMOOTHED the hem of the satin kimono over her stocking-clad thighs. Fortunately, the two pieces of pumpkin pie she'd indulged in last night at Sloan's sister's house hadn't made their presence known here— yet. The red FM shoes pinched the balls of her feet, but if they did their job, it would be worth it.

Tonight would determine whether Jenna and Sloan were going anywhere at all. If he could resist this plan, there was no hope and she'd have to forget about him, despite the sparks.

Candles flickered on the table set for two, and elsewhere in the apartment. The drapes were drawn. The meal she'd prepared waited. Princess was ensconced in Jenna's huge walk-in closet with her bed and a bone, so she'd be out from underfoot for the evening.

Now if only the guest of honor would arrive, the seduction could begin. When the door buzzer rang she jumped. The little security monitor Sloan had installed gave her visual confirmation—her prey awaited. "About time, Tex. I was starting to think you'd stood me up," she said into the intercom.

He held up a bottle of wine in one hand and a bundle of flowers in the other. "I'm sorry, and I have the gifts to prove it. It never fails that something breaks down right before I'm ready to leave work, especially when I have a hot date with a beautiful woman lined up."

"Well, if you're bearing gifts and compliments, I suppose I should let you in. Just come on in the apartment—the inside door's open."

She buzzed the door release, then hustled into the bathroom for a last check of her hair and a quick retouch of her lipstick. Besides, she didn't want to appear too keen.

She took a good look at her reflection and laughed. Yeah, right. Fat chance he wouldn't peg her as overeager the second he laid eyes on her.

Sloan let himself in, dropped the flowers on the island and poked under the cover of one of the dishes. The aroma of something spicy—curry?—wafted out. It didn't look too much the worse for wear, given his tardiness. And the leftover pumpkin pie Rachel had forced on Jenna last night sat nearby, answering the question of what was for dessert.

"Jenna?" he called. "Where'd you vanish to?"

The door to the bathroom opened. "I'm right here."

He turned, and all thoughts of dinner vanished. Jenna wore a fiery red satin kimono that barely reached her thighs. Black stockings blazed a shimmery trail down to a pair of red spiky shoes that gave her calves additional curve. He unglued his tongue from the roof of his mouth to stammer, "What are you wearing underneath that getup?"

A sultry laugh snapped his attention upward. She gave him a saucy wink, reaching for the belt. "I'll be happy to give you a peek, but only if you say the magic word…" She toyed with the ends of the tie at her waist.

He swallowed hard. "P-please?"

She shook her head. "Dessert, Tex. No peeking until you promise me that tonight, you're going to take the plunge, be impulsive, and finally eat dessert. First."

Knowing she didn't mean the pie, he nodded, struck dumb by the fact that his entire blood supply had already rushed south of his belt line.

When she dropped the kimono into a puddle of fabric at her feet, he groaned. A pair of barely there black lace panties. A matching push-up bra that did amazing things to her cleavage. And, best of all, a black garter belt with real, honest-to-God stockings, the kind he'd often fantasized about but never had the pleasure to encounter in reality.

"Well?"

"I've died and gone to heaven," he managed to get out.

Her throaty amusement shot straight to his crotch and caused his erection to swell even harder. She shook her head. "You've got it all wrong, Tex. No angels here tonight." She crooked a finger at him.

Without conscious thought, he moved in her direction, a sailor caught in the call of a beautiful siren. He stopped just short of her, drinking her in in ten-gallon gulps. Candlelight flickered over her, illuminating her porcelain skin with a warm glow. His hands trembled, but he fisted them, held them at his sides.

"What's wrong?"

"You're scarin' the hell outta me, sugar. I wanted this to be so perfect for you, and I'm terrified that once I touch you, I'm not gonna be able to stop."

"That's the idea." She closed the gap between them, reaching up to caress the back of his neck. She pressed her lips to his mouth and her lingerie-covered body to his at the same time, and the last remnants of clear thought fled. He gripped her hair in his hands, ravished her mouth like a starving man presented with a feast. The weeks of restraint snapped like an ancient, frayed wire.

He nudged her against the wall, fitting his form to hers. She arched her spine, driving her hips forward, brushing those black lace panties over the ridge in his jeans. She smelled of roses and tasted like tequila and lime. He plundered deeper, needing more. He palmed her breast, and she encouraged him with a groan that vibrated through his mouth. He brushed his thumb over the peak and she sighed, melting into him. "Yes," she whispered, grinding her hips forward again.

He obliged her, thrusting his erection against her, loving the way she moaned and moved. She reached up, pulling the cups of her bra beneath her breasts, then she arched again, offering them. He groaned, immediately lowering his head to accept her invitation. He drew his tongue across the nipple, making it tighten.

Jenna shuddered. "Yes, Sloan. More."

He lost himself completely then. Somehow her panties were removed, and she fumbled with the snap and zipper of his jeans. He shoved them down just far enough to free his erection. He inhaled sharply when she rubbed against him. "So wet."

"Yes, for you. Sloan, I need you."

He reached for his wallet. "Condom, wait—"

"No!" She brushed against him again, bare skin to bare skin. "I'm using the birth-control patch and I swear, I'm STD free. Tested and clean. I feel pretty safe with you as far that goes, too. Am I right?"

He gasped as she fisted him, stroking slowly down, then back up again. When he could manage speech again, he said, "Shoot, it's been so long since I had sex, the only STD I could possibly have is lackanookie."

She laughed, the warm sound reaching deep into his soul. "We're gonna take care of that right now." Hiking her knee over his hip, she took him inside her body with one easy move.

Her tight heat fried every circuit in his brain.

He pulled back, then pistoned into her. "Oh, sugar." She felt so good, so right.

She gripped his shoulders. "Yes. Harder."

The picture just over her head bounced in time with his tempo, her body pressed against the wall with every thrust. She clawed at his skin, crying out his name, demanding more and more until she shuddered around him, keening her pleasure in an unabashed way that triggered his own orgasm. "Jenna," he murmured, body shaking with the exertion. His knees trembled, and he took her down to the floor with him, spent. Their ragged breathing eventually slowed as they lay on the rug.

The full impact of what they'd just done hit him about a minute later—once his brain came back online.

So much for his fabulous restraint. So much for making it a slow, wonderful experience where she'd feel cherished. Hell, no, he'd done her standing up against a wall like a ten-dollar whore. "Jenna, hon, I'm sorry."

A sharp pain in his shoulder made him yelp. He grabbed the spot, rubbing it. "Hey! Why did you bite me?"

"Because. That may very well have been the most amazing sex of my life, and you're sorry for it?"

"Well, it's not exactly what I had in mind for our first time." Her words sank in. "Most amazing sex of your life, huh?"

"Don't let it go to your head." Her fingertips danced

down his chest, found the opening of his jeans. "Well, maybe this one."

"I thought it was pretty amazing, too." Joy filled him, so intense it scared him. She made him happy. Not happy-content, but happy-giddy. Like he could and should dance at a bowling alley. In front of people. And he wasn't quite sure how that fit in with the rest of his life. Giddy seemed so…irresponsible.

Not the right thing.

But her hand was making a particular part of him happy again, too. He cleared his throat. "So, how does a Texan measure up?"

"Well, I can't speak for all Texans, mind you, but so far, I'd say that this particular Texan measures up just fine."

"Fine? Is that all?" He flipped her onto her back, propped himself on his elbows over her.

"What?" she asked warily.

"The girls are with my sister for the weekend. How'd you like me to prove Texan stamina?"

"Ooh. Yeah. Prove it."

BY MIDNIGHT, the votive candles in the metal room divider that created the fourth "wall" of her bedroom space had burned to stubs but still cast flickers of light. Jenna resisted the urge to touch Sloan's face, to brush aside that stray lock of hair as he slept. Turned out that though Texan stamina was damned impressive, she'd still worn the poor man out. He'd proved to be well worth the wait. He'd spent several hours exploring every inch of her body. She shifted, limbs still languid from their lovemaking, although she wasn't ready to settle into sleep. Generally, she didn't let men stay over.

And she wasn't quite sure what to make of the fact that she was so willing to make an exception for Sloan.

She slipped from the bed, drew her robe over her shoulders and padded out to the kitchen. After a quick drink, she eased aside the sliding door's curtains. The shadows of bare tree branches shifted on her deck and the twinkle of snowflakes sparkled in the streetlight's glow.

Jenna opened the door just an inch, inhaling the sharp scent of cold, the first snow of the season. Not that it really counted as snow. Just flurries. She jumped when Sloan brushed his mouth over the curve of her neck.

"Hey. I missed you when I woke up and found you gone." Naked from the waist up, he shivered against her. "Brrr. Why do you have the door open?"

"Because it's beautiful. Can you smell the air? It's invigorating."

"No, you're invigorating."

She slid the door closed, then turned to face him, snuggling into his embrace. A buzz against her hip made her back up and look at him curiously as he cursed, then pulled his cell phone from his pocket. His eyes widened when he looked at the caller ID, and he flipped it open. "Rae? What's up?" He went quiet, listening intently, then he began to pace. "Did you ask Ashley? Sometimes she hears things she's not supposed to." He shoved the lock of hair from his forehead and sighed. "All right, I'll be there as soon as I can. Tell Ashley it's going to be fine, and no, she's not in trouble." He crammed the phone back into the little corner pocket of his jeans.

"Something wrong?" Jenna asked.

"Yeah." He retrieved his shirt from the floor near the sofa. "Seems that Brook has vanished from my sister's house." He bent to pick up a sock from underneath the coffee table.

"Oh, Sloan! Where do you think she is?"

"Well, Ashley said she thinks Brook had her boyfriend meeting her down there. Something about going into Pittsburgh tonight for some action." He glanced around the living room. "Have you seen my other sock?"

Jenna took it from the entertainment center's top shelf. He just shook his head. "How did that get there? Never mind." He finished getting dressed.

"Do you want me to go with you? I know Pittsburgh."

"No, thanks. I'm betting she'll be back in a few more hours. I plan on being there to catch her as she comes creeping in. Poor Rae was frantic."

"Don't be too hard on Brook, Sloan. She's just a kid. Surely you snuck out of the house more than once?"

His eyes narrowed. "What I did doesn't matter. And the point is that she's just a kid. She shouldn't be pulling this crap for a few more years at least."

"Maybe if you eased up on her a bit, she wouldn't have to go to such extremes."

"Jenna, I appreciate that you mean well. But I think I know how to handle my daughter. She needs strict rules and guidelines. And consequences when she breaks them."

"Maybe what she needs is a little bit of understanding. Did you know that Brook has incredible drawing talent?"

As he shrugged into his jacket, he looked at her as though she'd lost her mind. "What the hell does that have to do with this?"

"Never mind. Forget I said anything." Far be it from her to give anyone parenting advice. She leaned in, gave him a quick kiss on the cheek. "Thanks for the flowers, Tex. And dessert."

Pink flushed his cheeks. "Yeah. Really, it was amazing, Jenna, but—"

"No buts, Tex. No regrets. It was what it was, and let's keep it that way, huh? This is a dessert-only relationship—no heavy steak and potatoes. Keep it light, keep it fun."

He nodded. "Okay. Thanks."

As she closed the door behind him, Jenna couldn't help but think about Brook. Sloan was a good father, much like her own, but he also didn't get his daughter. It was as if they lived in the same space but hadn't connected at all.

And it was pretty sad that she was worrying about her lover's kid. But Brook reminded her of herself at the same age. Desperate for attention and love and willing to do some pretty stupid things in the pursuit of them. Luckily for Jenna she'd had Gram. And Dad hadn't been too bad. More understanding than Mother, anyway.

Too bad poor Brook didn't have a Gram-type person in her life. Sloan wasn't going to listen to Jenna's opinions on the subject.

"STOP HERE." Brook pointed to the curb about two blocks from her aunt's house. "I'd rather not take any chances."

"I'm not dropping you this far from the house. It's two-twenty in the morning. Who knows what kind of weirdos could be out and about?" Dylan moved one hand from the wheel to her leg, giving it a teasing caress through the denim.

A snort came from the back seat. "Weirdos like us, you mean?" asked Nick Garcia, one of Dylan's track teammates and his best hanging-buddy.

Kelly laughed. "We're not weirdos, you moron. Dylan meant psycho-killers, not a bunch of good-timers on their way home from Dave & Buster's."

Dave & Buster's had been a blast. An enormous video arcade for fun-lovers of all ages, along with a res-taurant and bar—not that any of them had pushed their luck by trying to get served—the place was fantastic for dates. They'd wanted to get down to Pittsburgh to try it out forever, but Brook had known there was no way in hell Dad would let her go all the way to Pittsburgh with Dylan and a bunch of other kids. So they'd made plans around her trip to Aunt Rae's. Dylan and the others had gone ahead to the action, and when the coast was clear, Brook had called Dylan's cell, and he'd picked her up.

More sounds drifted from behind her. Slurpy make-out sounds. Kurt and Amy, the other couple squashed into the back seat, couldn't keep their hands off each other, not even when other people were around.

Dylan stopped within eyesight of Aunt Rae and Uncle James's house. He pulled her into his arms, gave her a deep, long kiss that drew hoots of approval from Nick and Kelly. Dylan shot a quick glare over the seat. "Shut up." Then he returned his attention to Brook, leaning his forehead against hers. "I'm glad we did this. Although next time we're doing something *alone*."

Brook's cheeks warmed at his hint of how far their relationship had gone. He'd sweet-talked and seduced her out of her virginity. And though the first time hadn't been very good, she was starting to get the hang of it. "I'd like that. Thanks for tonight. I had fun."

"Me, too." He brushed his lips across hers one more time. "Night."

Brook pulled her coat tighter as she slipped out into the cold morning. A boatload of stars twinkled in the clear skies. She hustled up the sidewalk and climbed the front porch steps, breathing with relief when the doorknob turned in her hand. She'd left it unlocked, but worried that someone might check the door after she'd left. Inside, she slipped out of her shoes, nudging them under a table in the darkened foyer. She crept to the stairs and gripped the banister. When she was halfway up, the overhead chandelier burst into light. She blinked hard, then turned.

Her father, arms folded across his chest, lounged in the opening to Uncle James's office. Her backpack lay at his feet.

Shit. Busted.

"Nothing to say for yourself?" he asked.

She lifted her shoulders.

"Get down here."

With an exaggerated sigh, she descended the carpeted steps, leaning on the post at the bottom.

"No. Over here." He pointed to a spot right in front of him.

"Like you can't yell at me from there?" She moseyed across the wooden floor.

"Yell? I don't yell."

"Lecture, then."

"I just want answers. Where the hell have you been?"

"Out."

"Obviously. Where? And with who?"

"I was with some friends. We went to a game arcade."

"A game arcade? You expect me to buy that?"

Brook rummaged in her purse, pulling out her gaming card. She waved the plastic rectangle. "See this? It still has credits on it. And all my prize points, too."

The lights clicked on upstairs, and Uncle James appeared at the upper railing. "Thank God, she's home safe!"

A small surge of joy that someone cared about her faded quickly. Why couldn't that have been Dad's first response?

"Yeah. She's safe. And she'll be safe for quite a while, since she won't be leaving the house except to go to school or work."

"I'm grounded?"

"You're grounded all right."

"Until when?"

"Until I say otherwise." Her father grabbed his

leather jacket from a coat tree near the door. "Tell Rachel I'll talk to her tomorrow," he called up quietly to Uncle James. "I'm sorry for all this."

Uncle James shrugged. "Kids. What made us think being parents would be easy, huh? It's even harder to do by yourself. Give yourself a break."

Give me *a break.* Brook grabbed the backpack her father thrust at her and jumped back into her shoes. When he thundered out onto the porch, she called after him, "What about Ashley? Isn't she going home, too?"

"I see no reason to ruin the rest of your sister's weekend just because you can't behave." He didn't bother to look back at her, just kept going. "Aunt Rachel will bring her home on Sunday, just like we planned."

Brook scurried after him, following him down the sidewalk of the little town for about a block and a half—in the opposite direction she'd come with Dylan. Obviously the old man knew a thing or two about keeping secrets, too.

Sloan shoved his hands deep into his pockets, focused on reaching the truck without disturbing the peaceful slumber of his sister's neighbors. Without yelling at his daughter.

Once the wheels were rolling north again, he remained silent. Finally, he couldn't stand not knowing any longer. "You were with Dylan, weren't you? Did he drive all the way down here?"

"Yes."

"Your grounding includes him, Brook. You are grounded to the house and you are not to see that boy again. I can't believe he encouraged you to sneak out of the house. Your Aunt Rachel was worried sick. So was your uncle."

"Yeah, he's not even really related to me, but at least his first thought was to be glad I was safe!" Brook turned away, directing her gaze out the window. "Not like you!"

"Good grief, Brook. Of course I'm glad you're safe. Why the hell do you think I worry about you all the time?"

"Because you're afraid I'm going to screw up and make you look bad."

The kernel of truth in her statement embedded itself deep in his gut. "Well, maybe some. Not so much about looking bad, but I do worry about you making the wrong choices. Your track record isn't all that great, you know. I take all my jobs seriously, and being your father is the most important job I have. I want to do it right, but you sure don't make it easy for me."

"Whatever."

"You could help, you know. You could try doing the right thing for a change." He gripped the steering wheel harder. "Pick better people to hang out with. Did the rest of those kids' parents know where they were tonight?"

"Yeah, they did. They actually let their kids have some fun every now and then."

He shook his head. What kind of parent in their right mind let a bunch of kids drive from Erie to Pittsburgh on a Friday night? "Just remember what I said about the grounding and that boy."

"His name is Dylan. And maybe you oughta brush

up on your reading, Dad. It's hard to keep people who love each other apart. Remember Romeo and Juliet?"

"Is that some kind of threat, Brook? First of all, you're fifteen. Fifteen-year-olds think they know what love is, but they don't. And secondly, Romeo and Juliet ended up dead for no good reason. If they'd paid better attention, it wouldn't have ended tragically. But no, they were impulsive teenagers who didn't listen to their parents and so they ended up dead. Stop being melodramatic."

"I'm not the one being melodramatic," she muttered.

Sloan cracked the window open to change the air. The rush of cold smacked him in the face like Brook's words. She didn't really mean anything by the Romeo and Juliet crack, did she? Nah.

Jenna's comment about Brook needing some understanding echoed through his head. She'd tried to tell him something, but what? As far as he was concerned, all this understanding crap was for the birds. His brother-in-law's psychobabble amounted to a big waste of time.

Structure and rules. Discipline. That was what Brook needed.

And what he needed, besides a handful of aspirin to quell the pounding in his head, was another heaping dose of Jenna. Her warmth had the power to cure what ailed him.

Even if their impulsive relationship wasn't exactly the right thing.

CHAPTER SEVEN

A WEEK LATER Brook giggled as she ushered Dylan in through the back door. "If my father knew this, he'd go nuts."

Dylan glanced around the kitchen. "Y-you're sure he's not going to come home early or anything?"

"I'm sure. He just called to say he'll probably be late because something or other broke and he has to fix it. My bratty little sister is at a birthday party, so we have the house to ourselves." No way she was letting her father rule her life. She needed to see Dylan. He made her feel special. Loved. Stealing moments with him near his locker at school wasn't enough. Nick had dropped Dylan off two blocks away, then he'd hiked over to the house.

"You want something to eat?"

He stalked her, pressing her back against the kitchen counter. "Yeah. You." She laughed as he buried his face in her neck, nuzzling, tickling her shoulder.

Her breathing changed when he switched gears, kissing and licking the skin around her collarbone. Then he worked his way back up to her mouth, kissing her like he could never get enough. After that, he went back to her neck, concentrating on the spot where her pulse thundered. "Oh, Dylan," she murmured. "That feels so good."

"I know something that feels even better." He lifted his head to grin at her. "What better way to stick it to your dad? Let's do it in your bed. Or maybe his." Dylan laughed.

"I—I don't know…"

"Come on. You just said he wouldn't be home soon, not even at the regular time. I won't be here when he gets back, I swear." His eyes widened, and he cocked his head. "I thought you said you loved me?"

"Oh, don't give me that crap." She smacked his shoulder. "I do and you know it."

"Then come on. Don't live like the old man wants you to, all rules and no fun." His fingers slid down her side, stroked her hip. "I can make it fun for you." He waggled his eyebrows.

How could she resist him? "Okay. But if my dad catches you in bed with me, he'll kill us both. Just so you know."

"I'll chance it. You're worth it, my little hot Texas tamale."

He really cared about her. Enough to risk her father's wrath. With a broad smile, Brook took his hand and led him upstairs.

"THIS IS JUST SO WRONG," Sloan said, rolling over in the bed, throwing his arm over his face.

"Jeez, thanks for the self-esteem boost," Jenna said. "I had no idea sleeping with me was so awful."

"Oh, no, sugar, that's not what I meant." He forced himself to shift onto his side, propping his head on the heel of his palm. "You're wonderful. Addictive even. I was talking about the fact that I lied to Brook and ditched work early so I could spend time right here, in your bed. With your hot, sexy self." He trailed his fingertips along her arm, making the hair on it stand up. "If that's not proof I'm addicted, I don't know what is."

He'd even gone to the extreme of having her pick him up at the station so his truck wasn't in front of her place, where Brook was likely to see it. God, he was a disaster. One taste of her, one night in her bed, and it hadn't been enough. Now he was manufacturing ways for them to be together.

"There are worse things you could be addicted to." Her green eyes lit up, and he could barely breathe, she made him feel so damn good. "I'm low-carb and low-calorie. I have no dangerous additives like nicotine or tar. And I'm not likely to leave you with a hangover."

"Oh, you're wrong about that." He shifted closer, fitting his pelvis against her hip. "I can get drunk on you, no problem." He leaned down, nuzzled her hair, inhaling deeply. Today she smelled like coconut and other tropical scents. Things that made him forget it was heading for Christmas, making him picture the two of them alone on a deserted beach instead. "And you're definitely dangerous. The fact that I'm here right now, and the things I've done to be here, prove it. "

She reached up, caressed his cheek. "I think it's pretty neat you want to be with me that much."

"Neat, huh?" He murmured right next to her ear, causing her to squirm. She was sensitive to certain tones, an interesting fact he'd discovered last week. A low-pitched hum had her laughing in earnest.

"Stop! Stop! Ack! No fair!" She shoved at him.

He backed away to watch her. As she settled down, she looked up at him, her pleasure in him shining clear.

"You should come with a warning label," he said. "But any man with half a brain would ignore it, anyway." Leaning over, he brushed his lips over hers. "Breathe with me." He sealed his mouth over hers, captured her exhale as though he could inhale her spark, her very essence. Then he returned it to her.

Damn. Unlike a lot of men, he'd never been very good at doing the casual sex thing—one of the reasons he hadn't had sex in so long. And he was already in serious trouble with Jenna. *Lighten up.*

"Eat dessert first," he whispered.

She nodded. "Right."

He yanked the blue satin sheet from her naked body. "The question is, where to start?" He let his gaze travel the length of her, lingering on all the erogenous zones. By the time he returned his attention to her face, it was pink, and she shifted minutely.

Jenna tried to hold still beneath his frank appraisal, but when he licked his lips, she couldn't stop the low moan that rumbled deep in her throat. She arched her back just a bit, an invitation she hoped he wouldn't ignore.

"Maybe I should start here." He lifted her hand, turned it over, kissed her palm.

"You're going to torture me, aren't you?"

A slow grin curved his mouth, which he then pressed to her wrist in response.

Delightfully agonizing minutes passed before he worked his way to her shoulder, then down around her breasts. He teased the sides of them, licked the center of her chest, but never touched the now-peaked nipples that screamed for his attention. With an evil wink, he continued kissing down her belly, pausing over the sapphire-colored stone nestled in her navel. "This—" he flicked it with his tongue "—this is so damn sexy on you."

Then he continued onward, nipping at her hip, spending an eternity on her thighs. She moaned her disappointment when he moved lower and kissed her bony kneecap. And the man was heartless enough to ask, "Something you needed?"

She nodded as he trailed his tongue down her calf.

"What?"

"You missed all the good spots." A playful pout twisted her lips.

"I was saving those for later. Trying to get you good and primed." He slid a finger up the bottom of her foot, and she squealed, drawing it back. Then he straddled her ankles and crept up her body, caressing her with the skin of his chest.

She gasped when he brushed over the juncture of her thighs. Moving a little higher, he paused, staring at her breasts, his hot breath tantalizing. He lifted his head to look into her eyes. Shifting his weight onto his palms, he used his knee to spread her legs, then dragged his body higher, settling his erection in just the right spot. "So, are you good and primed?"

"Oh, yeah," she whispered.

When he took her breast into his mouth, she grabbed the sheets. He sucked and pulled, and she bucked beneath him. "Sloan, please."

"Such pretty manners, sugar." Just the tip of him eased into her.

She groaned, shifting beneath him, desperate for more. "Sloan!"

"Yes?" With a slow stroke she thought he'd never complete, he moved forward, burying himself in her bit by bit.

"Mmm." She raised her hips to meet him, sinking him to the hilt. "Better. Much better."

So he pulled back. And no matter how much she moved beneath him, no matter how she begged and pleaded, he refused to be hurried, setting a pace so languid, loving her so long she thought she'd lose every last scrap of her sanity. And when he finally brought her to the top, the orgasm made her shake and sob, calling his name.

Only then did he let go of the control he prized so much, quickening his pace. When he stiffened above her, he buried his face in the crook of her neck, murmuring, "Jenna, Jenna."

Spent, he relaxed, and his weight pressed on her. As if he realized it, he rolled to the side, pulling her with him, cradling her in his arms. "Amazing," he whispered, eyes still closed. "Completely amazing."

She stroked his face. "Still think it's wrong?"

His lashes fluttered open. "Without a doubt, sugar. It's wrong. I have guilt over lying to my kid and ditching work early. On the other hand, it's so damn right I don't know if you're an addiction I'm going to be able to break anytime soon."

"Why would you want to?" As long as he kept her as an addiction, they were both safe. Sex as an addiction between them was light. Nothing serious. Not a relationship.

They were friends. And incredible lovers. Nothing wrong with that, despite his guilt. Despite his kids.

"Why indeed?"

CHAPTER EIGHT

CHRISTMAS CHAOS REIGNED in Sloan's house. Molly and Ashley were in the living room near the tree, playing holiday music too loudly on the small boombox Ashley had gotten from Brook, so she'd "leave my stereo alone."

Jamey, clad in a black-and-red velvet suit with a tiny bow tie Sloan had given Rae hell over—poor kid—sat on the floor, tossing the crumpled gift wrap around while the expensive, batteries-not-included push toy his grandfather had bought lingered nearby, currently untouched and unappreciated.

Rachel and James were snuggled up on the couch, watching their son with bemused expressions. The old man was in the kitchen, whipping up another batch of his special eggnog. And though Brook hadn't eaten much and had scrammed back upstairs at the earliest possible moment—and, claiming illness, had stayed there, despite his and Rae's numerous attempts to bring her back into the festivities—all in all, it had been a wonderful Christmas.

In fact, it was the best one he could remember in a long time. No holiday madness at an airport in order to be with his family, no being home alone with just the girls.

So why did he have the distinct impression that something was missing?

The bottom stair creaked as he eased his weight onto it.

"Hey. Where are you going?" Rachel called.

"I'll be right back."

"Okay. Dad's eggnog will be ready soon, and you wouldn't want to miss that."

"Definitely not." Upstairs in his room, he pulled back the curtain, peered across the way. Her car sat in the parking lot, the three inches of fresh snow that had fallen for Christmas disguising the color she called Fusion Orange, and he called ugly. Damn it. She hadn't left her place at all today. Which meant she'd spent the holiday alone despite his invitation to join his family. He grabbed the phone, hit four on the speed dial.

It rang until the answering machine clicked on. He waited for the tone. "Jenna? I know you're there. Pick up." When she didn't, he hung up and dialed again.

And again.

On the third try, she answered, voice nasally. "I'll give you one thing, Tex, you're persistent. What can I do for you?"

"You can get your cute little butt over here and have some of my dad's special eggnog."

"That's sweet, Sloan, really, but I told you last night I wasn't up for Christmas with anyone."

"You know, I never would have guessed you were a Grinch. In fact, most of the time you're the farthest thing from it. So what gives?"

A long silence followed. Then she said, "I'm just not up for holiday cheer, Sloan. And I'm not up to facing your family right now. We don't have that kind of a relationship, remember? Dessert only."

"You had pumpkin pie at Rachel's on Thanksgiving. That was dessert, a holiday, and my family."

"Because I was on my way home from my parents' house and had to go right past her house. No, Sloan. I'm sorry." The phone clicked as the line disconnected, leaving him staring out the window at her place, listening to nothing.

He replaced the handset in the cradle. On his way back downstairs, he paused at Brook's room. The door was open just a crack and he peered in. Wrapped in a fleece blanket, she slept. He crept in, laid his palm on her forehead. No fever. She stirred, and he pulled back his hand. The distance between them had widened again, and he wasn't sure how to fix it. Some days being a father made neurosurgery look easy by comparison.

On the first floor, he passed through the noisy living room without a word to anyone. In the kitchen, he gathered a few items from the cabinet, then ducked into the dining room. He ladled some eggnog from the punch bowl into a sports bottle. Then he bagged a few chocolate-chip cookies and a couple of the green-iced trees Ashley had dusted with red sprinkles. For good measure he grabbed some of the Snickerdoodles he'd baked for Brook, even though the edges were a little on the over-brown side.

There. That covered the dessert angle.

"I have to go out," he announced to his family.

"Did something happen at the station, Daddy?" Ashley looked up from the board game she and Molly were now playing.

"No, Peach, nothing like that. I just need to go spread a little holiday cheer to someone who doesn't seem to have any. I won't be too long."

Rachel jumped from the sofa and followed him to the foyer. "You wouldn't happen to be going next door, would you? To see Jenna?"

"So what if I am, squirt?"

"Just asking. She seemed like a happy-go-lucky person when we met at Thanksgiving. Not the kind I figure to be lacking in holiday cheer. So maybe that's just a smokescreen for what you're really up to?" She waggled her eyebrows.

"I wish it were." He pulled on his boots. "Hold down the fort for me, okay?"

"Sure thing. Have fun." Rae gave him a smile and a wink.

Grumbling to himself about nosy kid sisters who never outgrew their butt-in-ski-ness, he trudged down the cleared sidewalk. The snowblower he'd bought himself for Christmas all the way back in November had proved to be the perfect gift—a necessity for life in Erie.

It took a little cajoling to get Jenna to let him in, but the cookies he promised did the trick. Princess met him at the door as usual, and he rumpled the dog's floppy ears. "How come *you* don't come to greet me like this?" he teased, shedding his wet boots and outer garments.

"Because you never scratch me behind my ears?" she answered from the couch.

"You don't like it when I mess with your ears."

"I don't like it when you *hum* in my ears," she corrected. "I don't mind some of the other things you do with them."

"Oh yeah? What things?" He poked through the kitchen cupboards, retrieving two round glasses. The eggnog just filled both of them. Clutching the bag of cookies under one glass, a few napkins under the other, he carried his offering to the coffee table in time to notice her shrug her shoulders.

"That's the best you can do?" A quick detour to the entertainment center let him flick on her stereo, tuning in a station playing Christmas music all day long.

She groaned. "Turn it off."

"Nope." He nudged her away from the corner of the sofa, claiming the spot she vacated. Then he pulled her into his arms, letting her settle with her back against his chest. He rested his chin on the top of her head. "Now, isn't this nice?"

"Mmm. I suppose."

"Such enthusiasm. I think you've damaged my ego."

"Sorry."

"And now you're giving me lip service, and not the kind I really enjoy." His concern level kicked higher when she didn't laugh or come back with a smart remark. "Jenna, what's wrong? Of all people, I expected you to be on the love-Christmas team, the kind that goes crazy with decorations and gifts and shopping." A small tree stood on top of her kitchen island, the cord for the lights dangling off the edge, unplugged. That was the only decoration in an apartment he'd watched change from floral summer decor to Halloween and Thanksgiving stuff all over the place.

"I don't want to talk about it."

"Okay." He just held her, waiting, knowing that most women couldn't resist talking about "it"—whatever "it" might be—eventually.

But he wasn't prepared when Elvis's version of "Blue Christmas" came on and she went board stiff in his arms, then yelled, "Turn it off! Off!" She clamped her hands over the sides of her head as he grabbed the stereo remote from the end table and stopped the music.

He lifted her onto his lap, cradling her against his shoulder until her trembling eased. "O-kay, now that really freaked me out. What in the hell is going on with you?"

"It's not the same this year," she whispered.

"Why not? Because your parents decided to go on that cruise? Is that why you're having a blue Christmas?" For the life of him, he couldn't imagine what possessed her parents to leave their only child alone at Christmas.

She shook her head against his chest. "Because of why they decided to go on that cruise."

"Why?"

A soft sniffle came from her. "It's not the same without Gram."

"Aw, sugar. Your grandma?" He tightened his arms around her. "Is this the first Christmas without her?"

Jenna nodded, lifting her head and wiping the sleeve of her sweater across her nose. "Last year was so different. The usual holiday fun with her. You never quite knew what she'd do next."

"Reminds me of someone I know."

She wanted to smile at that, but the tears swimming in her eyes wouldn't let her. "Yeah, I guess I take after her. No wonder, with all the time we spent together."

"The firsts after losing someone are always the hardest. First holidays, birthday, first anniversary of them passing. It gets a bit easier with time."

Jenna caught the inflection of experience in his voice. "I hope so. 'Cause this stinks."

"What happened?"

She clenched her teeth, trying not to melt into a mess of tears. "Christmas last year was fantastic. The day after, Gram and I hit the mall. She loved the crush of the crowd, the thrill of the bargain at the sales. We were there when the stores opened at the crack of dawn. By noon, our feet were killing us, and we were dragging an armful of bags." She paused, able to see Gram's animated face so clearly, every wisp of white-and-black hair, every wrinkle, each smile line.

She forced the lump in her throat aside, ignored the fact that her nose was clogging up again. "We went to her favorite restaurant for lunch. Gram had made a couple of comments about not feeling that great, but we'd both brushed it off. When the meal came, she praised it to the waiter, but didn't seem very hungry. She pushed it aside, ordered a hot-fudge sundae instead. We were talking about something—I don't even remember what—when her eyes got real big. She looked surprised." Tears rolled down her cheeks. That image would be one she'd never forget. The moment she'd learned to eat dessert first.

"Then what?" Sloan prompted, giving her a light squeeze.

"She—she keeled over. Boom. Just like that. Somebody did CPR on her, and when the paramedics got there, she had a pulse. But she'd had a massive heart attack. She coded twice in the ambulance on the way to the hospital and was pronounced dead on arrival." Princess nuzzled Jenna's knee, and she leaned over, scooping up the spaniel. The little dog turned around, licked the moisture off Jenna's face. "Gram was gone."

Sloan stroked her hair. "She must have been a special lady, and very important to you."

"She was. She—she always believed in me, no matter what crazy thing I wanted to try next, Gram always believed that I could do what I wanted to." Her shoulders began to shake with sobs she tried to mute, and her nose started to run again.

Sloan leaned sideways, taking her—and the dog—with him. His long arm reached over to the coffee table and yanked a napkin from beneath the cookie bag. He offered it to her.

"Thanks." She pushed Princess from her lap, then wiped her nose. When she tried to move away from Sloan, he just tightened his arms around her and shifted.

Before she knew it, they were snuggled on the couch, her head cradled on his chest.

After a few minutes, she relaxed into him, enjoying his warmth as he toyed with her hair. When his fingers drifted behind her ear and began to lightly scratch, one corner of her mouth twitched. She thumped her foot against his calf like a dog with a tickle spot.

His deep chuckle vibrated through her. "That's better."

"Definitely better." He'd already made her feel more normal, after she'd spent the whole day feeling like nothing would ever be right again. She caressed his stomach through the soft fabric of his brushed-cotton shirt. "I can think of something else that could help, too."

She raised her head, leaning in to kiss him.

"Mmm-hmm," he sputtered against her lips. He gently moved her away. "Easy, sugar." His fingertips skimmed over her cheek. "Not like that. Like this."

The tenderness he kissed her with made her heart go to pieces all over again. Though their sex life had always been incredible, she knew this time would be different. It was the way he looked at her, touched her. As if she was a precious thing, almost fragile. She'd never had a man treat her like that. He carried her to the bed, then made love to her.

And for the first time, she fully understood the difference.

A dessert-only relationship with him suddenly didn't hold the same appeal.

Fear followed fast on the heels of that discovery. Damn it. She was falling for him.

And that could only lead to heartache for both of them. *All* of them. Because she'd never stuck with anything in her whole life.

CHAPTER NINE

MID-JANUARY BROUGHT a blast of frigid temperatures. Snow pounded Erie every day, and every day Jenna wondered how to deal with her relationship with Sloan. For the most part, pretending nothing had changed the day he'd comforted her about Gram's death seemed to be working.

Or not.

But the misery she felt now had nothing to do with the confused state of her emotions. She huddled on the couch, a small empty garbage can on the floor beside her. An almost-full sleeve of crackers and a half can of flat ginger ale sat on the coffee table. An untouched cup of herbal tea courtesy of Margo, who'd stopped in before her Saturday-morning appointments, rounded out the "illness buffet."

Princess eyed her warily from the overstuffed chair, having learned early on that the stomach flu Jenna was battling for the second day meant the dog should stay away or risk getting dumped to the floor when Jenna grabbed the plastic can and raced for the bathroom.

Beneath the distress of feeling like crap, a niggling thought tapped at Jenna. Maybe…nah. Stomach flu. Had to be.

Still, this was her week off the birth control patch, and she hadn't really had a period to speak of. Could she…?

It's stomach flu, she insisted to herself. Everyone's got it. Someone probably came into the shop and passed it on.

The intercom buzzed. Princess shot from the chair, yapping at the visitor.

"Ugh." Flipping the purple-and-blue afghan onto the back of the couch, Jenna levered herself upright, taking the time to cram her feet into her fuzzy dragon slippers. Hopefully she looked as bad as she felt and whoever it was would go away. Quickly. *Please, don't let it be Sloan.* The last thing she needed at the moment was him seeing her looking like the undead. Wearing flannel pajamas to boot.

Jenna nudged Princess back with her toe, then groaned as the dog grabbed the dragon's crown. "No, Princess. Get away from the door." Having to chase the dog down the stairs was high on Jenna's Top Ten List of Things I Don't Need Right Now.

Princess growled, wrestling with the green slipper, thrashing her head from side to side.

"Oh, fine, just take it." Jenna pulled her foot free, letting the dog run away with her prey. "Why is it you leave them alone until I'm wearing them?" She glanced at the image from the security camera. The person wore a bulky coat and a white scarf around her head, but she felt confident it was Brook. What was she doing over here when Jenna had opted to close the shop for the weekend to recover from her stomach bug? She buzzed the lock on the metal door, then went into the foyer at the top of the stairs, waiting for the teen.

Brook trudged up, then unwrapped her face and pushed back the hood of the coat.

"I think I might be pregnant."

Jenna clamped a hand over her mouth, momentarily unsure which of them had spoken the damning words—the ones she hadn't even let fully form in her head, let alone on her lips. But then Brook's blue eyes filled with tears that threatened to spill over onto her cold-reddened cheeks. Jenna reached out and pulled Brook up the last stair, into the foyer and into her arms.

"Don't cry, sweetheart." After a brief hug, she guided the girl into the apartment. Shock prevented her from saying anything just yet. She helped Brook remove her coat, slung it over one of the stools at the kitchen island. They moved to the living area, where Brook threw herself into the soft cushions of the sofa.

Jenna eased down next to her. "Okay, so tell me what's going on. What makes you think that? Have you missed a period?"

Brook nodded. "T-two."

"Two?" The note of shock echoed off the ceiling.

"I—I just thought…"

"It's okay." Jenna took the girl's hands in her own, knowing full well what she'd thought. That it couldn't possibly be happening to her, that she was imagining it. There was some other explanation for it. *Like stomach flu.* "Anything else?"

"I don't feel sick or anything. But I'm real tired. I looked up pregnancy on the Internet and it said that's one symptom." The kid's voice faded to a whisper. "I'm so scared. My dad's going to kill me."

That makes two of us. The thought didn't help. Maybe both of them were worrying over nothing. "When did you miss your first period?"

"Somewhere in the middle of December. Like the week before Christmas, I think. I dunno exactly. I'm not always regular, and I don't keep good track." Brook pulled her hand free and ran the back of it across her cheeks to dislodge the tears tracking there.

Jenna offered her the tissues from the table. "Okay, since we're now in the middle of January, you should have had another period last week?"

The girl nodded. "Like Thursday."

"Okay. We need to know if you really are pregnant, or if something else is going on. I don't suppose you've done a home test?"

"No," she whispered. "I was scared to death Dad would find it in the house. And I didn't know who else to tell."

"All right. First things first. I'll run down the road to Quality—" the very idea of running anywhere made her stomach queasy, but she'd go "—and get a test, and we'll take it from there. Okay?"

Brook's eyes widened. "Not Quality! It's too close to the house! What if Dad decides he needs some milk or something?"

Jenna swallowed a groan, but she knew the girl was right. She added *"Sloan catching me buying a home pregnancy test"—the two pack, one for his kid, and one for her*—to the List of Things I Don't Need.

Her stomach pitched and she clamped her teeth, willing the queasiness to subside. Oh, God. If it were true, what would she do? How would Sloan react? She shoved aside her growing panic. Absolutely no point in either of them borrowing trouble. Yet. "Okay. I'll go to a drugstore farther away."

Princess jumped onto the couch, and Brook ruffled the dog's ears. Jenna slogged to the door, kicking off the remaining slipper and pulling on her boots. The long woolen coat concealed her pajamas. She wouldn't be the first one to go into a store like that. In fact, pajamas had become all the rage with teens. The one on her sofa stared into space, petting the dog, not acknowledging Jenna's leave-taking.

At the store, she faced an overwhelming selection. Who knew pregnancy tests came in so many variations? Blue lines, pink lines, two lines, plus signs. Dr. Seuss could have a field day writing a book about that. Heck, they even had a digital readout test that declared "pregnant" or "not pregnant." Given how she felt, that one looked the best. *Pregnancy Tests for Dummies and People Too Sick to See Straight.* Although on the other hand, anything computerized had too many things that could go wrong. Given how well she and computers got along…the stupid thing would probably accuse her of illegal operations. Maybe it would be better to go with the "two line" product. And it even came with a bonus test in the box—three instead of two.

She grabbed the box, holding it close so no one could read the package. Her face warmed at the cash register, and she chided herself for acting like a teenager buying her first box of tampons.

All the way home, bursts of fear warred with fits of optimism. No way either of them was pregnant. Okay, well, certainly not *both* of them. God couldn't have that warped a sense of humor.

Could he?

By the time she reached the loft, all she wanted to do was curl back up on her couch. But that wasn't going to happen.

She found Brook slumped in the same place she'd left her. The teen looked up as Jenna hung her coat on the oak coat tree near the door. "Did you get it?"

Jenna held out the plastic bag in response, kicking off her boots. She took out the box and tossed the shopping bag to the island as she passed. "You want to read the directions or should I?"

"You."

The insert paper unfolded like a tiny map. "Not too complicated. You take off the cap, pee on the stick for three seconds, put the cap back on, then set it on the counter and wait."

"Pee on the stick?"

"You can use a plastic cup if you'd rather."

"How long do we have to wait?"

"Three minutes."

Brook knew they would be the longest three minutes of her life. She shoved herself to her feet, then extended her hand. "Thanks."

In Jenna's bathroom, she completed the necessary

stuff, then put the test stick flat on the counter and tried to ignore it. She washed her hands with Jenna's tangerine soap, dried them with one of the fuzzy blue towels, then sat on the edge of the whirlpool tub. She glanced at her watch.

Great, she'd killed one minute.

"Please be negative, please be negative," she whispered. Her father would have a fit. And how would Dylan react? He planned on college next year. He said he loved her, but… A positive result would change everything. How could they take care of a baby?

Damn it, they should have been more careful, used a condom every single time. Still, it had only been that once that they hadn't…

Two minutes ticked by.

Brook jumped as a knock sounded on the door.

"Brook? You okay? What's the scoop?"

"I don't know yet." She glanced at her watch. The second hand swept past the seven. Almost. She stood and walked over to the counter. Her pale reflection stared back at her from the mirror. All she had to do was look down, and she'd know. "How accurate are these things? Are they ever wrong?" she called to Jenna.

"I suppose they are sometimes. What does it say?"

"I haven't looked yet."

"Well, for crying out loud, look! Find out what's going on."

Brook stared at herself in the mirror for a moment longer. "Please be negative," she mouthed. Then she tipped her head.

Two lines.

Shit.

She swallowed hard and braced her hand on the counter as her knees quivered.

Her father was going to kill her.

A watery haze blocked her vision, and hot tears spilled over, trickling down her face. She turned away from the mirror, sliding to the floor. Wrapping her arms around her legs, she pressed her forehead to her knees.

"Brook?" The door rattled, then Jenna banged on it. "Honey? Open the door." The handle jangled again. "Okay, I'm coming in there."

A few seconds later, Brook heard the door that led to Jenna's walk-in closet open. Bare feet swished across the linoleum, stopping next to her.

Jenna stared down at the test on the countertop. Two lines. Damn. That meant Brook's fears were real. She was pregnant. "Oh, honey." She dropped to the floor, pulled the child-woman now on the fast track to adulthood into her arms. "I'm sorry, sweetheart."

A sob wrenched loose from deep inside the teen, and tears spilled onto Jenna's plaid flannel top. "He's—he's going to kill me!"

"He's not going to kill you. I'm sure he's going to be disappointed and upset, but he's not going to kill you. I promise." Jenna rocked back and forth.

"You—you don't know. The night—the night my mom died, they had a big fight because she was pr-pregnant. I didn't hear all of it, but Dad was yelling. He…he never yells. Well, hardly ever."

"Shh. It's going to be all right." Jenna wasn't sure how it was going to be all right, but she also knew Sloan. He'd be upset, yes, but she didn't believe he'd turn his back on his daughter when she needed him most. "I don't know what happened that night, but I do know your father. He loves you. You can count on him."

And, hopefully, so could she, if it turned out she was pregnant, too. How would Sloan react to that? Hell, how would *she?*

Jenna held Brook for a while longer, letting the teen cry until she had no more tears. Then she helped her up, offered tissues for her nose and a warm washcloth for her face.

Back in the living room, they settled on the sofa once more. "I assume Dylan is the father?"

Brook nodded. "He's the only boy I ever…"

"Okay. You need to tell him. And you need to tell your dad."

Brook's eyes widened, and moisture welled up again. "I know. But…I'm not ready yet."

"Sweetheart, you're already two months pregnant. You don't have much time to waste."

"What do you mean?"

Jenna sighed. Her father should be the one having this conversation. "Hon, you've got three options here. You can have this baby and become a teenage mother. You can give the baby up for adoption. Or you can have an abortion. If you want to have an abortion, you're running out of time. You're down to one month left in the first trimester."

"Oh." Brook grabbed one of the throw pillows and clutched it to her chest. "I really hadn't thought about it," she whispered. "This is a baby. My baby." More tears spilled down her cheeks. "Dad is going to hate me. He already thinks I'm a screwup, and this is just going to prove it."

"You're not a screwup, Brook."

Brook sniffled. "Maybe not, but I sure got screwed in more ways than one, huh?" She offered Jenna a wavery smile. "Only once. We only had sex without protection once."

"Sometimes once is all it takes, hon. And no protection is foolproof." Jenna mentally crossed her fingers that her protection hadn't failed them. "It may not have been that time that you got pregnant. Who knows?"

"Not me, that's for sure." Brook rose to her feet. "Look, I want to talk to Dylan before I talk to my dad. Promise me you won't say anything to him?"

"How long?"

"I dunno. A couple days?"

"I'll give you until the end of the week. You can't put it off. I know you're scared, but you've got a huge decision to make."

"I know." Brook placed her hand in the middle of her very flat stomach. "Part of me still can't believe it. I don't feel sick."

That made one of them.

After Brook left, Jenna headed back into the bathroom. The extra tests and instructions were strewn about the countertop. Jenna shoved Brook's test to the side, letting it mingle with the bottles of makeup, the hair-brush and curling iron, and other assorted junk. She smoothed the papers flat, rereading them. Following directions had never been her strongest suit, but she didn't want anything to go wrong. Believing that two were better than one, she used the remainders of the trio at the same time. Once they were recapped, she carried them to the kitchen, laying them on the island next to the smoothie machine. Then she set the timer on the microwave and headed for the couch. Curled on her side, she contemplated the crackers and flat pop.

Her stomach rumbled.

No way *she* was pregnant. She'd been faithful with her birth-control patches. The fact that this was her week off them and she'd only spotted—barely—and that she felt like barfing at the mere thought of food meant nothing. She'd gotten the stomach bug. That had to be it.

Because Brook was pregnant. No way both of them would turn up pregnant at the same time. What were the odds?

And why the hell hadn't the timer beeped yet?

She raised her head but couldn't make out the numbers remaining on the microwave. Beep, beep, beep.

Time's up. But she didn't move. Couldn't. Maybe she'd just take a nap and look at the results after that.

But weren't you supposed to read those things at the right time? Forcing herself to her feet, Jenna slogged past the table, pulled out one of the island stools and slumped onto it. She covered the results window of the tests with her palm and dragged the plastic sticks closer.

With a deep breath, she lifted her hand just a bit and peeked under.

Then quickly slammed her palm back down.

Two lines.

Maybe the other one was different? Something wrong? She pulled her hand away completely this time. Eyes scrunched, she lowered her head. "Come on, stop being a coward. One, two, three." She opened her eyes.

Two sets of two lines.

Two pregnant women in Sloan's life.

Her stomach sloshed and heaved, and Jenna jumped from the stool to race for the bathroom.

God's sense of humor wasn't funny at all.

LATER THAT NIGHT, Sloan shifted from foot to foot, trying to stay warm. He glanced up into the security camera and leaned on the bell again. "Come on, Jenna, let me in before I freeze to death out here!"

The girls were both gone for the evening—Brook to Kelly's house, and Ashley for a movie and sleepover with Grandpa. He could have a sleepover of his own with Jenna.

The speaker box clicked on. "I'm sick, Sloan. Go away."

"Then let me come in and take care of you."

"No. I look like hell and feel even worse." Her voice softened. "But thanks for the offer."

"I've got a lot of experience with taking care of sick females. You're passing up a real opportunity 'cause you can have constant care all night. The girls are out."

"When I'm sick, I don't need anyone to take care of me. I just want to be left alone. Besides, I'm probably contagious."

"Stomach virus? It's been going around the station for a couple weeks. So far some people have had it twice, but not me. I think I'm immune to northern germs."

A weak chuckle came through the box. "So even the germs are bigger and badder in Texas, huh?"

"Yes. But this transplanted Texan is freezing out here! Take pity and let me in!"

Jenna groaned. "You're not going to leave me in peace until I do, are you?"

"No, ma'am."

"Fine. But not for long." The buzzer rang, and the lock clicked open. Sloan darted into the shelter of the stairwell. He knocked most of the snow off his feet, then climbed the stairs two at a time. Poor Jenna. Well, he'd help her out, offer some comfort and care. Not the evening he'd been hoping for, but still…

The upstairs door was unlocked, so he walked in, shedding his coat and scarf as he went. He toed off his boots and left them on the welcome rug. Princess scampered over and jumped up against him, standing on her hind legs. She swiped her tongue over the back of his hand while he tried to rub her head. "Hey, pup. Where's Jenna hiding?"

An afghan-covered lump on the sofa stirred. "Over here."

He knelt alongside the couch, gently pushing the dog

aside. Princess gave up on trying to get his attention and stalked to the far end of the sofa, jumping up onto what he suspected were Jenna's feet.

Only her hand showed from beneath the purple blanket. It waved in the direction of the coffee table. "As you can see, I have all my stuff close. Tea, soda, crackers, tissues. Margo stopped by to check on me before she left for Morgantown for the next week. I'm fine. Thanks for stopping by."

"Don't let the door hit me on the way out?"

The lump nodded.

"Sorry. Why don't you let me judge for myself if you need help or not?" He grabbed the edge of the afghan. She made a strangled, choking sound, and struggled to keep it over her head. But he eventually won, succeeded in pulling it away from her face. One hand flew to cover her tousled hair, the other her eyes. "I told you I look like hell."

"Sweetheart, you could never look like hell, not even if you were standing in the middle of it." He eased her hands away, stroked back her hair.

When she finally looked at him, he did his damnedest not to let his shock show. "Have you been crying?"

"No, no, not at all. Must have a cold, too." She pushed away his fingers as he brushed them over her forehead. "Sloan, please. Go. Leave me to suffer in peace."

"I guess you don't know me very well yet if you think I'd even consider walking out on a sick woman I care about." He rose to his feet. "I'm helping you, and that's final."

He headed for the kitchen. "How about a cup of chicken broth? Do you have any bullion?" Rummaging through the cabinets, he found the green-labeled jar. After prying loose one of two cubes stuck to the bottom of the container, he heated some water. When the broth was ready, he carried it over to her, setting it on the coffee table with all the other clutter. "Why don't you sit up? That will make it easier, and probably better for your stomach."

She pushed herself upright, tucking the blanket around her curled-up legs. He tried not to stare at her head but didn't quite manage it.

"What?" She reached upward. "Oh, no." She groaned. "I have Medusa hair, don't I?"

He grinned. "Is that what you call it?"

"I didn't want you to see me like this."

"Hey. I've seen you a lot of ways, from stark naked and flushed with passion, to sound asleep and drooling on your pillow."

Her eyes widened. "What? You have not."

He laughed. "Okay, so maybe not drooling. But Jenna," he said as he picked up the mug of bullion and sat down beside her, offering the hot drink, "no matter what, I think you're beautiful."

"Liar." She took the cup. "But you're sweet to say so."

"How about I go get your hairbrush and brush your hair?"

"Get it, yes, but I think I can brush my own hair, thanks. I'm not that far gone."

He scrambled off the sofa, crossing the living room toward the bathroom.

Jenna watched him go, warmed by his response to her illness. Surely a man who was this considerate to a woman with stomach flu would be even better about a woman carrying his child, right?

But she couldn't tell him. Not now. She hadn't decided what she was going to do yet. Besides, Brook needed his support and understanding far more than she did, so the teen had to tell the poor man first that he was going to be a grandfather.

She rubbed her eyes, damning them for giving away her tears. Margo had found her bawling, had held her while she'd blubbered her secret. They'd had a long discussion about the options, much like the one she'd had earlier with Brook.

The sheer terror she felt at the thought of being responsible for another human being when she was only now making progress with being the parent of a dog made her think maybe an abortion would be the right thing to do. Being a mother…wow. It was a huge step for someone like her. Someone who didn't do kids. Kids had to come first, no questions asked.

But, on the other hand, this was *her* baby.

What would Gram have advised her to do?

Keep the baby. She had no doubt Gram would tell her she'd make a great mother, and the baby would be lucky to have her. That they'd be lucky to have each other.

And Sloan already had two kids and had proved himself to be a good father.

One thing was sure—she wasn't going to make this decision impulsively, like many others she'd made in her life. No, she would consider this one for as long as she needed to. It was too important for impulse.

A crash in the bathroom startled her. "Sloan? Are you okay?"

When he didn't answer, she set the mug on the table, prepared to haul herself off the couch to see what had happened. But he emerged from the bathroom carrying something. Brows drawn down in a serious scowl that didn't mesh with the wildness in his eyes, he stalked across the room and held the object out to her. "Is there something you need to tell me?"

She stared at the two pink lines on the stick in his hand. *Oh, crap.*

"Well?"

"Where did you get that?"

"In the bathroom, next to your hairbrush."

"That's not mine."

"Oh, of course it's not yours. It's just in your bathroom, with your things—"

"I'm not lying to you, Sloan. That's not mine." Thankfully she'd tossed her positive tests into the kitchen garbage can. Had she covered them up with more trash? Shoot. She wasn't thinking straight, that was for sure.

"So, whose is it, then? I suppose it belongs to a friend of yours?"

"Actually, yes." *Your daughter.* Jenna swallowed hard, looking him right in the eye. "Sloan, I swear to you, that test is not mine." Great. She'd mastered the art of Clintonism. The truth—of a sort. Gram would kick her butt. On the other hand, her lawyer parents would probably be proud she'd learned to split threads of reason like that.

"Really?" His shoulders sagged with obvious relief. He dropped onto the sofa, tossing the stick to the table. "Oh, thank God. Phew. For a minute there, you had me worried."

"Worried?" Unease tingled across the back of her neck.

"Yeah. Don't get me wrong, Jenna, you know I love my girls. Even Brook when she's making me nuts. But I'm just as glad that my baby days are over. Hell, I'm having a hard enough time facing the idea of all the stuff I have yet to go through with Ashley, and I'm pretty sure she's going to be easier than Brook. But to start all over again?" He shook his head. "No thanks."

He cleared his throat. "Besides, look at Brook. I'm not so sure I'm doing a good job at this fatherhood thing."

"She's a good kid, Sloan. She's just different from you, that's all. And so she's done a few kid things. That doesn't mean you're a bad father."

"Yeah, well, I'm not fixin' to try it again just the same."

Moisture began to build in Jenna's eyes, and she blinked hard. No way would she cry over his words, no matter how much they twisted her. He didn't want any more children.

That certainly needed to be factored into her decision-making. But if she wasn't sure *she* wanted this baby, why did it hurt so damn much that he didn't?

"Jenna? You okay?"

She nodded. "Fine as someone with this damn virus can be."

He reached out, lifted her chin until she looked at him. "Oh, don't tell me. Your biological clock is ticking and you were thinking—"

"Hell, no." She jerked her face from his hand. "Hey, I understand about our relationship, Sloan. Nothing serious, right? Dessert only, no steak and potatoes?" Yeah, and she'd been the one to break the most important rule by developing feelings for him. And by starting to think there might be more with him.

That he might be The One, a man who wouldn't bore her after a while, wouldn't make her itch for a change of pace. A man she could compromise with.

"We've already broken the nothing-serious rule. I *care* about you. In fact, I care about you enough to say, sweetheart, if you do want a child of your own, you need to stop wasting time with me." His Adam's apple bobbed in his throat. "I don't want to stand in your way."

"Th-that's very considerate. I'll be sure to let you know when I feel the urge to trade you in on a newer model." She inched away from him, pulling the blanket tight around her body again. "Thanks for stopping by. I think I can take it from here."

"You sure you don't want me to stay?"

"Yes. I'm a big girl. I can take care of myself." And she could take of their baby without his help, too, if that was the way he felt about it.

If that was what she decided.

CHAPTER TEN

BY SUNDAY AFTERNOON, Jenna felt well enough to go down to the store and work on some jewelry. Thank goodness, it really had been a virus making her ill, and not the pregnancy. Nine months of feeling like that definitely didn't appeal.

Tomorrow she'd call her gynecologist's office. She needed input from the medical field. Margo had been feeding her multiple vitamins for years now, so that wasn't a worry. But she'd stopped taking the Saint-John's-wort this morning. She'd have to ask the doctor if that could have hurt the baby.

The portable phone she'd brought from upstairs chirped, and Jenna stopped the diamond-tipped drill, pushing her safety goggles up. "Hello?"

"Jenna?" A few soft sniffles followed. "It's me, Brook."

"Hey, honey. How are you today?"

"Still pregnant." Brook's dejection reached across the line. "I talked to Dylan last night."

Jenna held her breath and waited for the teen continue. When she didn't, Jenna prodded. "And? What did he say?"

"He—he said he wasn't ready to have a baby, and that I should get rid of it." Soft sobs now came from the distraught girl. "He said it would ruin his plans for college next year if I have this baby."

"Oh, sweetie. I'm so sorry." But not surprised. *Men.* "Where are you now?"

"I'm at Kelly's house. But I have to go home, and I—I was wondering…"

"What?"

"W-would you come with me when I tell Dad? I don't know what to say, but he probably won't freak out as much if you're there."

Jenna could relate to the fear in Brook's voice. "Sure, I'll be there with you."

"Thank you! I'm so scared."

"I know." After making arrangements for Brook's friend to drop her off at Jenna's building in about twenty minutes, Jenna finished drilling the piece of beach glass she'd started before the phone call, then cleaned up the worktable. Task complete, she headed upstairs to make sure Princess had a dry pee-pee pad, because heaven only knows how long this meeting would take.

She dreaded it as much as Brook did. How was Sloan going to react after his little "no more kids for me" speech last night? Well, this was his grandchild, and he'd just have to deal with it. Still, his acceptance of the situation would give Jenna some reassurance that he might just come around about her news, too.

If and when she decided to clue him in.

Bundled into her long woolen coat, Jenna stepped out

onto the sidewalk. The crisp, cold air invigorated her and made her nose tingle. She tilted her head, closing her eyes, enjoying the feel of the sunlight—a rare commodity in an Erie January—on her cheeks. The sound of a car in the slush at the curb made her open her eyes and turn. Brook stepped out the car, then waved off her friend. Jenna walked over to her. "Hey, kiddo. You ready for this?"

Brook shook her head. "But it has to be done."

"All right, then." Jenna held out her gloved hand. "Let's go do it."

Without another word they walked united toward the house next door. At the porch door, Jenna squeezed Brook's hand, then followed her inside. They shed their coats. The quiet house seemed to hold its breath, as though it knew what was about to take place. Brook squared her shoulders, then hollered up the stairs, "Dad? I'm home. You up there?"

"Yeah," came his muted reply.

"Can you come down here? I—I need to talk to you."

Less than a minute later, Sloan barreled down the stairs, legs a blur of faded denim. "Did you say we have to talk? That doesn't sound good." He came to an abrupt stop on the bottom step and stared at Jenna. "And why are you here? Not that I'm unhappy to see you up and about today. Glad to see you're feeling better."

He turned to look at his daughter. "Brook? What's this all about? Are you in some kind of trouble again?"

The kid burst into tears.

Puzzlement in his eyes, Sloan stepped down, then

reached for Brook, awkwardly enfolding her in his arms. "Hey now, Snickerdoodle, what could possibly be so bad it makes you cry like this?"

"Oh, D-Daddy. I'm so s-sorry!"

Jenna scanned the living room. A box of tissues sat beside the lamp on the oak end table. She pulled out a few, held them ready while Sloan soothed Brook. So far, so good.

"Why don't we sit down?" He turned Brook around and pointed her in the direction of the sofa. "I get the feeling that might be a good idea."

Brook took the tissues from Jenna with a quivering nod of thanks. While father and daughter settled next to each other on the couch, Jenna perched on the edge of the oversize chair.

"Okay, now. Tell me what's going on."

Brook wasn't sure how she'd get the words out. Her stomach filled her throat and for sure, any second now, she'd hurl all over the living room floor. The pregnancy didn't make her sick, but telling her father about it was going to.

"Brook?" Her dad's eyes were soft, understanding. As soon as she told him, that would change, and he'd probably never look at her like that again.

She opened her mouth but closed it again quickly.

"Jenna? What in the hell is going on? What's so horrible that my daughter can't even bring herself to tell me? I mean, I've been called to a store to pick her up for shoplifting. We've had it out over my catching her with pot. Somebody tell me—and I mean *now*."

"I—I'm pregnant," Brook whispered.

"What? I don't think I heard—holy shit. Did you just say you're pregnant?"

Staring at her hands twisted in her lap, Brook nodded.

"Pregnant?"

"Yes."

With a string of curses she'd rarely heard him utter, her father shot off the couch and began pacing the room like the leopard at the Fort Worth Zoo. Brook kept her head down, terrified to see what filled his eyes now.

"I'm going to kill that boy," her father growled.

Brook snapped her attention up as he yanked open the front hall closet and dragged his leather coat on. He strode to the door. "D-Dad?"

Jenna stood up. "Sloan? Where are you going?"

"For a walk," he replied through clenched teeth. "I want you both right here when I get back." The slam of the door rocked the whole house.

Brook jumped. The tears began to flow down her face again. Jenna sank to the sofa next to her and pulled her close. "Don't cry, kiddo. It's going to be okay. The hardest part is over. Give him some time to get used to the idea. See, he didn't even yell."

"D-do you think he's going to Dylan's house?"

"No. He just had to say that. I think it's part of the father code of ethics and machismo."

The door burst open again, and her dad came back in, tracking snow across the rug. Hand in his hair—was he *pulling* it?—he stalked back and forth, emanating enough bottled-up energy to run every light in the city for several weeks. "I cannot believe this. First, I've told you a million and one times to *wait* because you're not old enough, not ready for sex. Do the right thing, I said. Second, what's wrong with you? Didn't the two of you know anything about protection? I know the schools hand out condoms, give me a freakin' break. You get a decent allowance and you work. You could have bought some. Hell, in a pinch, you could have lifted some! Third, I'm going to kill that boy!"

Jenna tightened her arm around Brook's shoulder.

"How could you be so irresponsible?"

"I didn't do it on purpose."

"That doesn't make much difference right now, does it?"

She shook her head.

"I don't know why I'm surprised. This is so like you. I should have expected it."

"Now, Sloan—" Jenna said.

"You. Don't even talk to me right now."

Brook had had enough. She jumped from the sofa. "Don't you talk to her like that! She's my friend. And what do you mean 'this is so like me'?"

Her dad shook his head. "Never mind."

"No, I want to know. You mean 'cause I'm more like Mom, don't you?"

"Do not mention your mother to me. Not right now."

"Don't give me that righteous, controlled bit, Dad. I know how you are! I know that Mom was pregnant when she died and that you didn't want the baby! I heard you yelling at her that night! Hell, the whole damn neighborhood should have heard, except we didn't have any neighbors."

Her dad stalked over and stood toe-to-toe with her. He leaned down and spoke in a very soft voice that worried her more than his yelling had. "Go to your room. Now. We'll discuss all this later, after I've had a chance to get a better grip on myself." He paused. "Now, Brook!"

Sloan waited while she scampered up the stairs, then he went into the kitchen. Fingers closed around the handle of the fridge, he leaned his forehead against the freezer. He scrunched his eyes shut to keep the hot tears from leaking out.

His little girl was pregnant.

He swallowed hard and lightly banged his head on the cool white door.

Pregnant.

No matter what choice she made now, her life would never be the same again.

And his heart ached for that.

He kicked himself for being so rough on her. But damn, this had been one hell of a shock. His anger had been aimed only partly at her. More of it belonged to the boy—and to himself. Somehow, he'd failed as a father.

Had his own father felt this way when Rachel had announced her surprise pregnancy? The distance between them at the time had prevented Sloan from knowing a lot about what went on in that period of Rae's life. But at least his sister had been an adult with a college degree already, and a career of her own. Brook was still just a baby herself.

A warm hand on his shoulder had him twitching. "Sloan?"

He whirled around. The hum of the refrigerator vibrated through his back. "Jenna. I kind of forgot you were here."

"I imagine you have a lot on your mind right now."

"That's the understatement of the year." He sighed. "One of the things on my mind is your part in all this. That positive test I found in your bathroom last night was Brook's, wasn't it?"

"Yes."

"Do you really think that was your place?"

"She showed up on my doorstep, crying, terrified that she was pregnant but not sure. Should I have turned her away?"

"Just tell me this. If the test had turned up negative, would you have clued me in on the fact that my teenage daughter was sleeping with her boyfriend, Mr. Horn-toad?"

She pressed her lips together, apparently considering it. Then she shook her head. "Probably not."

"And that's because you're not a parent."

Jenna's eyes widened a bit, lifting her eyebrows.

"You should have come to me immediately. I can't believe you looked me right in the face last night and didn't tell me my daughter was pregnant!"

"I made her promise she'd tell you soon. And she did."

"That doesn't excuse what you did." Needing some distance, he stalked to the other side of the kitchen, propped his hip against the counter. "Look, I think it's safe to say I'm going to be pretty busy for the next while, so…"

"Don't give me that, Sloan. You're calling it quits, aren't you? Had enough dessert, right?"

His throat tightened at the thought of not having her vibrancy, her light, in his life. Especially now, when he'd probably need it even more. But he needed to focus on Brook. "Yeah. I guess I am. I'll call you though, okay?"

For a long moment, she just looked at him. Then she nodded. "Sure. You do that." With her head held high, she turned and strolled from his kitchen. A few minutes later he heard the front door click shut.

Gathering his courage, and resolving to stay calm no matter what, he made his way upstairs. He knocked on Brook's half-open door, then entered her room. The perfume and lipstick on the dresser, and the posters of the latest teen heartthrob on the walls, clashed with the collection of stuffed animals perched in the cargo net in the corner over her bed. A lacy bra lay on the floor next to a pair of Curious George pajama shorts. Even the room couldn't decide if it was more child or woman.

On the bed, Brook pressed her face against the wall, shoulders shuddering. His guts twisted. The twin mattress shifted as he eased himself onto the edge. He cleared his throat. "Brook? I'm sorry for yelling at you. I was just…well, surprised is too mild to describe it. Stunned might be better."

She pressed tighter against the wall.

He reached out, stroked her arm. "Somehow—and I honestly have no idea how at the moment—it's all going to work out, I promise you. But there are some serious decisions to be made here, Brook, so we need to talk. Roll over."

She did, bringing with her a yellow teddy bear clutched against her chest. She scooted away from him so her spine pressed against the wall. "Are—are you going to make me get an abortion?"

"What?" He reared back. "I'm not going to *make you* do anything. Especially not have an abortion. Why would you think that?"

She sniffled. "Be-because of that night with Mom. I heard you tell her to get an abortion and she said no."

"Oh, Brook. That conversation was definitely not meant for your ears." Sloan dragged his hand over his face. "Well, if you're old enough to be carrying a baby of your own, I guess you're old enough to know the truth of what happened that night. But this is between us, Brook. Your little sister doesn't even remember her momma, and I don't want her thinking any less of her."

Brook looked puzzled.

"Your mother was pregnant all right. But the baby wasn't mine."

"What?" Her mouth dropped open for a moment before she snapped it shut. "No way! That's a lie! Mom would never do that!" She hugged the bear tighter.

"Yes, way. She'd told her lover and hadn't gotten the response she'd expected. In fact, he'd told her no matter what, he wasn't taking responsibility for a kid. It took her a few days to get up the courage to tell me. Needless to say, since I knew the baby wasn't mine, I wasn't too keen on the idea that she'd been steppin' out on me. On you. And on Ashley, who was only a little mite at the time."

"H-how did you know it wasn't yours?"

Sloan groaned. "Brook, I didn't want to know about your sex life—hell, I didn't want you to *have* a sex life until you were long married and out of the house—so I certainly don't feel like discussing my sex life with you." His face warmed. "Let's just say when I told you abstinence is the best birth control, I was speaking from experience, okay?"

Beth had discontinued their lovemaking while pregnant with Ashley, saying she felt unattractive and not interested in sex. He'd counted down the weeks after their second child's birth, waited for her to get the okay from the doctor, but their sex life had never gotten restarted. His ego had been horribly bruised when he'd discovered that it wasn't sex his wife wasn't interested in anymore but, rather, sex with him.

"Huh?" For a moment, confusion filled Brook's face, then the pieces fell into place. "Oh. You mean you weren't getting any?"

"How did this become about me?" Sloan tried to remember where the conversation had derailed. Right, the night of Beth's death and their argument over the child she carried. "I was angry, and I said things that night to your mother that I shouldn't have. I regret that every day. But Brook, I'm not about to force you to have an abortion. That's one option in front of you. We have to figure out what the right thing is." He'd always considered himself staunchly pro-life. But the reality of his pregnant teenager had him thinking about the possibility of an abortion. Life sure had a way of smacking you in the face and making you really consider what you believed deep down.

"Jenna said abortion, adoption, or motherhood were my three choices."

"She did, huh?" He sighed, partly out of regret—he was already missing Jenna—and partly out of sadness. None of the options were much of a choice for a fifteen-year-old. "Well, that about sums it up. And one of the first things we need to do is get you to a doctor."

"Are you still mad at me?"

"I'm not mad, sugar. I'm disappointed. I'm hurt that you didn't listen to me. How many times I've said 'I don't talk just to hear myself,' I don't know. I'm upset and I'm sad, and I wish I could change things for you."

"What about Dylan? You're not really going to hurt him, are you?"

"Right now we're going to focus on you. But we will be having a talk with Dylan and his parents, don't you worry about that. Does he know?"

Arms still clutching her bear, Brook nodded.

"And what did he say?"

She shrugged.

"Brook, I want to know what that boy said when you told him you were pregnant."

"Are you gonna make him marry me?"

"What?" His indignation made his voice squeak like an adolescent's. Like the way he imagined Dylan might squeak when Sloan applied a little pressure. "I swear, where do you get these ideas?"

"You always say to do the right thing. And Granddad made Uncle Roman marry Aunt Rachel when she got pregnant with Daniel."

"Yeah, and just look how that turned out. No, Brook, you're far too young to be getting married. I don't think that's the right thing at all."

"I'm far too young to be having a baby, too."

Unfortunately, that point was already moot.

CHAPTER ELEVEN

LATE THURSDAY afternoon, Sloan pulled up in front of a large Tudor house in one of the upper-crust neighborhoods. He'd often wondered who could afford these expensive places the builders kept cranking out. Answer: the parents of the kid who'd knocked up his daughter. Brook shifted in the passenger seat and tried, without success, to stifle a long sigh.

"You okay?"

She nodded. "I suppose. This is going to be bad. I just know it." Brook turned to face him. "Dad, promise you're not going to go all psycho, okay?"

Sloan held up his hand. "I promise I am not going to go all psycho. We just need to know where things stand on their side of the issue." He'd taken Brook to an ob/gyn yesterday. So far, both she and the baby were healthy. His head still spun with all the information the doctor had loaded on them, from the risks Brook faced as a pregnant teen, to nutrition, diet and exercise tips, along with places they could go for help no matter what Brook chose to do.

"Come on. Let's do this." Sloan jumped from the pickup's cab. Brook followed more slowly. On the front porch, he rang the doorbell. His daughter slipped her hand into his and he squeezed it. As he schooled his expression, the door opened. Dylan's face lost all its color when he recognized him. "Oh, Mr. Thompson. Hey. What's going on?"

"Cut the crap, Junior. I think you know why we're here. Are your parents home?" Sloan pushed his way into the marble foyer of the house, leading Brook in by the hand.

"Dylan? Who is it?" A woman in a pair of black dress slacks and a beaded sweater came down the curved staircase, fastening an earring as she descended. "Oh, Brook, how lovely to see you, dear." At the bottom she extended her hand to Sloan. "And you must be Brook's father. Very nice to meet you."

"You may not think so in another minute or two." Sloan shook her hand.

"Excuse me?"

"Is your husband home?"

"He is, but this is really not a good time—"

"No kidding. It's not a good time for me, either, but there's an issue that we all need to discuss."

Dylan shuffled his feet, then cleared his throat. Sloan shot him a squinty-eyed glare.

Mrs. Burch looked from one to the other. "I can see that something's going on here. Dylan, take our guests to the parlor and get them something to drink. I'll go hurry your father along. Perhaps we can clear up whatever the problem is and still not be late for the club dinner." She turned and glided back up the stairs.

"Uh, this way." Dylan ushered them from the foyer to an intimate room with cream-colored upholstered sofas and dark wooden end tables. "Can I take your coats?"

"We're not staying that long."

Junior looked relieved at that. "What can I get you to drink?" The kid jammed his finger into the knot of his tie, loosening it.

It took every ounce of self-control Sloan had not to grab the blue silk and tighten the knot to the point where the kid's eyeballs would bug out. "We're not here on a social call, and you know it. Apparently you haven't clued your parents in on the 'situation' yet, have you?"

Face blanching again, Dylan shook his head. "N-no, sir. Look, I'm really sorry—"

"Save it. If you're smart, you might want to run along upstairs and give them an idea of what they're facing down here."

With a quick nod, Dylan darted from the archway.

Sloan turned his attention to Brook, who looked paler than the cream brocade furniture. "Sit down, honey."

Without a sound, she eased onto the edge of the sofa.

"Sit back, relax. You're not going to break it." Sloan plopped himself next to her and took her hand. "I promise, Snickerdoodle, it's going to be okay. The boy has to own up to what he's done, and I want to be sure that these people aren't going to make trouble for you."

They sat in silence for several minutes. Then from upstairs, raised voices could be heard, followed by the slamming of a door. Sloan gave Brook's fingers a squeeze. "Sounds like the polecat's outta the bag now."

Another few minutes passed before the Burch family appeared together in the archway. Mrs. Burch's face was flushed, and there were faint tearstains on her cheeks. Mr. Burch had his hand gripped around the back of Junior's neck. The woman scurried to a chair in the corner of the room and lowered herself into it, hands fluttering on her knees. Mr. Burch urged his son into the room. "I believe Dylan has something to say to both of you."

"M-Mr. Thompson, Brook, I'm really sorry about this."

"*This?* You mean the fact that my daughter is about to turn your parents into grandparents?"

Mrs. Burch gave a little moan of dismay.

"Whoa, there." Mr. Burch held up his hand. "No one said anything about us becoming grandparents. Now, it's unfortunate that the kids messed up. But surely you're not intimating that Brook's going to go through with this pregnancy, are you?"

Sloan stood. "Brook is going to do what she decides is the right thing for her. Period."

"Surely she can see that it's in her best interests to have an abortion?" Burch reached into his jacket, pulled out his checkbook. "And we will be happy to pay the full costs for the procedure."

Brook covered her face with her hands. The heavy padding of her jacket twitched as her shoulders shook with muted sobs.

"Like son, like father," Sloan muttered. Brook had told him Dylan had pretty much said the same thing when she'd told him she was pregnant. "If Brook decides that's what she's going to do, then we'll take you up on whatever my insurance doesn't cover. But what I really want to know is what kind of support we're going to get from you if Brook decides to keep the baby. Or if she puts the baby up for adoption, we want to know if Dylan will sign the relinquishment papers."

"Adoption?" Mrs. Burch gasped. "Strangers raising the baby?"

"Lydia," Mr. Burch barked. "Get a grip on yourself." He flicked a nonexistent piece of lint from his jacket. "Mr. Thompson, if your daughter decides to keep this baby, then we'll let our lawyers handle the situation of support. And if she wants to put the child up for adoption, Dylan will go along with that. He has a track scholarship waiting for him next year, and he's not about to lose that opportunity. Not to mention he's too young to be a father."

"I guess he should have thought of that before he unzipped his pants, huh?"

"There's blame enough to go around. It takes two, Mr. Thompson."

"No kidding. Now I can see how you acquired this house. You're a rocket scientist."

Mr. Burch sputtered. Sloan reached down and helped Brook to her feet. "Come on, sweetheart. We're leaving." In the foyer, he turned to look at Dylan's dad. "Don't worry. We'll be in touch."

Dylan glanced at Brook without lifting his head. Hand at his side, he wiggled his fingers at her in a gesture so subtle Sloan almost missed it. Then he wished they both had, when Brook sniffled and burst into a fresh batch of tears. But at least the kids seemed to have feelings for each other, and in some way, he found that comforting.

Even if he did still want to wring Junior's neck with the blue silk tie.

Outside, he dragged vast quantities of cold air into his lungs, hoping to chill the anger he felt at the people inside the house. Obviously Mr. Burch didn't understand that support meant more than just money.

Do the right thing obviously had no meaning to them.

He helped his daughter into the truck, pulling some napkins from the glove compartment and offering them to her. She gave him a wavering, watery smile in return. "Thanks, Dad."

"You're welcome."

"No, I mean it. For everything." She blew her nose, then crumpled up the tissue. "I—I really am sorry I let you down." Fresh tears spilled down her cheeks.

Oh, Lord have mercy, he'd forgotten what pregnancy hormones did to women. He pulled her into his arms. "I know, sugar. I'm sorry I let you down, too."

She pushed him away, looked up at him with surprise in her eyes. "How did you let me down, Daddy? I'm the one that got pregnant after you told me a million times to wait to have sex. To do the right thing. B-but…I really thought he loved me!" She ended on a piercing wail, and threw herself back into his embrace.

"I know you did, sweetie."

HOURS LATER, with both girls asleep, Sloan prowled the house, unable to settle down. The scene at the Burch household kept replaying itself over and over, along with Brook's tears, her options, and…Jenna's stunned face when he'd basically told her he'd be too busy for her now.

The next day at work, people had to keep repeating themselves, he was in such a fog. Fortunately, most people just assumed his distraction was normal behavior for an engineer. With a quick word to the station's GM, he left early.

After parking the truck in front of his garage, he shoved his hands deep in his pockets, trying to ignore the pull of the girl next door. But he couldn't. A few stray snowflakes drifted from the sky as he trudged down the sidewalk and around to the front of her building.

There, he was met by the Closed sign on Elementry's door. Despite that, he wrapped his gloved hand around the doorknob and gave it a hopeful twist. No luck. Cupping his hands around his eyes against the glare, he peered through the window, but saw no movement, nothing to indicate Jenna was in the shop. He rapped on the door, hoping if she were working in the office, she'd at least come to take a look.

Nothing.

He went around to the side and stabbed the buzzer. Her car sat in its normal parking space, so unless she'd ridden with someone, she had to be home. He waved at the security camera. "Come on, Jenna, at least let me apologize for the other night. I don't want it to end like this."

In desperation, he climbed the snow-covered outside staircase, gripping the banister. On her deck, he tapped on the sliding glass door. Princess nosed aside the curtain to bark at him, her plumed tail wagging when she recognized him.

But no Jenna.

She must really be pissed at him. Not that he blamed her after his little rant. He went home, hoping in time she'd forgive him. He'd try again tomorrow.

Family Fun Night had been canceled due to a decided lack of family fun at the moment. Still, the routine of getting dinner, helping Ashley—who'd noticed the increased tension in the house and kept asking questions he wasn't ready to answer for her—practice her reading, even listening to the pounding thud of Brook's music from her room gave him some comfort. The world might be somewhat upside down at the moment, but life went on. He'd learned that lesson through all the tough times.

Shortly after he'd tucked Ashley in for the night, the phone rang. And rang. And rang. Without Brook answering it. He darted into the kitchen and grabbed it. "Hello?"

"Sloan?"

"Yes. Jenna? Is that you?"

"I need help," she whispered, voice hoarse.

The hair stood up on his arms. "What's wrong?"

"I need help," she repeated.

"Jenna, you're scaring the crap out of me. What's going on?"

"Brook has a key. Please…" Her voice faded away.

"I'll be right there." He slammed the phone down

and took the stairs two at a time. Brook looked up, shocked, when he burst into her bedroom. "I need your key to Jenna's place. Something's wrong over there."

"On the top of my dresser." Brook pushed back the chair from her desk. "Do you want me to come, too?"

"No. I have no clue what's going on. Besides, someone has to stay here with Ash." He grabbed the key and headed back down the stairs, jumping into his boots. On the way out the door, he shrugged into his coat and ran to her place. His fingers fumbled with the lock. In the stairwell, his military training kicked back in as though he hadn't been discharged a day, and he climbed stealthily, ears straining to hear anything going on in her apartment. He paused at the top, ear pressed to the door.

Nothing.

He eased it open and slipped inside. The living area was illuminated only by the glow from the television set. The low murmur of an old movie came from it.

Princess yapped at him from the open bathroom doorway.

"Jenna?" he called, moving in the direction of the dog.

The spaniel barked again and vanished behind the door.

"Pulling a Lassie, Princess?" Reaching the room, Sloan flipped on a light, eliciting a weak groan from Jenna, who lay on the floor between the huge tub and the sink. The dog lapped her owner's face.

Sloan knelt beside her, pushing a portable phone out of his way. "Jenna? What happened?"

"Sick. Can't keep anything down," she whispered.

"Sorry. Didn't know who else to call. Margo's away. Never felt like this."

"How the hell long have you been like this?"

Her shoulder twitched. "Day or so."

He scooped her into his arms, concerned at the lack of muscle tone she displayed. Her head lolled against his chest; her limbs flopped. "I think we need to get you to a doctor. Which, at this hour, means the emergency room." He placed her on the sofa, pulling a blanket off the back and tucking it around her. "I'm gonna go get my truck. I'll be right back."

Fifteen minutes later, he carried her through the emergency entrance of St. Joseph's Hospital. The waiting room was blessedly empty save for one woman. A triage nurse took one look at Jenna in Sloan's arms and led them to a private exam room.

He eased her down onto the gurney. The nurse picked up Jenna's wrist, checking her pulse. "What seems to be the problem?" she asked Jenna, jotting the information on a chart.

"She's been vomiting," Sloan supplied when Jenna didn't answer. "Can't keep anything down."

"How many times?"

"I don't know."

"Sweetheart, how many times did you throw up?" the nurse asked Jenna, pinching a bit of skin on her forearm. "She's definitely dehydrated."

"Dunno. Lost count."

"Probably that horrible stomach virus that's been going around. We've had a lot of folks in with that. In fact, tonight's been our slowest night in the past two weeks, lucky for you." The nurse bustled around the room, taking Jenna's blood pressure and temperature. "You're going to need to see the receptionist out front," she told Sloan. "Fill out the paperwork and such."

"Uh…I don't know if I can do that. I doubt I know all the answers."

"Isn't this your wife?"

"No. She's—" He fumbled for a second. "My girlfriend." Lover sounded so…California-ish. And he wasn't sure what they were anymore, but she was a girl, and hopefully still his friend, so girlfriend would do. She hadn't protested the label.

"Well, then away you go anyway. See the receptionist, fill in what you can for her. Someone will be out later to let you know how she's doing."

"Okay." He brushed Jenna's hair back from her face. "I'll be nearby in the waiting room, all right? If you need me, just have someone get me."

Her eyes fluttered open, and she offered him a feeble nod.

"Rest," he told her. "And don't give the doctor a hard time." He eased through the door, then followed the corridor back to the emergency room waiting area. A quick call home reassured Brook that everything was under control—no intruders, just a very sick Jenna.

After getting a clipboard and a stack of papers from the receptionist, he sat down in the standard uncomfortable chair. Pen poised, he filled out what he could, disconcerted by how much about Jenna he didn't know.

They'd been sleeping together for several months, and while he knew exactly what could make her moan with passion, he didn't know basic things. Like her birthday. Did she have a middle name? What about allergies?

Okay, he scored points for knowing she used a birth-control patch. Of course, that shouldn't count, because it related to the sex issue.

The forms didn't ask things like hobbies, which he could have answered, or if the person had a killer smile that made everyone around her feel like the sun had come out after a week of rainy days.

When he'd completed all he could, he took the clipboard back to the front desk and settled in to wait. The low drone of CNN came from a television bolted to the ceiling in the corner.

But after watching the same blasted headlines for about the gazillionth time, he got up. The woman at the front desk didn't have—or wouldn't share—any information on Jenna's condition. Two hours seemed a long time for a stomach bug. Without seeking permission, he snuck back down the corridor to the exam room. Inside, Jenna still lay on the gurney, but now an IV dripped fluids into her arm. He crossed the room quietly to stand at her side.

A barely perceptible splash of color graced her cheeks again. That had to be a good sign. He skimmed his fingertips over the faint pink.

She opened her eyes, shifted her head to look at him. "Hey."

"Hey, yourself. How you feeling? Any better?"

She nodded. "The IV is helping."

"Good. Any idea how much longer we might be? I should probably call Brook and give her an update."

"No."

"Okay." He headed for the door.

"Sloan?"

He turned. "What?"

"Please stay." She held out her hand. "I don't like being alone here."

He took her still-cold fingers in his, rubbing them. "Sure, I'll stay. And listen, while we've got the time, there are some things I need to say to you. I'm real sorry for the way I treated you last weekend. I know you were just trying to help Brook. I'm sure you can understand that I was pretty freaked out over everything and—"

"Sloan—"

"No, let me finish."

"But, Sloan—"

"Shh. Jeez, give the woman a little IV fluid and she's ready to talk your ear off again instead of listening." He pressed his fingertip to her lips. "I shouldn't have pushed you away. I don't want you out of my life, Jenna. In fact, right now, you're the brightest spot in my life, and I don't know if I can face going through this with Brook without your sunniness to help."

Her mouth quivered beneath his fingers. She looked at him with soft eyes. He lowered his hand. "You're not gonna cry, are you?"

She shook her head. "Can't. Don't have enough fluids yet." She choked on a chuckle. "Oh, Sloan, I'm so glad. Because there's something I have to tell you."

"Okay."

The door to the exam room burst open, and a lab-coated doctor, who looked too young to drive let alone practice medicine, rushed into the room.

Damn, I'm gettin' old. Sloan shook his head at the thought. Old enough to be a grandfather. He sighed.

"Well, Ms. Quinn, no wonder you're feeling so sick. Your HCG levels are through the roof! You know what that could mean, right?"

Both Jenna and Sloan stared at him.

"Twins! Of course, that's not certain. It's only one possibility, so we'll have to do an ultrasound to see—"

"T-twins? Did you just say twins?" Sloan asked. His stomach twisted itself into an intricate slipknot as he turned back to Jenna, unraveling the implications. "Y-you're pregnant?"

She nodded. "That's what I needed to tell you."

A Texas heat wave stormed over him. His face flushed, and the room seemed too hot to tolerate. His legs shook and he groped for the chair. "With twins? Oh good grief."

"Sir? Sir?" The kid doc rushed forward as Sloan sank down, just managing to make it into the orange plastic seat alongside the exam table. "Put your head between your knees, sir." The physician shoved his head down. "Try to relax. I need some smelling salts in here!" he bellowed.

"I don't need that crap. I just need a minute," Sloan

muttered. Pregnant. Jenna was pregnant. Maybe with twins. Several beads of sweat popped across his forehead, and the room threatened to spin.

"Sloan?"

He looked up. And as if the note of concern in her voice wasn't enough, the fear in her eyes, the same fear he'd seen in his teenage daughter's eyes—completely undid him. He took her hand and gave it a reassuring squeeze. "It's gonna be all right, sugar. I'm just…"

Shocked. Worried. Freaked-the-hell out!

Holy shit. He was going to be grandfather *and* a father. At the same time.

Jenna searched his face, which had gone slack again. At least he hadn't run screaming from the emergency room. This wasn't exactly the way she'd hoped to break the news to him. "Surprised?"

"Yeah, you could say that."

The bigmouthed doctor eyed them. "Sorry. Didn't mean to scare you both. Hey, maybe it's not twins," he offered.

"You said something about an ultrasound?" Sloan asked.

A few minutes later, a nurse helped Jenna into a wheelchair, which made her stomach pitch and roll as though she were on the deck of the *Brig Niagara* in the middle of a horrible storm. Jenna clamped her mouth into a tight line and willed the feeling to go away as Sloan followed her, holding a just-in-case plastic pan in one hand and guiding her IV pole with the other.

While he waited in the hall, she got settled on yet another gurney. Once they had her all situated, with her pajama bottoms slipped low and some goopy stuff on her stomach, they let Sloan back in. He took up a position behind the other two men.

"Now, what are we looking for?" the technician asked.

"Multiple pregnancy," the doctor, whom Jenna had mentally nicknamed Doogie, replied. "She's only five weeks, but her HCG levels are really high."

The only thing Jenna could make out on the screen was static. "Looks like we're off the air," she said to Sloan.

He gave her a quick glance, no humor in his blue eyes. Stung by his silent rebuff, she turned her head toward the wall.

"Well?" Sloan asked. "How about interpreting this for me?"

"So far, I only see one heart."

"You can see the heart?"

"Sure. Look right here. See this? That's the baby's heart, beating."

"Wow. That's amazing." The note of awe in Sloan's voice zinged her straight in the chest. "Look, Jenna, you can see the baby's heart." He cleared his throat. "Uh, there is only *one* baby, right?"

The technician moved the little sonar thing around her stomach some more. "Looks that way."

Sloan exhaled with a rumble, and she turned to look at him. His still-stunned expression perked up a bit. "One. Well, good."

"Okay, we're done." The technician wiped the goopy stuff off her skin, then pulled down her T-shirt.

Jenna wiggled her pj bottoms into a more respectable position.

"Here you go, Dad. Baby's first video." The doctor popped a tape from the machine, handing it to Sloan. The nurse came back and helped Jenna into the wheelchair.

Sloan fell into step beside her as they returned down the corridor. "How are you feeling?"

"Moving. Not good."

Back in the exam room, Jenna curled on her side, hoping the waves of nausea would once more subside if she stayed still.

"Okay, so what now?" Sloan demanded of the physician. "It's not twins. Why is she so sick, and why are her…whatever levels so damn high?"

"Could be hyperemesis gravidarum."

"And in English, that means?"

"That means it's going to be a very rough start to this pregnancy. At least the first trimester. In most cases, it eases up around the twelfth week."

Oh, wonderful. Only seven weeks to go. Jenna kept her eyes shut, grateful for Sloan's take-charge attitude with the doctor. Right now, she just wanted to concentrate on not heaving again. Eventually, she drifted off to sleep.

She woke to the painful sensation of the hair on her arm being tugged as a nurse removed the IV. "I'm done?"

"You're done, hon. We're going to let you go home, and hopefully we won't have to see you again. Try ice pops, flat soda, bland crackers. You've got to keep something down to nourish yourself and that baby. No more getting dehydrated."

Jenna nodded. "Where's Sloan?"

"He went outside to make a phone call and warm up the truck for you." The nurse smiled. "That's a good man you've got there."

"Yeah, I think so." The proof, though, would be in how he reacted after he got her out of the hospital. So far, she didn't have a clue what the man really thought about her being pregnant with his baby. After signing numerous release forms, instruction forms, and who-the-heck-is-going-to-pay-for-this forms, she sat in the wheelchair near the wide electronic doors. Sloan's black pickup rumbled to a stop just outside. He jumped out and came around the front of the truck as she tottered out. The blast of frigid air made her feel more alert. He helped her up into the seat and handed her a plastic bucket. "Just in case. No throwing up in my truck, right?"

"I'll do my best." She held the pail on her lap. The motion of the pickup wasn't quite as bad as the wobbly wheelchair's had been, but still, it wasn't smooth sailing. They rode most of the way in total silence, only the fan on the heater filling the gap.

Finally, Sloan blew out a long breath. "How did this happen?"

"The usual way, I guess. Although maybe not. Could be it was that time I was on top. Or the time we did it on the stool. Or the time in the tub." Oh, yeah. The night they'd made love in the tub had been magical, surrounded by candlelight, taking turns washing each other…phew. Maybe they didn't need the heater on at all. Her stomach clenched. And maybe she shouldn't be thinking about things like that right now, damn him.

"That's not what I meant, and you know it. I meant, what happened with your patch? Did you forget it one week or something?"

"No." Jenna cleared her throat. "Margo's really sorry."

"What the hell does Margo have to do with the fact that you're pregnant?"

"She did some research after I told her. Seems that Saint-John's-wort may interfere with hormonal forms of birth control. She didn't know that when she told me to take it."

"Wonderful. Freakin' wonderful. She couldn't have done that research *before* this happened?"

Jenna's chest tightened. Her nose tingled, and a slight haze filled her eyes. She blinked it back. "I'm sorry."

"When were you planning on telling me?" Sloan gripped the steering wheel so hard his knuckles creaked. How could she have kept this from him?

"When I figured out what I wanted to do."

"Do? What do you mean, do?" A cold chill crept down his spine, and he shuddered. "Whoa, Jenna, I hope that doesn't mean what I think it does. Are you thinking about not having this baby?"

"You said the other night you didn't want any more kids."

He swore softly. "Sugar, that was hypothetical. But

now we're talking about reality. Did I want to have more kids? No. But now that there's one on the way, that's a whole nother thing." The videotape from the sonogram lay on the seat between them. He shoved it closer to her. "I saw the little heart beating. You can't want to stop that."

"I don't know what I want."

"You're scared." He could hear it in her voice and had seen it in her eyes at the hospital.

"T-terrified. I don't do kids. I don't know anything about taking care of a baby."

"Well, you're in luck, because I do." He reached for her hand. "You'll be a good mother, Jenna, because you have a very loving heart. You reached Brook when no one else could."

They fell back into silence.

The truck's tires kicked up slush as they turned off the main road. He passed her place and pulled into his driveway.

"Sloan? Door-to-door service would be good tonight."

"I gave you door-to-door service. I can't take care of you if you're over there and I'm over here. And I can't leave the girls alone all night." He slid from the truck, coming around to her side. Cold air rushed in when he opened the door and offered his hand. "Welcome home."

"Tex, I'm a big girl—"

"Don't argue with me. It's not open for debate. I'm not willing to find you lying on the floor in front of the toilet, dehydrated and damn near unresponsive again."

Her breath clouded around them as she exhaled.

"Look, Jenna, this isn't what either of us had in mind.

But now we've got to play the cards we're holdin'. We've got to do the right thing." His warm palms framed her face. "I'm going to support you in this. And support means more than just money. If you don't want to stay for yourself, then…do it for the baby. Our baby."

"Our baby? That sounds so…weird."

He wanted to make her see the tiny life inside her for what it was—a child. Something to be cherished, even though neither of them had intended this to happen. "I'm picturing a little girl with red hair and her momma's quick smile and warm laugh."

Jenna's eyebrows twitched. "I hadn't thought of it that way."

"I know."

She offered him a half smile. "Maybe she'll have her daddy's blue eyes, too."

"I'd like that." When he leaned forward as if to kiss her, she shot her hand up between them and covered her mouth.

"Don't," she mumbled. "I'm disgusting."

He pressed his lips to her forehead instead. "Let's get you inside and settled, huh?"

"What about Princess?"

"She'll be okay at your place until morning. We'll deal with her tomorrow. We'll deal with all of it tomorrow. Now you need some rest."

As he guided her into his house, he crossed his fingers that tomorrow she would agree to do the right things.

To have his baby.

And to marry him.

CHAPTER TWELVE

WITH JENNA ASLEEP in his bed, Sloan found himself prowling the first floor of the house, walking circuits through the living room, dining room, into the kitchen, and back around.

He was going to be a dad again. That took some getting used to. More disconcerting was Jenna's refusal to acknowledge that she was going to carry the baby to term. The small victory of getting her to picture a little girl with his blue eyes wasn't something he could count on to tip the scales.

He dug in the front hall closet and pulled out the old VCR buried on the top shelf. After hooking it up, he popped in the tape the doctor had given him.

The tiny flicker of their baby's heart in the silvery static made doing the right thing clear. On all accounts. Shutting it off, he climbed the stairs and headed for Brook's room. He stepped over the discarded clothes on the floor, drew closer to her bed.

The soft lines of her face in sleep made her look even younger. It was still so hard to believe that his baby carried a baby of her own. The mattress creaked as he perched on the edge.

Brook stirred, opened one eye. "Dad? W-what's wrong? Is Jenna okay?"

He nodded. "She'll be fine." He tucked her hair behind her ear. "It's just…I've been doing some thinking tonight. Brook, sweetheart…" He sighed. "I don't know that an abortion is the right thing. A baby is a precious thing, no matter how it comes into being."

Both eyes open now, she nodded. "I already figured that out, Dad. I just can't do…that. You're right. It wouldn't be the right thing. I don't think I could live with myself. I mean, what if Mom had decided to abort me? No, I just can't do it."

"You figured that out already, huh?"

"Yeah."

The half smile he gave her felt bittersweet. "Guess you're growing up already, Snickerdoodle."

"Da-ad." The silver brow-ball wiggled. "Please. Don't call me that. I'm going to be a mother."

Sloan pressed his hand to his chest. "And I'm going to be a grandfather. God help me. Maybe you'll learn a thing or two yourself about how hard it is to be a parent. I can only hope." He leaned over, pressed his lips to her forehead. "Now go back to sleep. You're sleeping for two."

SATURDAY MORNING Brook woke, pondering the weird late-night visit from her father, and with the urgent need to pee. Definitely the worst side effect of being pregnant. Well, that and the fact that her boobs hurt like hell. Even putting on a bra was uncomfortable. But this pee-itis was the pits, especially at school where the teachers didn't want to give her too many hall passes. Eventually she'd have to tell them. The school had special programs for pregnant teens. She groaned, rolling out of bed.

Bleary-eyed from staying up until Dad had called to let her know that Jenna would be okay, Brook stumbled into the hallway and ran smack-dab into her father, clad in a pair of sweats and an old T-shirt, knocking gently on the bathroom door. "Jenna? You okay? You want me to come in there?"

A weak "no" was followed by the unmistakable sounds of ralphing.

"Eww, gross. Why is Jenna upchucking in our bathroom?" Brook asked, shifting from foot to foot. "I've gotta pee."

"I guess you'll have to use the toilet in the basement, then."

"Ick. I told you we should have gotten a two-bathroom house. Why is she here? Did she sleep over?" Brook rapped on the door. "Jenna? You almost done? I really need to go!"

"Brook, for once, stop thinking about yourself. Jenna's in there, sick, and all you care about is yourself. I thought you claimed Jenna was your friend?"

"Well, why can't she puke in a garbage can or something? I can't help it if I'm pregnant and it makes me have to pee!"

Her father's face darkened. "And Jenna can't help that she's—" he stopped short, then finished "—sick, either. Have a little compassion for someone else."

"Jeez, whatever." Brook circled around him, heading for the basement and the horrible lopsided toilet in the laundry room that passed as the house's half bath.

"Brook?"

She paused on the second stair. "What?"

"When you come back up, we…we need to talk."

"Great, something to look forward to." She whirled and continued her trip to the basement, wondering what he needed to talk about now. Hopefully it would not be a repeat of last night's little "please don't have an abortion" speech, since she'd already told him she wasn't going to do that.

She flipped the basement light off and headed back into the kitchen. Was Dad going to give her a big lecture about how he'd slept on the couch last night while Jenna'd had the bed? Did they think she was stupid? She could tell they'd been "sleeping together" for a while. A *woman* knew these things.

Starving, she rummaged in the fridge. After a bowl of chocolate puff cereal only took the edge off, she made herself a peanut butter and marshmallow sandwich. With a glass of milk in one hand, and the sandwich in the other, she finally trudged back upstairs.

She hesitated a moment in her father's doorway. Jenna was curled in his bed, tucked beneath his navy-blue comforter. Dad held a glass of clear liquid in his hand. "Just try, Jenna," he coaxed. "You don't want to have to go back to the hospital and have them stick an IV in you again, do you?"

Jenna shook her head.

Brook sauntered closer, chomping on the sandwich. "Man, you look horrible, Jenna," she muttered around the peanut butter and bread gummed to the roof of her mouth.

"What's that smell?" Jenna moaned. "Get it out of here!"

"Brook! Are you trying to make her throw up again? Take that to your room and I'll be there in a minute."

"I'll be waiting breathlessly."

"What did you say?" Her dad glanced up at her, his eyes narrowing.

"I said, I'll be waiting." Jeez, what the hell was his problem today? Jenna was sick. So what? Big deal. She'd get over it. And he needed to. She turned and stalked from the room.

Sloan watched his daughter leave. He had no clue how his girls would react when they found out Jenna was pregnant. Shoot, Ashley didn't even know that Brook was pregnant yet.

Jenna shifted on the bed, and he returned his attention to her. "Come on, just one teeny, tiny sip, and then I'll leave you alone for a bit."

"You're annoying when you're being considerate."

He laughed. "Brook would tell you I'm annoying, period. Here. Just a sip." He lifted her head and bent the straw to her lips. Satisfied when she drew in a small amount, he eased her back down to the pillow, then set the glass on the night table. "Good. That will do for now."

Rising from the bed, he laced his hands together, lifted them over his head and stretched. The joints in his shoulders popped. "Try to get some rest. Ignore any hollering you hear from next door. I'm going to give Brook the…news."

"News?"

"About you being pregnant? Let's just get that over with."

"But I don't know—"

"Pregnant?" piped a small voice from the doorway. "You mean, like having a baby? Like Aunt Rae did?" Ashley, clad in her bathing suit, of all things, clapped her hands. "Oh, goodie! We're having a baby!" She barreled toward the bed at full speed. Sloan reached out and caught her just as she launched herself at Jenna's reclining form. "I won't be the littlest anymore! Waahoo!"

"Easy, Peach." Sloan closed his arms around his younger daughter, relief filling him. Her positive attitude was something he needed at the moment. At least someone was thrilled over this unexpected turn of events. "No jumping on Jenna right now. She's not feeling too well."

"Because of the baby?" Ashley squirmed, craning her head to look down at Jenna.

"I guess."

"This is so cool. Does that mean you're gonna be my new mom, too?" Ashley asked.

Jenna's face went another shade paler. "Uh, uh…"

"What's going on in here?" Brook demanded, storming back into the room, minus the offensive sandwich. "A new mom? You two are getting married and you didn't say anything to us first? I didn't know it was serious."

"Well, I don't know if we're getting married because

I haven't had the chance to ask her yet." Sloan winced at the flicker of fear in Jenna's eyes. Didn't she want to marry him?

"Jenna's having a baby," Ashley announced to her sister. "We're getting a little sister. Or maybe a little brother." She trapped Sloan's face between her hands, forcing him to look at her. "Right, Dad? It could be a brother?"

"What? Jenna's pregnant?" Brook's expression registered shock, which quickly twisted into anger. "You freakin' hypocrite! You get all over me about not being careful, having sex when I shouldn't be, and you've knocked up your own girlfriend! Sure, that's doing the right thing! What's the matter, Dad, didn't have enough money for condoms?"

Sloan set Ashley down and whirled on his teenage daughter. "That's enough. Let me remind you that I am the adult here—"

"Could have fooled me. Most adults are more careful when they have sex. It's just us stupid kids who get 'caught'!"

"I said, that's enough. Go to your room. I'll be in later and maybe we can have a civilized discussion about all this."

"I doubt it." She flipped her hair. "And you," she said to Jenna. "Some friend you are. I knew you were screwing my dad, but this really tops it all. If you think I'm going to welcome you with open arms, think again. I don't need a new mother! Especially not one who joins the family by accident."

"Enough!" Sloan bellowed. Ashley squeaked and ran from the room. His arm trembled as he raised it, pointing in the direction of the door, a silent order that Brook should do likewise. Keeping his anger tightly in check, he just waited. Eventually she turned and left.

He lowered his arm with a long exhale.

A soft sound caught his attention. He looked over at Jenna. Tears trickled down her cheeks. "Aww, sugar. Don't cry." The headboard creaked as he sat on the bed and pulled her against his chest. "But I'm glad to see you've got enough moisture in you to make tears."

She choked on a cut-off laugh. "I'm supposed to be the rosy optimist, not you."

"You mean to tell me all this has knocked off your rose-colored glasses? You're not having fun yet?" *He* sure as hell wasn't. Two pregnant females, pumped full of whacked-out hormones, making them both even more emotional than usual.

In his head, he heard the blat, blat, blat of the Emergency Broadcast System. "This is a test," the drill went.

Yeah, this was one doozy of a test all right, as though the universe had decided, *Hey, let's put the screws to Thompson.*

A few quiet sniffles faded into his T-shirt.

He held Jenna close, resisting the automatic urge to rock her, given the way her stomach reacted to motion lately.

"I want to go home. I can't stay here."

"Why not?"

"Because Brook hates me now. I feel bad enough. I don't need to be antagonizing her just by my presence."

"I didn't see you doing any antagonizing." He stroked her hair, savoring the softness, the vibrancy—a vibrancy that was lacking in the rest of her. He missed that. "Tell you what, when you prove to me you can drink a whole glass of flat pop and eat some crackers and keep it all down, then you can go home. I'll make house calls." He shifted her away from him so he could see her better. "Damn lucky I got involved with the girl next door, huh?"

Her bottom lip quivered. "I guess."

Retrieving the glass from the night table, he held it out to her. She accepted it, took a small sip, then wrinkled her nose. "Blah. I hate flat soda."

Downstairs, the doorbell rang. Sloan cursed. "Now what?" He rose. "I'll be right back. You see if you can't get more of that into your stomach."

Jenna closed her eyes as he left the room. Damn him and his Texas-size mouth. She felt more trapped now than she had when she'd seen the positive test stick. Little Ashley had been so excited about the idea of a baby brother or sister.

And Brook…

Jenna hadn't expected the teen to turn on her like that. But given how hard she'd been trying to get her father's attention, Jenna could see how this would tick her off. She'd probably be ticked off, too, in the same situation.

Still, it felt like Sloan had forced her into the position of having this baby after all. How did you explain to a seven-year-old that you'd decided having her little sister was a bad idea so you'd simply…

Bile and flat ginger ale rose up in her throat, and Jenna threw back the covers, dashing for the bathroom.

WHEN SLOAN OPENED the front door, his sister bustled into the house, greeting him with a kiss on the cheek. In her arms, Jamey looked like some kind of weird winter scarecrow, his arms and legs sticking out, stiff and bulky, in a powder-blue snowsuit. Molly and James followed on her heels, and Sloan's father brought up the rear. "What's going on?" Sloan asked over Jamey's loud cries as they shed their coats. "Not that I'm not glad to see y'all—" Okay, so he wasn't really. They were the last thing he needed at this very moment. "But why are you here?"

Rachel laid Jamey on the couch, opening the zippers on his suit. She glanced over her shoulder at Sloan. "You forgot, didn't you? I'm taking the girls and Jamey to Splash Lagoon today, and you and Dad are taking James to the shooting range to teach him how to handle that pistol he just had to have."

"Splash Lagoon, right." The trip to the indoor water park explained Ashley's mode of dress.

"You did forget," Rae accused.

"Uh, well—"

"So what if he forgot, honey?" James said. "We're here now to remind him."

A pair of feet tromped down the stairs. Ashley stopped halfway down. "Hey, Molly! Hey, Aunt Rae!"

She did a little wiggle. "Check out my bathing suit. I'm ready to go."

"That's great, Ashley. Did Brook decide if she's coming with us or not?" Rachel peeled the snowsuit from Jamey, whose sobs quieted as she hefted him against her shoulder.

"Brook's in a mood," his younger daughter announced, as if that were some big news flash to the family. "She says she hates you, Dad, and she's never speaking to you again."

"I should be so lucky," Sloan muttered, earning him a sharp look from his father.

"Oh, and Jenna's throwing up again, and she said she's not real happy with you right now, either."

Every pair of adult eyes in the living room snapped to him. Rae arched an eyebrow. "Jenna's here?"

"Yeah. She's…sick. I had to take her to the E.R. last night. I couldn't very well let her go home alone, could I?"

"Jenna's sick because of the baby! I'm gonna be a big sister!" Ashley shouted, descending the last few stairs.

Sloan resisted the urge to put a hand over his own stomach, which didn't feel so well right now, either.

His father shook his head.

Sloan cleared his throat. "Well, now that that polecat's outta the bag, I suppose I ought to tell you about the other one. Brook's pregnant, too."

If not for Jamey's cries, the room would have been absolutely silent as they stared at him. Then everyone started talking at once. Bits and pieces filtered through the chaos. "This family needs better instruction on proper condom use," his father muttered.

"Oh, Sloan." Rae's eyes filled with concern as she set her son on the floor, then came to offer Sloan a hug.

"Cool," Molly chirped, grabbing Ashley's hand. "You'll be a big sister and an aunt. Being a big sister is neat. Well, except for the stinky diapers."

"Oh, ick!" Ashley pinched her nose shut.

James just gave him a slap on the shoulder and an expression that said he was available for consultations.

The stairs creaked. Sloan looked up to find Jenna making her way down. The oversize clothes he'd given her last night—his Rangers jersey and a pair of his sweats—made her look vulnerable as she glanced over the railing to find the living room filled with his family. Her face went two shades lighter, and Sloan bolted up the stairs to take her by the arms. "What the hell do you think you're doing?"

"Going home," she whispered, leaning against him. "Brook's locked in the bathroom. I *need* a bathroom."

"I'll chase her out—"

"I want to go home." Jenna burst into tears, pressing her face against his chest.

Sloan smiled weakly at his family. "Hormones."

Yeah, it was going to be a great day.

CHAPTER THIRTEEN

SLOAN TOOK a long pull from the dark bottle in his hand. Legs sprawled over the arm of the chair, he watched his father eye him. "Go ahead, Dad, say whatever it is that you need to."

The day had at least provided some distractions. After he'd settled Jenna back in at her place, they'd gone on as planned. Rachel had taken the girls to the water park. He and his father had taken James to Bob's Gun Shop and taught him to shoot, although Sloan had questioned the wisdom of cold steel in his own hands at first, given his state of mind. But the focus on something as mundane as target shooting had helped him loosen up a bit.

Now his sister was upstairs, getting Molly ready to spend the night with Ashley. Jamey snoozed on a blanket on the floor. And his brother-in-law feigned patience, when Sloan could tell that all he wanted to do was get Rachel to the hotel room they'd booked for the weekend.

"I'm still in shock," the old man said, pointing his beer at his son. "Your girlfriend and your daughter. Hellfire, I'm gonna be a granddad again, and a great-granddad. That takes some getting used to."

"Tell me about it," Sloan said.

"You should," James offered. "Tell us about it, I mean."

"I can't. You and Dad are sitting on the couch."

"Couch jokes. Wow, there's something a psychologist rarely hears."

Sloan shrugged, taking another drink of his beer. "I'm not in top form tonight."

"Have you thought about what you're going to do? How you're going to handle all this?"

His father grunted. "He's going to do the right thing, that's what he's going to do. He's gonna marry that girl."

"The hell he is!" Rae's voice came from the staircase. They all glanced over at her as she thundered down into the living room. "Unless he's madly in love and was planning on marrying her already, that would be a huge mistake. I should have never let you bully Roman and me into getting married, Dad."

"You can't blame me. The boy had a wandering eye."

"That's exactly it, Dad. Roman wasn't marriage material. Hell, he wasn't even good boy-toy material. And I endured three-and-a-half years of trying to make something work that didn't have a snowball's chance in hell to start with. Always wondering why I didn't measure up, why I couldn't get it right."

James edged forward on the sofa to reach for Rachel's hand, but she brushed him off, turning to face Sloan. "Daniel wasn't 'an accident,' Sloan. You know I always said he was a surprise, not an accident, or a mistake. I cherish every moment I had with him. My marriage, however, was a mistake. A huge mistake. Don't make the same one."

"Jeez, Rae, don't hold back, tell us what you really think." Sloan tightened his grip on the bottle.

"There is such a thing as right and wrong," the old man said. "He needs to make things right. A baby needs a mother and a father."

"The baby has a mother and a father, Dad," Rae said. "Or else it wouldn't exist right now."

Their father scowled. "I raised you kids with morals. What would your mother think?"

Rae propped her fists on her hips.

Uh-oh, Sloan thought. Here it comes. He'd never seen his kid sister stand up to the old man like this.

"She'd probably think that you're barking orders like you were still in the army. News flash, Dad. We are not, and never were, under your command. And you're retired. Give it a rest."

Their father harrumphed. "You don't ever retire from being a parent."

Rachel plucked Jamey's snowsuit from the back of the couch, then knelt on the floor next to her sleeping son. "I know that, Dad. But you have to let us make our own decisions now."

James moved to retrieve their coats, held Rae's out for her. She shrugged into it, then bent over and lifted Jamey into her arms. "Now, if you'll excuse us, my husband and I have an appointment with a Jacuzzi tub."

A small growl rumbled in the old man's throat and Rae chuckled. "I know, Dad. Too much information."

Sloan rose from his chair and accompanied them to the door. "Maybe you should go warm up the car first. It's pretty cold out there."

James dangled a remote starter fob with a grin. "Already warm." He stuffed the keys in his pocket, then took his sleeping son from Rachel. "Don't keep me waiting too long, hon." A blast of frigid air entered the house as he went out.

"That was pretty impressive, Rae-Rae," Sloan whispered. "Standing up to the old man like that. Wow."

She giggled. "Yeah. Didn't know I had it in me, did you?"

He shook his head.

"Me, either." Her face went somber again. "But seriously, Sloan, don't compound the problems you're facing. Look at me."

He locked his gaze with her blue eyes. It was like looking in a mirror.

"Do you love her? Madly, truly love her?"

Sloan lifted one shoulder. "I like her—a lot. She makes me laugh. I've enjoyed life more since being with her than I have in years. But love? That's a strong word. A serious word. And what we've shared has been anything but serious. Until now."

"There you go. Take it slow. If you change your mind, there's no rush. You can always marry her later. But divorce is messy." Rachel reached up and patted his cheek. "I'll be here for whatever you need. I love you."

He shuffled his feet. "Yeah," he muttered. "Me, too."

She grinned. "Say it. I'm not leaving until you say it."

"Your husband's waiting."

"And he's going to be mad at you when he finds out it's your fault."

He pulled his sister into a tight embrace. "I love you, brat," he murmured into her hair. "Thanks."

"Lace your boots tighter and carry on, soldier." The admonition had a long family history, going back to their father's stint in Vietnam. Following a helo crash in the jungle, he'd laced his boots tighter over a pair of broken ankles and carried an injured buddy several days to safety.

"Yes, ma'am." And not only would he carry on, but he'd do the right thing. Just like his daddy had taught him. His sister would just have to get over it.

"See you in the morning."

After she left, he went back to his father and beer in the living room. The comfortable old chair sighed beneath him as he threw himself back into it. "So," he said, retrieving his bottle, "James has sure made a difference in our little Rachel, hasn't he?"

To his great surprise, the old man laughed. "I always knew that girl had it in her. She's a strong woman. Just usually she's quiet about it."

"She told me to lace my boots tighter and carry on."

"Exactly. But I still say she's wrong about the big issue. You ought to marry that woman. This world's difficult enough. A child needs two parents working as a team. Hell, Brook and Ashley could use a mother. I've been telling you that for years. Maybe if they'd had a mother…"

"Are you trying to tell me that if I'd gotten married again and given my girls a mother, Brook wouldn't be pregnant right now?"

He shrugged. "Your sister got pregnant after we lost your mother. Maybe it's like they're looking for some kind of connection to replace what they lost."

"Wow, that's deep, Dad. I'm sure James would be impressed. It's also bullshit and you know it. Accidents—or as Rae would say, surprises—happen."

"Obviously."

Sloan jumped from the chair. "Look, I need to go check on Jenna. Can you stay a while and keep an ear open for the girls? Somehow, I don't think James would appreciate me leaving Molly alone, even if Brook's in the house and I'm only next door."

"Sure."

HE SLIPPED into Jenna's apartment using Brook's key—his key now, since after the morning's ugly outburst, he figured confiscating it was only right. Besides, he needed it more.

Sloan found Princess snoring on the sofa. After giving her a quick pat, he headed around the entertainment center to the bedroom portion of the apartment. The curved metal room screen's collection of votive candles was unlit. He glanced over at Jenna's bed. The rumpled covers indicated she'd been there at some point during the day.

He rapped on the bathroom door. Water hissed, but Jenna didn't answer him. Inside, steam spilled over the top of her oversize shower and hung thick around the high ceiling. "Jenna?"

Approaching the fogged shower door, he got a strong whiff of her rose-scented body wash, which generated some pretty steamy images that had little to do with hot water. He tried to push the tantalizing memories of making love to her in this room, beneath those same showerheads, from his mind. Sex had gotten them into this mess, and the woman wasn't exactly up to it, anyway.

He fingered the fluffy yellow bath sheet draped over the towel warmer. "Jenna? Everything okay? How are you feeling? Obviously well enough to get a shower, so that's good."

When she still didn't respond, he pressed his nose against the glass to peer inside, but the coating of moisture made it impossible to see. "Jenna? If you don't answer me, I'm opening this door and letting all your heat out."

"Go 'way." Her weak voice was barely audible over the water, and came from—the bottom of the shower?

"Nope. Tough cookies." He yanked open the door, sending droplets of water all over the colorful bath mat. "What's going on?"

Jenna sat, legs drawn up to her chest, back pressed against the shower wall, water cascading over her.

"Good gravy, Jenna, are you tryin' to drown yourself or what?" He leaned inside and turned off the knobs.

She glanced up at him, a bedraggled sight that just tore into his chest. Were some of those moisture tracks tears? "Can't drown in a shower."

"Yes, you can, but let's not test the theory, okay?" He grabbed the towel off the rack, eased her forward and wrapped it around her, then lifted her into his arms.

"When I need rescuing, cowboy, I'll let you know." Despite her words, she settled against his shoulder, seeming content to let him carry her to the bedroom. "Water felt good. Made me forget I feel like hell."

"I'm sorry, sugar."

"You should be."

Shoving aside the mussed jade-colored bedspread, he set her on the edge of the bed, then returned to the bathroom for another towel. He dried off her hair, then eased her back against the gold-tasseled throw pillows. Starting with her toes, he worked his way up her calves to the edge of the huge bath sheet. "Mmm," she purred, then sighed. "Too bad I'm not up to having you follow through on that. You do have the best hands, Tex."

"Thank you, ma'am. I do aim to please."

"Don't I know it," she murmured.

"Yeah, well, I think I'd better leave the rest of the drying off to you, or we may find ourselves discovering if you really are up to it or not." He certainly was. Or was well on the way to being up for it. A half-mast erection already strained toward the fly of his jeans.

He dropped the second towel at her side and moved toward her dresser. "What do you need from here?" His own shirt clung to him as if he'd been caught in a sudden cloudburst. He peeled it away from his chest. The Texas Rangers jersey she'd worn home earlier lay on the floor nearby, and he scooped it up, quickly exchanging it for his wet garment.

That was a mistake, because it smelled of roses.

Of Jenna.

"I'd like a pair of my flannel pj's, please. Bottom drawer. And don't forget the fresh undies. Top drawer on the left."

"Oh, Lordy." He rummaged through the scraps of silky material, a peach thong here, creamy lace panties there. Red string bikinis. Black satin boxers. A bustier he had fond memories of. Her garter belt. "Why don't you have any old granny underwear?" This wasn't helping reduce the tightness in his pants. He settled on the black boxers.

"This is more like it." Down in the bottom drawer, blue fuzzy pants and a matching oversize shirt boasted black-and-white cows jumping over the moon. He offered them to her, then turned his back while she finished drying off. But not even boxer shorts or flannel pajamas could hide the fact that Jenna Quinn was one sexy woman.

"Granny underwear," she scoffed. "You're the grandpa-to-be, pops."

"Thanks heaps." His libido drained away like the final dregs of dishwater circling the drain. "For a moment there, I almost forgot that my fifteen-year-old is pregnant."

"Sorry. Misery loves company."

He faced her. "Are you miserable, sugar?"

The cows on her shoulders shifted upward. "Yeah. I feel queasy every minute."

"That's God's way of getting you ready for parenthood, 'cause trust me, sweetheart, it doesn't get any easier. In fact, queasy is one of the milder sensations of parenthood."

"Thanks heaps." She replicated his drawl as well as his words. "If I wasn't sold on parenthood before, I sure am now."

He ignored the sarcasm and the jolt of panic that raced through him at her comment. *Stupid.* He was supposed to be convincing her that parenthood was going to be great, not giving her more ammunition to consider an abortion.

"So, what have you had to drink today?" He wandered out to her living room and checked the coffee table. A white wrapper and a wooden Popsicle stick sat next to a nearly full sleeve of crackers and a half can of soda. He swirled the soft drink around as Jenna crawled onto the couch. "Please tell me this is the second or third can you started today."

She pulled the blanket over her, then shifted back to make room for Princess, who jumped up next to her. "Uh, okay."

"Jenna," he scolded. "You need plenty of liquids if nothing else."

"Tell that to my stomach."

"Did the ice pop work better? Stay down easier?"

She nodded. He glanced over at her kitchen, then snapped his fingers. "I've got an idea. You just kick back, relax, and let me take care of you."

The concept actually appealed to her. Jenna settled

deeper into the sofa cushions, absentmindedly running her fingers through the dog's long hair. Sloan clattered around the island, opening cabinets, the fridge and freezer.

"What are you up to?"

"It's a surprise." A few minutes later, the whir of the smoothie machine grinding up ice filled the loft. The clink of a spoon followed. Sloan eased into the chair beside her. He extended a margarita glass.

"You know I can't drink."

"It's virgin. I'll push liquids into you in whatever form it takes. I figured the cold helps. You can just take small sips and let it melt in your mouth."

The frosty glass chilled her fingers. She rolled the icy drink over her tongue. Fortunately, it had little odor. She'd discovered her condition made her extremely sensitive to strong smells—like her favorite body wash, which had triggered her slide to the floor of the shower. Or Brook's peanut-butter sandwich.

Jenna tried not to gag at the thought, but ended up coughing.

"You okay?" Sloan's eyes widened.

"Yeah." She returned the green-stemmed glass to him. "That's enough for now." Princess jumped from the sofa to the floor so she could paw Sloan's knees. He scooped her onto his lap, and sharp, irrational jealousy pierced Jenna. She cleared her throat. "How did it go with your family today?"

"Oh, we all walked around like a cowboy with a heat rash along the chaps line."

"Stiff, huh?"

"Pricklier than a cactus doesn't begin to describe it."

"I'm sorry."

"Not exactly your fault, is it now? As I recall, we were both fully engaged in what brought this about. Although I dare say Margo might want to steer clear of me for a while." He shook his head. "You know, the whole expecting-a-baby-and-a-grandbaby-at-the-same-time was a damn sight funnier when it happened to Steve Martin in that movie. 'Course, his daughter was at least married." He lifted the glass he still held in his hand, took a swallow, then looked at it with surprise. He leaned forward and put it on the table. "Speaking of married..." He rose, set the dog back on the floor, then came over to the sofa and sank down on one knee.

A quick flash of panic tightened Jenna's throat. "Oh, you're not—"

"Jenna Quinn, will you marry me?"

"M-marry you?"

He nodded. "Yes. Marry me. I meant it this morning when I said I hadn't had a chance to ask you yet."

"Why?"

"Why what?"

"Why do you want to marry me?"

"Because you're carrying my baby and it's the right thing to do."

"Oh." Jenna swallowed her disappointment. Of course, he was doing the right thing. She had no right to feel slighted in the least. Their dessert-only relationship had gotten a whole lot more serious than either of them had expected.

Ugh. Food metaphors had to go, given the state of her stomach. "I—I think I'd like to sleep on it, okay? Maybe for more than one night. I mean, this is like the biggest decision of my life." After deciding to actually *have* their baby, that was. "I don't want to rush into anything as important as marriage."

"You mean, like you're not rushing into parenthood?" He raised his eyebrows. "Besides, tell me one thing in your life that you haven't rushed into."

"Bed with you?"

"Only because I slowed it down."

"You want a medal?"

"No. I want you to say yes."

"I'll think about it." Marriage. She stifled the shiver that crawled along her arms. Another big commitment thing. She was going to break out in hives, for sure.

The phone rang. They both glanced around the living room, trying to place the source of the sound. "I think it's in the bathroom," Jenna said.

His knee popped as he climbed to his feet and headed for the other room. Jenna heard him answer, then strained to hear more of the conversation. He came out with the phone cradled between his shoulder and ear, nodding. "Okay, hold on just a minute. Here she is." He covered the speaker with one finger. "It's your mom. She says she and your dad are thinking about coming up for a visit."

Jenna clamped a hand over her mouth and bolted for

the porcelain god to whom she'd been offering up way too many sacrifices of late.

"Mrs. Quinn? Jenna can't talk right now. Can I have her call you back?"

ONE WEEK and one more trip to the doctor's office (under protest but at Sloan's insistence) later, Jenna sat in Element-ry's office. Waiting.

Dread made her stomach feel even worse than usual, so she pressed against the plastic balls in the elastic bands around her wrists, courtesy of Margo. Between that, small bits of soda and crackers every hour, and some ginger, the vomiting was at least under control. When the front door chime sounded, she whipped off the bands, stuffing them into the middle drawer of her desk.

She strolled onto the shop floor. Robert Quinn stood near the door; her mother, Mallory, perused the glass cases. "Hi!" Jenna chirped. "It's so good to see you." A peck on her dad's cheek earned her a pat on the shoulder in return.

"Hello, honey."

Her mother moved away from the case and gestured around the shop. "I love what you've done with the place. It's so—" a pause while the normally word-efficient woman searched for the right term "—cute."

"Thanks, Mom."

Mallory Quinn opened her arms and turned her face, offering her cheek. Jenna walked into the embrace. The fur of the mink coat tickled her skin, and the strong scent of floral perfume forced her to clamp her teeth together.

She backpedaled. "So, what brings you to my humble place?"

"We need a reason to visit our daughter?" her mother asked.

"Usually, yes. And since it's not my birthday…"

"Your father and I have light caseloads right now, so we thought we'd come up and see how you're doing with the business, that's all." Once again her mother's eagle-eyed gaze swept over the room. "Things slow right now, dear?"

"Post-holiday quiet, I guess."

Her father nodded. "Makes sense. I imagine you'll see it pick up again next week, just before Valentine's Day."

"Oh, yeah. I'm also thinking about a Web site. That ought to increase sales. And did I mention when we talked yesterday that the Maritime Museum and the gift shop at the airport are willing to take some of my pieces?"

"No. That's great news, honey." After shooting a warning glance her mother's way, her father smiled at her. "Sounds like you're on the road to success."

"This time," her mother murmured.

Jenna ignored it. "Thanks, Dad. I think so. I've finally found my niche."

"At thirty, that's a good thing."

"Well, not all of us map out our lives at age twelve and never deviate from the plan, Mother."

Her dad looked at his watch. "Two minutes. I think that's a new record." He winked at Jenna. "So where would you like to go to dinner?"

Her stomach rolled at the mere idea. "Oh, Dad, that's not necessary, really."

"I know it's not necessary, but it's something we want to do. So what will it be?"

Her mother sniffed. "Not that chain restaurant we went to last time, dear. Somewhere with real napkins and tablecloths, okay?"

"Is that place down by the bay open in the winter?" her dad asked.

She nodded.

"Let's go there, then. I love the view."

For her father, who'd run interference with her mother for Jenna her whole life, she'd do just about anything. Even sit in an upper-crust restaurant and try like hell to be civilized to the Ice Maiden who'd given birth to her.

The front door blasted open. Sloan stomped his feet on the rug, shaking loose snow from his boots. "Wooiiee, it's cold out there today." He glanced up. "Oops. Sorry, Jenna, I didn't realize you had customers. Although I suppose the car in front should have clued me in, huh?" He pointed to the office. "I'll just wait for you in there." But before going through the archway, he detoured to her side and gave her a quick kiss on the cheek. "You look better today."

"Well, he's certainly a smooth one," her mother said.

Jenna pasted a smile on her face and grabbed his hand. "Mother, Dad, I'd like you to meet Sloan Thompson. Sloan, my parents, Robert and Mallory Quinn. Mother, you talked to him on the phone last week when you called me. He's my neighbor and he's, uh, very important to me." She leaned close as if to repay his kiss in kind and whispered, "I need rescuing now, cowboy."

Sloan's eyes widened, a brief flash of panic chasing through the bright blue. "Mr. and Mrs. Quinn." He cleared his throat. "It's a pleasure to meet you."

"Important to you, huh?" Her father stuck out his hand. "Coming from my daughter, that's quite an endorsement, Mr. Thompson."

"Please, sir, Sloan." He disconnected from Jenna and moved to shake her father's hand.

Her mother arched a cool eyebrow, giving Sloan a slow perusal. "Well. If you're important to Jenna, then perhaps you should join us for dinner. We'd love to get to know you better."

"Oh, you're going out for dinner, huh?"

Jenna begged silently.

"Well, thank you, ma'am, I'd love to join you. Let me just make a few phone calls, take care of some business, and we can go."

AFTER DROPPING their coats with the clerk and pocketing their claim stubs, Sloan offered Jenna his arm. She'd been quiet the whole ride over, and he knew she'd been fighting the effects of the swaying car. Poor thing.

He held her back as her parents approached the maître d'. Sloan could hear her mother request a good table with a view. "They don't know, do they?" he whispered.

"No, and I'd like to keep it that way for now."

"How the hell do you expect to do that? You're turning green already, sugar."

"Whispering, while cute courtship behavior, is not polite." Her mother arched that damn perfectly groomed eyebrow at them again. The irrational urge to muss her hair rode him hard. She probably rolled from bed in the morning completely made-up. Where a woman with such a ramrod up her ass had gotten a daughter as free-spirited as Jenna was beyond him.

"Sorry, ma'am. You're right."

"This way," the maître d' said. He escorted them to a table by the front window and presented them with embossed leather menus that weighed a ton. Sloan barely heard the spiel of the specials because he was peeking at Jenna around the edge of the menu. The pallor of her skin set off the highlights in her hair and the soft green of her eyes. She'd applied more makeup than usual in a blatant attempt to cover up the signs she'd been sick as a dog lately. He still found her attractive as hell, and sort of fragile.

The urge to put his arm around her—to shelter her from the probing stares of her mother and the questioning looks from her father—shocked him.

"Sloan?" she said, apparently repeating herself.

"Yes?"

"To drink?"

"I'll have a scotch. Straight."

"I'll take ginger ale, please," Jenna said.

"What? No wine, dear?" her mother asked. "The meal is on us. No need to be chintzy. Have whatever you like."

"What I'd *like,* Mother, is ginger ale." Jenna smiled at the waiter. "Thank you."

Ordering and initial small talk out of the way, the lawyer in her parents came out clear as day as they took turns cross-examining him. Where was he from with that delightful twang? What did he do? What did his parents do? When he whipped out pictures of the girls, causing her mother to sputter on her wine, Jenna pinched him on the thigh beneath the cover of the linen tablecloth.

"I had no idea you had children."

"Yes, ma'am. Ashley's seven, and Brook's fifteen."

"They're great kids," Jenna offered.

Her dad looked pleased. As the waiter approached the table with a tray of appetizers, her mother looked at Jenna. "Somehow I never expected to see you dating a man with children, dear."

Mrs. Quinn leaned back to allow the server to place a plate of escargot swimming in butter before her. "You do realize," she said to Sloan, "that my daughter has only ever dated the same man for a period of—what was it, dear?—four months?"

"It was six, Mother." Jenna stared at the crock of potato soup set in front of her.

"Nevertheless, it's not fair to children to have them get attached to you only to have you not be part of their lives again."

"You should know," Jenna murmured.

"How do those coconut shrimp look, Sloan?" her father cut in with a smooth change of subject. "My frog's legs look excellent."

Jenna pushed back her chair, dropped her napkin to the table and scooped up her purse. "Excuse me. I'll be right back." With a quick glance of apology at Sloan, she scurried off, in search of the restrooms, no doubt.

He half rose as she departed, then eased back into his chair, offering her parents a weak smile. She was going to owe him big-time for this.

Jenna lingered in the bathroom as long as she dared. No point in giving her mother more ammunition. She re-applied some blush and lipstick, then headed back to the table. Sloan stood, pulling out her chair. "Thank you."

The empty plates in front of her parents made her feel much better. She nibbled at the crackers provided with her soup and made a show of lifting her nearly empty spoon to her mouth, though she didn't eat much. The now-cool soup didn't carry as much scent as it had when steaming hot.

"Sloan was telling us about his sister and her step-daughter, Molly," her father said. "About her heart trans-plant. Sounds like quite an amazing family."

"They're a tight-knit bunch. Sloan moved up here just so he could be closer to them." Jenna pushed the brown crock away from her. A busboy swooped in, asked if she was finished, and whisked it away at her nod.

"Wasn't the soup any good, dear?"

"A little salty," Jenna lied. Salad proved more diffi-cult to fudge. She spent a lot of time babbling about ideas for the store, moving the romaine around her bowl as she did. Oil and vinegar, her most bland dressing op-tion, didn't bother her, but the lettuce itself proved harder to deal with. Once again when the others finished, she pushed hers aside.

So far, so good.

Or not so bad, anyway.

"Did you know Jenna was valedictorian of her high-school class?" her mother asked Sloan.

"No, ma'am. I didn't know that. Although I'm not surprised. She's always struck me as a bright lady."

"Yes. The girl has an IQ of 146, and instead of taking an opening at Princeton, she chose to go to Penn State. To get a degree in art."

"And business, too, Mallory. Don't forget that," Dad said.

"And my mother will never get over the fact that I have a mind of my own, a very sharp one as she has pointed out, and I'm not afraid to use it to think for myself."

"Ah, look, here's our dinner," her father said as their server approached. "Saved by the cuisine."

Lemon butter swamped her plate, nearly floating her chicken piccata. She tried to ignore the aromas wafting from the other plates being set on the table. But her father's Louisiana catfish and her mother's poached salmon didn't give her much choice.

The temperature in the room dipped, then shot up. Her fork trembled in her clammy hands. Parting her lips just a crack, she tried shallow mouth-breathing.

Didn't help.

"Are you all right?" her father asked. "You've gone a bit pale. Is there something wrong with your food?"

"I—I haven't been feeling well, Dad." She eased her

chair away from the table a bit. Sloan's fingers closed around her knee, offering a covert squeeze of support.

Her mother stared at her. Then she set her fork down. Leaning forward, she looked closer. "You're sweating. And you've turned the most unattractive shade of gray." Her eyes narrowed, and Jenna could see her mentally compiling the list of evidence. "No wine. Ginger ale." She sat straight up in her chair. "Oh, God, you're pregnant!"

Jenna opened her mouth to say something—what, she had no idea—but her mother raised her hand. "No! Don't say a word. We will not speak of this here." She glanced around the room, as if to be sure no one in the restaurant had heard the horrible news about her daughter's unexpected pregnancy.

"Mr. and Mrs. Quinn—" Sloan began, only to be silenced by another wave of the commanding hand and her mother's "shh."

It was the uncertain expression on her father's face that made Jenna want to weep. His eyes glistened. "Daddy—" she began.

"Don't 'Daddy' him. You're not going to wrap him around your little finger this time. Once again, you prove how selfish and self-centered you are, Jenna. Why can't you think about someone else for a change?"

Sloan jumped from his seat and threw his napkin onto the chair. He reached down to help Jenna up. "That's enough. Nobody talks to her like that. Not even her mother. Come on, sugar, we're leaving."

Mallory Quinn's mouth opened for a split second. "But-but we drove."

"We'll get a cab." He wrapped his arm around Jenna's shoulder and eased her away from the table. "Should you decide to be more reasonable, you know where to find us." On the way out, he had the maître d' call a local taxi company. Jenna rushed away from him, heading to the coat check to reclaim her jacket. He caught up with her in front of the restaurant, with tears coursing down her cheeks and puffs of dragon smoke issuing from her mouth and nose.

"I hope that steam coming from you doesn't mean you're pissed at me."

She turned to face him and broke into laughter that alternated with sobs. "No. That was the best rescue ever, Tex." She threw herself against his chest.

He wrapped his arms around her, once again struck by his need to protect her. "Don't cry. Your face will freeze. Think how you'll look with little icicles hanging off your chin like an old woman's whiskers."

Another snort-laugh was muffled by his coat. "Don't. Don't make me laugh."

"Why not? I'd rather hear you laughing than crying."

"Because." She shoved him away and straightened up, her palms against her belly. "I'm not puking out here."

"Why not?" he asked again, grateful the banter was keeping her mind off the ugly scene that had just played out—and thoughts of what came next where her parents were concerned. "The hospital's just up the street."

"That's why not." She stomped her foot into the coating of snow on the sidewalk. "I'm not going there again until it's time to have this baby, mister."

"Fine by me."

In the dim light of the streetlamps, her face grew somber. "On the other hand," she murmured, "maybe I really ought to reconsider having this baby at all."

The sucker punch drove the air from his lungs, and he struggled to appear impassive. "Why? Can't take feeling like crap every day for a few more weeks?"

She shook her head. "Children have to come first, Sloan. Always. What if I can't do that? What if I screw up? Look at my role model. Not exactly Mother of the Year, although she did get Lawyer of the Year once." She knuckled her eyes.

"Jenna," he chided. "You are nothing like that. You're warm and caring. Hey, look at how you dealt with Brook when she came to you, in trouble."

"I recall you didn't appreciate how I handled that."

"You know I changed my tune about it."

A taxi eased to a stop at the curb. Sloan opened the back door and helped her in. After getting in himself and giving the driver directions, he pulled Jenna against his side. They rode to her building in silence. Once inside, he helped her with her coat. She stalked to the sofa and flopped down, gathering one of the throw pillows in her arms.

Twenty minutes later, he'd managed to get her to drink some ginger tea. He sat at the end of the sofa with her head cradled in his lap, stroking her hair and the soft skin of her forehead. Like a contented cat, she hummed her approval. Eventually she slipped into sleep. Sloan eased off the couch, substituting a pillow beneath her head, tucking a blanket around her. He pressed a light kiss on the tip of her nose. When the doorbell rang, she stirred, shifted, then burrowed deeper under the cover.

The monitor showed her father, clapping his ungloved hands together, waiting for a response. Sloan left the apartment door open and descended the staircase to the outer door. A private chat with Robert Quinn, well out of Jenna's hearing range, was called for. "Come on in."

In the stairwell, they appraised each other. Sloan swallowed hard. "Look, sir—"

"Son, I don't think you have a clue what I'm feeling right now."

"Oh, I'm pretty sure I do."

"I'm not a very physical man, Sloan, nor prone to violence. But right now, I'm sorely tempted."

"I understand, sir."

"And do you understand how much I love my daughter? You've got two girls. What would you do if one of them turned up pregnant? How would you feel?"

"Like I wanted to strangle the son of a bitch who knocked her up before the time was right."

He nodded. "So, I need to ask. What are your intentions toward my daughter?"

"You mean, like marriage?"

"If you don't intend to marry her—"

"Actually, sir, I've asked her to marry me. She hasn't given me an answer yet."

"Ah. Somehow I'm not surprised. My daughter has always followed her own mind. If she decides not to marry you, then I expect support of some kind for the child. Assistance for Jenna." His lips quirked. "I am, after all, a lawyer."

"I assure you, sir, neither Jenna nor the baby will want for anything. I'm already covering her medical bills since she doesn't have any insurance."

Her father groaned. "No insurance?"

"She couldn't afford it and figured she was healthy. The doc is giving us a break for cash payment."

"All right. As long as you behave well toward her, I'm sure we can handle this in a civilized manner." Her father thrust out his hand. "I have your word you'll take care of them both?"

"You do."

"Good. I'll hold you to that." With a final shake, he released the firm clasp. "Now, I need to speak with my daughter."

"She's sleeping. On the sofa." Sloan followed him up the stairs. Once in her apartment, he took her father's coat, then puttered around in the kitchen, trying to appear uninterested in the scene unfolding a few feet away in the living area. Robert bent over, just looking at her for a moment. Then he caressed her hair. "Jenna?"

She stretched. "Hmm? Dad?" She sat up, rumpled and adorable like a sleepy kitten. "What's up?"

Robert eased himself onto the couch beside her. "I need to talk to you, hon. First of all, try to give your mother some slack. She's a little…overwhelmed right now. I figured with her on the edge, putting the two of you together wasn't a good idea, but she wouldn't let me drive up here alone. And I needed to talk to you. In person."

The sleepiness vanished, replaced by wariness. "About what?"

He took her hand. "I'm having surgery next Wednesday."

"What kind?"

"A double bypass. But don't worry. I have the best cardiac surgeon in the area, and she says it's going to be a snap. No problem."

"Oh, Daddy!" Jenna sniffled.

Her father drew her into his arms. "Don't cry. I'm sure it's going to be fine. Believe me, doctors are extra careful when treating lawyers." He laughed. "And besides, the news you just gave us is the best reason I can think of for getting healthy fast. I'm going to be a grandfather." A note of awe flickered in his voice.

"Th-thanks, Daddy."

"For what?"

"For being good about the whole thing. For not lecturing me."

"Lecturing won't change anything. I'll finally have some photos to brag about at the firm."

"Wh-what did Mother say?"

Robert cleared his throat. "She said to let you know that ice pops are a good idea for the nausea. She threw up damn near every day for the first two months with you."

"She did?"

"Yes, she did. But the idea of becoming a grandmother is going to take some time for her to get used to. Says it makes her feel old."

Jenna giggled. "Well, if you want something to really tweak her with, to distract her from your surgery, you can tell her that if Sloan and I get married, she's not only going to become a grandmother, but she'll be a great-grandmother first."

Sloan froze in the midst of dropping a strawberry into the smoothie machine. Robert glanced over Jenna's head at him. "Ah. So he does understand how I'm feeling."

Sloan nodded. "I do."

The words caught in his throat.

CHAPTER FOURTEEN

THE LAST DAY of school before April vacation hadn't gone well at all, with two tests Brook hadn't been prepared for. And now she had a meeting with her father and the guidance team. Yippee, she could hardly wait.

The chaos and confusion of dismissal swirled around her: the press of the bodies in the hallway, the chatter of voices once again glad to be free—temporarily. In the process of reaching for her English book, she caught a glimpse of her reflection in the locker-door mirror. She grimaced, then tugged on the hem of her sweater. Despite the loose clothes, the small swell of her stomach was becoming unmistakable.

At the far end of the hall, Dylan's lanky form appeared. He looked in her direction. His head bobbed and he gave her a little wave—the only acknowledgment she ever got from him, since the scene at his house. His father's orders to stay away from her had been obeyed.

Wuss boy.

She pulled her coat from the locker and draped it over her arm. Her backpack was lighter than normal because only Mr. Davidson had been cruddy enough to assign a project over the vacation.

The noise died away as kids filtered out of the building. Brook trudged down the hallway, passing the custodian pushing a dust mop over the tile. Her dad stood outside the guidance counselor's office, face drawn and tired. But he smiled when he saw her. "Hey. Do you have any idea what this is all about?"

Brook lifted one shoulder. "No clue."

"All right. Let's get on with it, then." He took her backpack from her hand.

The scent of stale coffee greeted them, along with Ms. Sheldon, the school psychologist; Mr. Berger, the guidance counselor; and Mrs. Jackowski, one of the Family and Consumer Science teachers. They all introduced themselves to her dad. Then, after everyone settled in the cushy chairs at the round table in the middle of the office, awkward silence descended. Brook resisted the urge to squirm. What the hell had she done now?

"Mr. Thompson," Ms. Sheldon began, "we've asked you here today because we're all concerned about Brook's future, as we're sure you are. We wanted to be able to come up with a plan of action."

"Okay," her dad said. "Sounds reasonable. But what exactly are we talking about? I mean, is she disrupting classes, or do you see a special talent in her you want to nurture? What?"

"Oh, Brook's a fairly good student—"

"When she wants to be," Mr. Berger injected.

Ms. Sheldon frowned at him and continued. "But we're more concerned right now with helping Brook make decisions regarding her pregnancy. We have a variety of programs in place to assist teen mothers, but it seems that every time any of us tries to discuss these options with Brook, she tunes us out. It's as if she's still in denial."

"Welcome to my world," her dad said. "She tunes me out anytime I want to talk about something she doesn't want to hear."

Brook stared at the purple nail polish on her fingernails.

"See? Just like that."

"Oh, for crying out loud," Brook said. "Give me some papers to read on whatever programs we're talking about. I'll read them over spring break and we can figure it out when school starts up again."

"Actually," said Mrs. Jackowski, "we had a different sort of project in mind for you for over vacation." She leaned over in her chair to pick something up. She laid it on the table. "This is an infant simulator. Have you ever seen one of these before?"

A knot of dread formed in the pit of Brook's stomach as she shook her head.

"This computerized baby will give you a real taste of what it's going to be like to have a baby of your own, Brook. It will cry to be fed, changed, rocked, or just because it feels like it. It requires constant care, either from its mother—you—or from a designated babysitter. The computer chip inside it will report you for abuse if you don't respond to the baby's cries or if you handle it too roughly."

"That's pretty neat," her father said, reaching for it.

A little pink romper showed it was a girl. "The technology to accomplish all that is amazing."

"I don't think they'll let you take it apart, Dad, to see how it works. I'm guessing that would be abuse, too, right?"

Mrs. Jackowski retrieved the baby, cradling it in her arms. "It most certainly would. Mr. Thompson, we will hold you responsible for replacing this simulator if anything happens to it."

Her dad chuckled. "I wouldn't actually take it apart."

"Good. Then if you both agree to participate in this program, we'll run the training video, and you can be on your way with your baby."

"Oh, joy," Brook muttered. "It's a girl."

BROOK STRUGGLED with the car seat, yanking on it with growing frustration. Her dad stood beside her, holding his "grandbaby" in his arms. A cold wind blew across the deserted parking lot of the high school.

"Brook, do you want me to do that? Those things can be kind of tricky."

"Fine." She stepped aside and accepted the baby, whom she'd named Rebecca, from him. He maneuvered the car seat into position and got it strapped in.

Brook then gingerly placed the baby into the restraints. The last thing she needed was an abuse report before they'd even left the parking lot. The simulator had a sensitive neck that required the same gentle handling a real baby did. Mrs. J. had demonstrated proper holding several times before Brook had gotten the hang of it.

Brook climbed into the truck's front seat, slamming the door. "Okay, let's go. Vacation, here I come."

Her dad gave her a weirded-out look.

"What?"

"Nothing."

They weren't halfway home when the baby in the back seat began to cry, starting soft and slow and working up into a rip-roaring pitch in no time. Her stomach started tumbling, and she was pretty sure it wasn't caused by her real baby. "Crap. What do we do now?"

"We? What's this we stuff, sugar? You're the momma. Just remember, if you let the baby cry for more than thirty seconds without doing something, it's considered neglect."

"Then pull over!"

Dad jerked the truck into the parking lot of the tire place at the end of Powell Ave. Brook jumped out, quickly vaulting into the back seat. The blue diaper bag with the *Baby Think It Over* logo—a wailing baby, cute, very cute—sat on the floor. She grabbed it and started digging through it. This was going to be some vacation.

THE BABY HOWLED from the room next door. Sloan groaned. When the bleary red numbers on the clock snapped into focus, they read 2:47 a.m.

The crying grew louder, and the door to his room burst open. He sat up. Brook held the infant simulator in his direction. "I can't get it to stop. I tried changing, burping, feeding, rocking. Daddy, make it stop!"

"Did anything happen to it?" He took the computerized baby from her.

"You mean, like, is it defective or something?"

"I don't know. Sounds like something's wrong."

Brook pulled on the bottom of her pajama top, twisting the fabric. She shuffled her feet. "Well, um…"

"Um? Brook, what happened to the baby?"

"It kinda, sorta, fell out of my bed."

"Brook!" He clicked on the small nightstand lamp, examining the baby for any obvious damage. A few seconds later the unit stopped crying, and he slumped with relief—apparently the crying jags had a cutoff time, fortunately shorter than some he'd experienced with his own kids. He laid the simulator on its back on his bed and swung around to his daughter.

Who had tears streaming down her face.

His heart twisted. "What's wrong, honey?"

"I—I haven't been a mother for twelve hours yet, and already I've let her get hurt. The crying is making me crazy, I'm tired, and I need some sleep." She placed a hand over her rounding tummy. "If it's not the fake baby, it's this one, rolling around in here and keeping me awake."

He opened his arms to her. "C'mere."

She sat sideways across his knees, locking her hands behind his neck and burying her face against his shoulder. Sobs broke loose from deep inside her, and her hot tears dampened his T-shirt and the skin beneath. He rocked her as he had when she was little. "Shh."

"You're—you're supposed to tell me it will be all right," she choked out.

He hesitated only a second. "It will be all right, Snickerdoodle."

"H-how? I don't know anything about babies!"

"Neither does any other first-time parent. You'll learn the hard way, just like your mom and I did." He caressed her shaking back.

"Re-remember when Mom and I used to play tic-tac-toe? And sometimes we'd just scribble out the boards and yell 'Do over'?"

Sloan nodded, recalling his wife's laughter as she and Brook competed with purple and red crayons.

"I wish I could have a do-over."

So did he.

JENNA PROPPED the portable phone between her ear and her shoulder, reaching into the display window to reposition the terra-cotta pots of silk daffodils and tulips. The early May sunlight glinted off the pieces of gold jewelry she'd chosen to feature this week. Soon that sunlight would have real flowers popping up in the landscaped beds along her sidewalk.

She sighed. It felt great to be back in her shop fulltime instead of sneaking down the stairs when she could manage it. "Yes, Dad, Sloan's been great," she said into the phone.

And he had been. He'd been there when she needed him—and sometimes even when she hadn't. There was no way she'd have gotten through the weeks of intense nausea without his help, without his making smoothies and urging her to drink something, not to mention the million other things he'd done to make her more comfortable. Fortunately, although the doctor's prediction had been off a little, by fifteen weeks the nausea had stopped.

"So why haven't you given the man an answer about his proposal? If you're going to say no, then say no. But don't leave him hanging like this indefinitely. What are you doing, waiting for the baby to go to school before you make a decision?"

"Hey, whose side are you on?"

"I like Sloan, honey. He seems to be a very good man. You could do a hell of a lot worse."

She knew that. But still…she'd sworn off impulsiveness. "Didn't your doctor tell you to avoid stress? Doesn't meddling in my life constitute stress?"

Her father laughed, a sound that warmed her far more than the rays of the sun through the window. She'd heard more laughter from him since his bypass surgery than in the rest of her life put together. "I'm in great shape now, Jenna, no need to worry on my account."

"That's good, Dad. So, when are you going back to the firm full-time?"

"I'm not."

Jenna lost her grip on the phone. It knocked over two pots of red tulips and clattered to the floor of the display window, narrowly missing a pair of dogwood-blossom earrings. She scrambled to retrieve it. "Sorry. Didn't mean to drop you. You're not going back to the firm full-time?"

"No. I think I'm going to make time to do some of the other things I've always wanted to do."

"Really? Like what?"

"Never mind. Let's get back to the focus of this discussion. You and Sloan. Do you love him?"

The baby chose that moment to make its presence known, a soft fluttering deep in her stomach. Jenna pressed her hand over the long sweater that hid the little round swell.

"Jenna? I asked if you loved him."

She'd never been involved with a man like Sloan. Part bluster and hard on the outside, but soft and squishy on the inside. He had a heart as big as the state he came from but didn't want anyone to know it. "I think so. I've never been in love before, so I'm not certain."

"What are you afraid of? It's so unlike you. You've never in your life been afraid to take a chance, afraid to fail and have to pick yourself back up and start over again."

Jenna considered it as she drew the curtain on the display window. "I guess…I'm afraid to lose myself. To end up compromising who I am. To have to be accountable to someone else."

"Oh, Jenna." Her dad's voice softened. "You're going to be accountable to someone else from now on. Your child."

Her chest tightened. "Yeah. There is that. I'm not just making decisions for myself anymore, am I?"

"No, honey. You're not."

"That terrifies me, Dad. What if I make the wrong decisions? I mean, it's one thing to make a mistake for myself. Like you said, I'm an expert at starting over. But this isn't just about me now."

"Listen to yourself, Jenna. You're already showing signs of being a great mom. You're thinking not about yourself but about your child."

A long stretch of silence passed along the phone line. She had to do the right thing for her child—which meant facing her fear and giving Sloan the trust he'd earned from her. Goose bumps popped along her arms. The one man who hadn't been fitting her for an apron might just be the one to tie one around her waist. She'd come to adore Ashley, who'd been visiting her at the shop at least twice a week, sometimes more. And she'd cared about Brook long before she had really known anyone else in the Thompson family, even though she and the teen still weren't back on good terms.

Laughter floated from the earpiece of the phone. "What are you chuckling about, Dad?"

"Oh, I just had a thought. What are you going to do if your child turns out to be an introverted bookworm who wants to be a lawyer?"

"Ack! You bite your tongue! Why, the horror of it!"

"Seriously, what would you do?"

"Well, I guess I would want her to do whatever is going to make her happy. Even if that means being a lawyer."

"Despite what you may think, that's all I've ever wanted for you, honey. And that's what I want for you now."

She couldn't resist tweaking him. "You still want me to be a lawyer?"

"No! I want you to be happy."

"That's all I've ever wanted, too. Thanks, Dad." She

said her goodbyes and disconnected, carting the phone back to the office. Cheryl, the teenager she'd hired to replace Brook, was putting away the glass cleaner and paper towels.

"I'm done wiping down the cases," Cheryl said. "If you don't mind, even though it's a little early, I'd like to leave."

"Sure thing. Go ahead. I think I might close up a little ahead of schedule tonight myself." And she did just that, turning the sign around and locking the front door behind the girl. Then she used the connecting door to go from her office into Margo's, but her friend wasn't there. Jenna wandered down the hallway, peeking into the empty treatment room, then continued to the main shop. Margo sat behind the front counter, staring into space.

Jenna snapped her fingers. "Earth to Margo. Come on, let's go."

"Go where? I'm supposed to be open for another hour."

"Do you have another massage client?"

Margo shook her head.

Jenna made a big production of scanning the room, peering down the two aisles of naturopathic products. "Well, since I see other customers are swarming you tonight, like they are me, I propose we ditch this lemonade stand. I'm going stir-crazy. Besides, I'm starving."

"Now that your appetite is back, you'd better watch it. You'll gain back all the weight you lost at the start of this pregnancy, and then some. You'll be as big as a house by the time that baby is born, at the rate you're going." Margo left the counter area, brushing past a display of essential oils, to secure the front door.

"Thanks so much. You're a barrel of laughs these days."

Her friend scrunched up her face. "Hey, I really thought Phil was going to be The One. Excuse me for sulking for a few days. You're supposed to sympathize with me for getting dumped again."

Jenna reached out to rub Margo's shoulder. "Poor baby. Phil was obviously a toad, not worthy of a fantastic woman like you."

"That's better."

CRUISING DOWN 38th Street, work behind him, the night ahead, Sloan reached for his cell phone to call Jenna, then changed his mind. Instead, he gripped the steering wheel with both hands to prevent himself from waffling again. He'd been doing his damnedest to give her some space.

It wasn't an easy task, when every moment he spent with her gave him a natural high—especially now that she was back to her old sparkly self.

Passing Crazy Eights Pub and Pool Hall, he did a double take, looking over his shoulder. Was that ugly orange thing in the parking lot *her* ugly orange thing? Or were there more people in Erie with horrible taste in car color?

At the next intersection, he turned, making a trip around the block and coming up the side street by the pub. A closer look at the car assured him it was Jenna's. No one else would have the red furry sneaker monster from Bugs Bunny dangling from the rearview mirror. He pulled the truck into a space three spots down before he even realized what he was doing.

Should he? Would she feel he was checking up on

her? Hell, he had a good enough reason to be checking up on her. She was carrying his child, for God's sake. And it wasn't as if he'd gone out looking for her—she was the one who'd picked a place on his route home from work.

He swung from the truck. Inside the building, the odor of stale cigarette smoke and beer greeted him, along with classic rock blaring from the ceiling speakers. The stools along the bar were all full, as were the majority of the tables. The place had to be a gold mine on Friday and Saturday nights if it was packed like this on a Wednesday. Happy-hour specials—dollar drafts and twenty-five-cent wings—were posted in neon print on a board by the door.

Sloan made his way around the perimeter, scanning the crowd for Jenna. Finally spotting her, he ground to a stop. Bent over a pool table, poised to take a shot, she didn't seem to realize that the plunging neckline of her tunic exposed the newly expanded cleavage she sported thanks to the pregnancy. And she couldn't notice the guy with the broad grin, leaning on a pool cue behind her—checking out her ass, no doubt.

Sloan's guts tightened and his hands clenched. Fiery pain blossomed in his chest.

He searched his memory of the night they'd gone out to dinner with her parents. Six months, she'd said, had been her longest relationship. If you counted from their dinner date back in October, they'd already been seven months. He was on borrowed time.

Was the guy drooling over Jenna's luscious backside

his replacement? Was she tired of Sloan now and already looking for a new playmate?

Hellfire. He'd promised himself he'd never again put himself in a position where he'd doubt the woman in his life. And what had he done? Gotten involved with a natural-born flirt—a woman who not only could hurt him like Beth had, but likely would.

Jenna straightened from the missed shot with a shrug. Then she caught sight of him. Her eyes widened with recognition. A slow smile curved her mouth, turning into a huge grin as her whole face brightened.

He felt like a total heel for doubting her.

"Tex!" she mouthed, waving him over.

He wove through the scattered tables and chairs around the pool-playing area. When he got close, she came to meet him, throwing her arms around his neck and pressing a kiss to his lips.

That made him feel even lower, the dust beneath somebody's boots, never mind the heel.

He snaked his arm around her waist and drew her closer, aware of the other guy's attention on them. He kissed her firmly, making sure there would be no doubt in any onlooker's mind that she was his woman.

"All right, knock it off or get a room," Margo growled at them.

Sloan separated from Jenna, glancing at her friend. "What's with her?"

"All men are scum tonight, Tex, so don't mess with Margo, okay?"

"All men? Even me?"

Jenna nodded solemnly, but her eyes twinkled. "Even you."

Sloan jerked his head in the other guy's direction. "What about him? Is he scum, too?"

"Who, Johnny?" Jenna laughed. "No, he's not scum."

"Why the hell not?"

Jenna's face grew red and she laughed harder as she motioned the dark-haired man closer. "Johnny, come meet Sloan. He wants to know why you get a free-pass on all-men-are-scum night."

Sloan eyed the hand Johnny stuck out, grudgingly taking it, squeezing a little harder than necessary.

Johnny joined Jenna in chuckling. "I wondered why he was giving me the evil eye from the other side of the room. Jenna, you're naughty. You've never told your man about me. And here I thought we were friends."

"We don't count Johnny as scum because he's one of the girls, not a man," Margo called out, sizing up a shot.

"And you know, I'm not quite sure how to take that," Johnny said, placing his palm in the middle of his chest. "Compliment or dig?"

"Johnny used to run a hairdressing place in the empty part of my building when I first bought it, but then he got too big for us and moved. Hey, maybe you are scum," Jenna said. "I still haven't rented that out."

"Don't be bitchy, dear," Johnny replied.

The bells went off in Sloan's head, and his face warmed. Gay. The guy was gay. "Guess you weren't scoping out Jenna's uh...never mind."

The man laughed. "No, while Jenna has a very nice

ass, especially bent over a pool table, I'm more likely to be checking out yours. Especially since I, like Margo, find myself recently dumped." He craned his neck as if to see around Sloan. "Do you wanna play in the next game?"

Sloan shifted his weight from foot to foot, resisting the temptation to either turn away or slug the guy.

"Don't be hitting on my man, Johnny, or I'll have to get out my claws." Jenna arched her hand at him, displaying her pink and yellow nails. "Besides, I can vouch for the fact that he's not your type. Look at him. You're making him uncomfortable. Cut it out."

"*Your* man, huh?" Sloan murmured near her ear. "I think I like that. You'd better watch it, though. I might just mistake that possessiveness for some form of commitment."

"Hey, I'm having your baby. How much more of a commitment do you want?"

He arched an eyebrow at her. She held his gaze for a moment, then looked away.

A bitter zing of disappointment shot through him.

"Are you guys going to actually play, or just talk all night?" Margo asked, taking a swig of her beer.

"Here are your hot wings." A waitress dropped an overflowing bucket of chicken wings, a pile of napkins, and an empty, paper-lined basket on a nearby table. "Does anyone need anything else?"

"Food! I quit for now. You can shoot for me, Margo." Jenna pulled Sloan toward the steaming bucket. "Want some wings?" He shook his head but ordered a draft.

"If you're smart, you won't get between her and the

chicken," Johnny said as he passed Sloan on his way to the pool table. "She's liable to bite you."

"Would you really?" Sloan asked her as they perched on the tall stools that encircled the table.

She didn't answer, just sank her teeth into an orange-coated wing. Sipping his drink, he watched her devour one after another until a small pile of bones filled the once-empty basket. Her obvious delight gave him great satisfaction. "It's good to see you eating again. And enjoying things again."

"Let me tell you, it's good on this side of it, too." She wiped her hands, then her mouth, with a napkin.

"You missed a spot." He took the crumpled paper from her and brushed at the corner of her lips. "You know, I really need to get going. The girls are expecting me."

Jenna nodded. "I'll follow you. I wanted to talk to you tonight anyway. Just let me make sure it's okay with Margo, and see if Johnny will drive her back to the shop when they're done commiserating on the scumminess of men."

"Talk, huh?" In his experience, it was never a good thing when a woman announced she wanted to talk.

CHAPTER FIFTEEN

JENNA'S HANDS SHOOK as she shut off the car. For several long minutes she just sat there, trying to calm the quivering in her stomach that had nothing to do with the baby.

Well, not exactly.

A tapping sounded on the window next to her ear, and she jumped. "Sloan! Jeez, you scared me. Don't do that." She grabbed her purse from the passenger seat and climbed out.

"Why don't you come over to my place? We can be together while I get the girls' dinner. Otherwise I have to wait, and I don't want to. I want to be with you now."

"Do you really think that's wise?"

"Why? I thought you wanted to talk to me?"

"I meant Brook." The thought of facing the teen made her palms damp. But if she and Sloan were going to have any kind of a future together, she had to make sure his older daughter was going to eventually accept her again.

"Brook's been a little more…mellow lately. I say let's do it. Ashley will be thrilled to see you at our place." Sloan extended his hand. "Come on. I'll feed you something else, too."

"Dessert?" She grinned at him as they strolled down the sidewalk, fingers entwined.

He skidded to a halt, turning to her. "Has that appetite returned, too?"

"Absolutely."

He lowered his head, gave her an easy kiss that had her insides going gooey. "Mmm. Spicy. Just like you." He brushed his lips over hers one more time. "I'll have to see what I can do about taking care of both your appetites."

Apprehension filled her as they resumed their trek to his house. "Well…maybe not. I'm getting kind of round, you know. And I had to take out the belly-button ring."

"Hey." He stopped on the top porch step. "I've told you before. I think you're beautiful no matter what. I certainly don't want to stop making love to you just because your body is changing. In fact, I've been dying to get you naked again, okay?"

"You say that now, but what about in another few months?"

"You'll still be beautiful and desirable. Sugar, sexy isn't just about the outside. It's an attitude. Trust me when I say you are probably the sexiest woman I have ever known, right now, and always. You have to believe me when I tell you that."

She searched his face, finding concern and a bit of uncertainty in his eyes. "This is important to you, isn't it?"

"Yes."

"Okay, then I believe you. And I'll be looking forward to you backing up your sweet-talking words with some action." She winked at him.

"Good." He kissed her again, then led her into the house. "Girls, I'm home!" he called up the stairs.

In the kitchen, Jenna sat in one of the chairs at the little dinette while Sloan poked around in the refrigerator. They heard a set of small feet clatter down the stairs to the living room. Ashley barreled into the kitchen a few seconds later. "Daddy!" She threw herself at Sloan, who scooped her into a hug, then set her down.

"What do you want for dinner, Peach?"

"Can we have chicken quesadillas?"

"Hmm. Do you think Jenna can take the heat of the pico de gallo?" Sloan nodded in her direction.

"Jenna! You're here!" Ashley forgot about her father, rushing over to throw her arms around Jenna's neck and squeezing. "You like spicy food, right?"

"Yes, I do."

"Does the baby?" Ashley untangled her arms to stoop over and pat Jenna's stomach in a gesture she found oddly moving.

"As far as I can tell."

"Then you'll love Daddy's quesadillas."

"Okay, it's settled," Sloan said.

The kitchen filled with the smells of chicken, onions and peppers as the food sizzled in a large frying pan. Ashley brought her reading book out, asking Jenna to listen to her read a story for part of her homework. Sloan bustled around the stove, ignoring Jenna's requests to see what he was putting in the meal.

The whole scene gave Jenna a warm fuzzy. Being with him, even with Ashley, just felt so damn right. But when she thought about Brook, Jenna's hands started to tremble again.

Sloan sent Ashley to fetch her older sister, but the little girl returned quickly. "She's asleep, Dad, with a whole bunch of papers spread around her on the bed."

"Let her sleep, Sloan. Trust me when I say pregnancy takes a lot out of a person." Jenna could deal with waiting a while to see how Brook responded to her presence in the house again.

Dinner and cleanup breezed by. Jenna was surprised how natural it felt, given her several months' absence from his home. After Sloan sent Ashley upstairs to take a bath, he took Jenna's hand and pulled her down onto the sofa, placing an arm around her shoulders. "Now," he said, "why don't you tell me what's going on in your head?"

"That obvious, huh?"

"Well, when I asked for the butter for a tortilla you left the table and brought me back a beer. Not that I'm complaining about the beer, mind you. I appreciated it."

"Wow. Guess I was pretty far away. No wonder Ashley giggled when I came back from the kitchen." She snuggled into him, pressing her cheek against his chest.

"So, what's on your mind, sugar?"

The rehearsals she'd imagined had all been easier than this. But maybe the moment wasn't right. Somehow there should have been candlelight and music, and maybe she should tell him after they made love, naked in his arms, tangled in her sheets…

"I love you." There. She'd said it.

The house shifted and the pipes rushed with water, evidence of Ashley's filling the tub. But Sloan remained silent. Jenna wiped her palms over her jeans. "Uh, a response of any kind would be good."

"Could you repeat what you just said?"

She sat up and slapped his chest. "This is no time to be funny! I've never told any man that. Well, my dad, but he doesn't count."

"I'm serious, sugar. I want to be looking at you when you say it again."

"Oh, Sloan." She cupped his cheeks with her hands. "I love you."

He smiled, turning his face to kiss the heel of her palm. "Hot damn. No wonder you couldn't think straight tonight. But I have to ask—what brought you to this stunning conclusion? Especially now?"

"What's not to love about a guy who takes care of a woman while she's sick as hell? Who loves his kids so much that he uproots his whole life to do what he thinks is best for them? Who even goes as far as asking the mother of the latest child to marry him when he's not sure it's what he really wants?"

Sloan's breath caught at the honesty of her comment. Marrying her was the right thing to do, but he had to admit to moments of relief that she hadn't answered his proposal yet.

But the admission that she loved him…now that put a different spin on things. He leaned in and took her lips with his.

"Dad?" The banister creaked and a set of footsteps

came down the stairs. "I have to talk—what the hell is she doing here?"

Sloan turned to face his daughter, settling a protective arm around Jenna. "Watch your mouth. It's about time you got over it, Brook. Jenna and I didn't plan for this to happen any more than you and Dylan did. If you want people to give you a break, then you have to offer that same break to others. Before you found out she was carrying your brother or sister—" he held up his hand as Brook opened her mouth "—you counted Jenna as your friend. How would you have felt if Kelly had decided to stop being your friend when you found out you were pregnant?"

"Totally different. I'm not having Kelly's father's baby. And if I were—major eewwww—but if I were, I'd expect Kelly to be pissed at me."

"For how long, Brook?" Jenna asked softly. "I didn't mean to betray you. And I don't want you to think that I'm trying to bust into your family and take your mother's place. I'm not. But I really would like for us to be friends again. I've missed you."

Brook snorted, folding her arms over her chest. "Sure. It didn't take you long to hire Cheryl."

"You quit. And so did Nicole. I really needed help because I was so sick. Without Cheryl, Margo, and even your dad helping me out, I might have had to close the shop completely."

Brook's defiant look slipped a little. "So?"

"So that business and the building is all I've got right now to support myself and my baby."

"That's not true. You've got my dad, too."

Sloan started to speak, but Jenna tightened her fingers around his thigh. "I didn't set out to steal your father away from you, Brook."

Brook's hands slipped to her sides, shoulders drooping. Her lower lip trembled. "But you did," she whispered, her voice just audible on the far side of the room. "When I needed him the most. And just when he'd started to love me. *Me!*"

His chest constricted at his child's revelation. "Brook, honey, I've always loved you." He fled the sofa, striding in her direction. "I haven't always understood you, I haven't always liked the things you've done, but I've always loved you."

Brook rushed down the final two stairs and threw herself into his open arms. "Oh Daddy!"

He held her tight, stroking the hair she'd stopped coloring like a chameleon since finding out she was pregnant.

"I—I hope you still love me when I tell you something."

"Sweetheart, no matter what, I'll always love you."

Brook raised her face from his chest. Tears flowed down her cheeks. "G-good. Because for once, I'm going to do the right thing. I—I've decided I'm going to put my baby up for adoption."

A small sound of shock mingled with dismay came from behind him, from Jenna.

His brain heard the words, but it refused to process them. Or maybe it was his heart that wouldn't do the processing—or couldn't, given that it felt like it was being crushed in a huge vise grip.

"D-Daddy?" Brook's tears continued to flow, and the uncertainty in her eyes proved his undoing once again.

"Let's sit down, honey." Numbly he guided her to the couch, where she settled down beside Jenna without a squeak of protest. He sat on the other side of her. "What—" he cleared his throat, hoping to sound unflustered by her announcement "—what made you decide that's the right thing to do?"

Brook took the tissue Jenna offered, mopping at her face. "I had a meeting with Mrs. Jackowski today. We went over the results of the infant simulator. We talked for a long time. I'm just not ready to take care of a baby!"

She blew her nose, then clenched the tissue in her fist. "It was a lot harder than I thought it would be—and that baby wasn't real." Brook's hands splayed across her belly. "I want something better for her, Dad. I want her to have a mother who knows what she's doing. Someone who's ready for her, who's waiting for her. Not someone like me. And I want her to have a dad in her life, too. Dylan doesn't want to be a dad."

"There's no need to be hasty, Brook. You've still got time—"

"I'm not being hasty! I've been thinking about it and thinking about it. I can't take care of her." A fresh set of tears streamed down her face. "She deserves better, Daddy. I'm not good enough for her. Not now."

"Oh, Brook." Sloan pulled her into his embrace, blinking hard. "Don't say that."

"It's true, Dad, and you know it. I'm a screwup. I need to make sure I have myself together before I worry about someone else."

"Sounds to me like you've got yourself amazingly together right now. Like you're putting the baby first." But he didn't have to like the fact that her first mature decision meant his grandchild would be raised by strangers. Suddenly he found himself relating to Dylan's mother's outburst when he'd mentioned adoption as one of Brook's choices. Funny, it didn't feel like much of a choice at the moment.

Over Brook's head, he locked gazes with Jenna, finding tears filling her eyes, too. Good. "Don't give her away to strangers, Brook. Give her to me and Jenna. We'll raise this baby together with our own."

Jenna's mouth dropped open. Brook went dead still in his arms. For a long moment, none of them moved. Then Brook shoved from his embrace, bolting to her feet. She whirled to face him. "Are you *crazy?* Do you know what that would do to me, having to see my baby every day but not being able to say she's mine? To hear her call Jenna momma and not me? Hell, for that matter, have you even thought about how much it's going to kill me to give up this baby and then see yours every day?"

Brook ran to the stairs but paused halfway up. "Who's being self-centered now, Dad? I can't believe you said that!" A sob broke free from her throat, and she bolted up the rest of the steps.

Sloan turned to Jenna, his own shock mirrored on her

face. She waved toward the staircase. "Go. Go to her, Sloan. Make it right."

"How?"

Jenna shrugged.

JENNA WENT HOME, giving Sloan the space and time he needed to work things out with Brook. But the house next door continued to draw her attention, sending her out to prowl the edge of her deck, which butted close to the top of the fence between their properties. The inch-or-so opening of Brook's bedroom window allowed Jenna to catch some of the emotion spilling out, but not the actual words.

About an hour after she'd left, a silver SUV pulled into the driveway. Sloan's brother-in-law, a psychologist if she remembered correctly, climbed out and entered the house through the back door. Apparently Sloan had felt the need for professional reinforcement.

Jenna's stomach knotted, and she swiped the back of her hand across her cheeks. Poor Brook.

The sliding glass door resisted her tug, but Jenna yanked harder. Inside her apartment, she poured herself some cold water, wishing she could have something stronger.

But the little one inside her deserved better.

Just like Brook felt her baby deserved a better life than she could provide.

Jenna flopped on the couch, staring at the tiny lump just under her tunic. Breathing gently, she calmed herself and waited. Sure enough, the faint fluttering began, the palpable proof of her child's existence. "You know, when I first found out about you, I wasn't sure what to do. Wasn't sure I was ready to be a mother. I'm still not sure what kind of mother I'm going to be. But to even think about giving you up, now that you're on your way…"

Brook's words about how it was going kill her to give up her baby and then see Sloan and Jenna's child every day echoed in Jenna's head. The teen's plan of action would probably be the hardest thing she would ever do in her life. And she was doing it at sixteen.

How could Jenna live with herself if she inflicted further pain on the grieving girl?

Brook's willingness to sacrifice deserved to be honored. Reciprocated. Kids needed to come first—and that included Sloan's oldest child. Thank goodness Jenna hadn't managed to tell him everything she'd wanted to earlier. Because her plans had changed again.

New tears welled up in her eyes, and Jenna cursed the pregnancy hormones that seemed to make her cry so much these days. But she had to face the facts.

She couldn't marry him.

SLOAN SLUMPED at the kitchen table, head propped on one palm, the other hand wrapped around a mug of coffee that had gone cold an hour ago.

"You look like you could use some fresh air."

He jumped at James's voice. "I didn't hear you come back down."

"So I gathered." James picked up his fleece jacket

from the back of a chair. "Grab a sweatshirt or something and let's go outside. We can talk out there."

Sloan followed his brother-in-law down the back porch steps. James dragged a pair of battered lawn chairs to the corner of the garage. "Sit."

"Well, don't keep me waiting all night. How did Brook seem to you?"

"Brook seems to me like a young woman going through a very rough time. But I have to tell you, she's definitely matured a lot in the past few months. I honestly feel that she's given this adoption decision a lot of thought, Sloan."

"What? Come on, how can that be?"

"She's been reading Internet stories on open adoptions for weeks now. Give her some credit. This is definitely not an easy decision."

Sloan rubbed his hands over his face. "No kidding."

"She needs your support and your strength to do this, Sloan. She has to know that you're in her corner here. In a lot of ways, she's trying desperately to measure up to your standards of 'do the right thing.' Your approval means everything to her."

"*Now* she wants my approval?"

"She's wanted it all along. Brook feels like you disconnected from her when her mother died. Ashley was a toddler and needed more of your attention. I think a lot of the things Brook's done in the past have been all about getting your attention. Look, Sloan, I know your father raised you and Rachel to keep a stiff upper lip, to control your emotions. But Brook really needs you to try to share your feelings with her."

Sloan shifted, uncomfortable in the chair—hell, uncomfortable in his skin. He'd spent the recent part of his life trying to compensate his girls for the loss of their mother, trying to do the best he could for them. And it turned out that his best had left his older daughter doubting the basic foundation of their family—the fact that he loved her.

"I must be the world's worst father."

James snorted. "Hardly. Hey, where would I be if all kids, even the long grown-up ones, didn't have issues with their parents?"

"Unemployed?"

"Pretty much." James launched into more detail of how Brook had researched her decision, and her emotional state regarding giving the baby up for adoption.

"It's going to hurt her bad," Sloan said. He already felt the sting of even thinking about giving up the baby, and he wasn't the one carrying the child.

"Yes, which is why she needs you. This isn't something she's ever going to 'get over,' Sloan, any more than Rachel's 'gotten over' losing Daniel. But Brook will learn to live with it just like your sister has, and she'll move on with her life. Open adoption is a much better system, in my opinion, because it lets the birth mother have control—from choosing the people who will raise the baby, to getting updates and future contact, if both parties are comfortable with that."

Sloan slouched lower in his chair, crossing his ankles. "So she'll know who has the baby?"

"Absolutely. She'll pick the parents."

"Hmm." Sloan considered that for a while. Occasional cars zoomed by on Twelfth Street, and a plane landed at the nearby airport, engines roaring as it slowed on the runway.

How could the whole world continue on as normal when his life was so damn upside down?

"Now let me tell you what I'm worried about as far as Brook's concerned."

"What?" That brought him upright fast, making the webbing of the old chair creak in protest. "There's more?"

James nodded. "The whole 'Jenna's baby' issue."

"Jenna's baby *issue?*" Sloan rubbed the back of his neck, where the muscles had contracted into two-by-fours.

"Not only does Brook feel she's going to have to compete with another baby for your attention now, but she's jealous of Jenna in so many ways. If not for Jenna being pregnant, I think Brook would have been okay with your new relationship. But the fact that Jenna's having your baby twists everything for Brook."

Sloan sighed. "What the hell am I supposed to do about that? It's not like I can take it back."

"No, you can't. But you can go out of your way to make sure Brook feels secure in your love. Give her the attention she needs. I think it's really good that you didn't let your old man pressure you into marrying Jenna."

"Ha! Let me tell you what. It's not me that's the problem there, it's Jenna. Nobody pressures her into doing something she doesn't want to do." Which made him damn glad she'd decided to have his baby. A shiver crawled down his spine as he suddenly got a flash of insight into Brook's dilemma—what if Jenna had aborted his baby, and he'd been forced to see Brook's child, a constant reminder of what he'd lost?

"Oh, God." He thumped the heel of his palm against his forehead. "I am such an idiot."

No wonder she'd reacted the way she had when he'd offered to raise her baby with Jenna. And no wonder she predicted such pain in seeing her baby sister—he firmly believed they were having a girl—every day.

He slumped forward in the chair. "Help me, James. I need to know the right thing to do. Jenna's child is as much my responsibility as Brook is. I want to marry Jenna and be one big family. *Happy* at some point in the future would be nice. But having our baby around is going to hurt Brook. What's the right thing?"

His brother-in-law gave Sloan's shoulder a quick squeeze. "Sometimes there really isn't one clear, right thing."

CHAPTER SIXTEEN

AFTER JAMES LEFT, Sloan went next door and let himself into Jenna's dark apartment. He dropped the keys on the kitchen island, then slogged toward her bedroom. Sound asleep, she sprawled in the middle of the bed, one arm over her head.

His stomach tightened as he watched her. The woman loved him. Her revelation earlier had hit him like an eighteen-wheeler without brakes.

And God help him, he loved her. She'd taught him to laugh again. She carried his child. And yet, he didn't know if he should be campaigning for her to accept his proposal, or, given Brook's frame of mind, be grateful that she hadn't accepted.

Torn in too many directions, he didn't know what to do. Part of him felt as though he owed Brook far more loyalty—sixteen years' worth—than the new baby. And yet, how the hell fair was that? It wasn't the baby's fault that her presence was going to hurt her older sister so much.

He closed his eyes, fighting tears. Brook wasn't the only one the whole situation was hurting.

Guess you should have thought of all this before you unzipped, old man.

Princess crept across the comforter, cramming her nose under his elbow and giving it a flip. He patted her with one hand while he toed off his shoes, then he scooped the dog from the bed and set her on the floor. "Go on," he whispered. "Bunk on the couch for now. I'm not staying that long."

The dog gave him a reproachful look, then turned and padded away.

Sloan lifted the comforter and slipped in between the sheets, cuddling up alongside Jenna's warm body. She stirred, and he pulled her into his arms.

"Mmm." Her leg sprawled across his hips and her hand caressed a circle on his chest. "You're dressed."

He pressed his lips to her forehead. "I just need to hold you for a while."

"Bad time with Brook?"

"You could say that. Shh. Go back to sleep."

"No. Talk to me." She shrugged off the arm he'd slung around her, then climbed from the bed. The nightstand drawer squeaked as she opened it. A lighter appeared in her hand, and she turned toward the metal screen. Soon the glow of candlelight cast flickering shadows around the room.

Sloan groaned. "Sugar, really, I just needed to hold you for a while. Don't go to all that trouble. Blow them out and come back to bed."

"I'll come back, but I want to see you." She duplicated his slide between the sheets. "So tell me."

Instead, he tightened his arms around her. A deep inhale brought the scent of the rose body wash she favored. He burrowed his fingers into her silky hair. "I hope our baby is a redhead."

She pushed herself up on one elbow, staring deep into his eyes. "Sloan, I can see you're upset. Why don't you want to tell me what's going on?"

"Why did it take you so long tonight to tell me that you love me?"

"Because I wanted to do it right. Instead I just blurted it out."

A small smile fought its way to his lips. "It was perfect. Very you. I wish I had more of your jump-right-in-and-forget-the-alligators attitude."

"Hey, I don't mess with alligators, mister." She brushed her fingertips over his cheek. "But you know, there's something else I need to tell you."

"Well, ladies first."

Jenna blinked hard against the moisture already gathering in her eyes. Damn it. She wasn't going to blubber on him. *Think light. Think dessert.* While part of her mourned the loss of their easygoing relationship, she wouldn't change the way this man had taught her to dig deeper. To give more of herself. To compromise and put others first. But he'd only been able to do that because of who he was. "There's those lovely manners, Tex."

"Spill it, sugar."

"Okay. I…I can't marry you."

"What?" He recoiled from her, brows drawing together. "Why not?"

She pretended not to see the quick flash of pain in his eyes. "Because. It's not the right thing to do."

"Because of Brook?"

She nodded.

He closed his eyes, drew in a deep breath, then let it out.

"Hey." She tapped on his nose with her finger. "Just because I'm not marrying you doesn't mean I'm cutting you loose. I figured we'd carry on kinda like…"

"Like we've been carrying on?" His blond lashes fluttered open and he offered her a lopsided half smile that tugged at her heart.

"Yeah. I mean, I'm still right next door, and you can come over whenever you want, and so can Ashley. I still expect you to be a good father to our baby. I'll be calling you when I need help or a breather. But this way Brook…"

"Won't have to face our child every day?"

A tear slipped down Jenna's face as she nodded again. "I—I can't do that to her, Sloan. The pain…"

"Oh, Jenna." His voice quivered. "Look at you, sugar. You're crying over my little girl's broken heart. Have I told you how amazing you are?" He took her hands in his and leaned closer, kissing her tenderly. The covers tangled around them as he rolled her over so she lay on her back, looking up at him. "Remember on our first date, you said you didn't do kids?"

"Yeah."

"Well, I think you do kids just great. You're going to be a fantastic mom. Ashley loves you. And so do I."

Jenna shut her eyes, swallowing the huge lump threatening to clog her throat. "W-what?"

"I love you, Jenna."

He *loved* her. They both felt the same way. "I'm beginning to think love is highly overrated. It hurts," she whispered.

"Sometimes." He brushed the hair back from her face. "And sometimes it makes you feel like dancing in a bowling alley. Or making snow angels." The warmth of his mouth pressed against hers. "Or making love to the angel next door." With his tongue, he coaxed her lips wider, kissed her deeper. A low groan rumbled in his throat. "I wasn't going to do this, I swear, but one taste of you, and I'm lost. I was lost on our very first kiss."

"Do it. Make love to me, Sloan."

As if they had all the time in the world, he did just that, exploring the changes in her body, making her feel every inch a sexy and desirable woman. When they were both sated, she rested in his arms. One of the votive candles sputtered and went out, sending a plume of smoke spiraling upward. "That's probably my cue to leave," he said.

"I wish you could stay." That was one of the things she'd been looking forward to if they married—sharing a bed with him every night, always having his warmth at her side.

"I wish I could, too, sugar." He rolled from the bed, retrieving his clothes from the floor and putting them on.

"I'll walk you to the door." Jenna pulled on her red kimono, stuffing her feet into the dragon slippers. In the silent darkness of the night, she followed him through her apartment. At the island, he picked up his keys, jangling them in his hand before cramming them into his pocket.

When they reached the little braided rug near the coat tree, he pulled her into a tight embrace, resting his chin on the top of her head. "Thank you," he murmured.

"For what?"

"Being with you, loving you, has taught me to look at things from a very different point of view. Especially Brook. I'm sorrier than you'll ever know that she's coming between us, but I can't explain what it means for me to be able to reconnect with her, to see her for who she really is, instead of who I've wanted her to be."

"You're a good dad, Tex. I told you that."

He slid one hand to her belly, caressed the firm roundness through the satin. "I swear, Jenna, I'll be here for this baby. And for you. I'm just a phone call and a short jog away if you need me."

"I know." The man had proved that all the weeks she'd been sick.

A quick kiss, and he slipped out the door. Jenna flipped on the security monitor in time to catch a final glimpse of him as he shut the metal door at the base of the stairs. He paused just outside, shoving his hands deep in his pockets, head hung low. For a moment, he stood there, shoulders slumped. She pressed a finger to the screen, wishing she could touch him, ease the obvious turmoil he felt. Then he turned and jammed the buzzer. "Jenna? You still there?"

"Yes."

He looked into the camera. "I just have one more question. Give me a straight answer, okay?"

"Okay."

"Earlier tonight when you came to my place, before we knew about Brook's plans, and her feelings, were you going to say yes?"

Grateful the video transmission only worked one way and he couldn't see her fresh batch of tears, Jenna cleared her throat, working hard to keep her voice even. "Yes. I was going to say yes."

CHAPTER SEVENTEEN

"DADDY! Make the pain stop!" Brook squeezed his hand until Sloan thought his fingers were going to turn black from lack of circulation.

"I would if I could, sweetie. You can do it. Breathe!"

"Grrr, you breathe! I just want it to stop!"

Alarmed, Sloan glanced over at the monitor, finding comfort in the technology that let him know more about his daughter's labor than she did. The digital numbers began to descend. "The contraction is almost over, honey. Hang on. Not much longer."

When she relaxed back into the birthing-room bed, he sank into the chair at her side.

Being her birthing coach hadn't been a great idea, in his opinion. But she'd insisted the only person who could help her get through it was him. She'd begged and pleaded.

And given that they'd made so much progress with the assistance of the family counselor James had hooked them up with, he hadn't really had much choice. The counselor had thought Sloan supporting his daughter through the birth of her child was the perfect opportunity for him to prove his love.

Fortunately the Lamaze teacher—who'd eyed him rather suspiciously the first time he'd shown up at the second course with Jenna in tow instead of Brook—had told him he might feel more comfortable at the head of the bed.

"Dad! I think another one's coming!"

Sloan stood up, checking the monitor. Sure enough, the numbers were rising again. "Yes, okay, get ready. Take a deep breath."

"Oh! I think I have to push!"

He glanced around the birthing room. Shift change had left him on his own. "No, no, don't push! There's nobody here but us. No pushing! I'll go get the nurse and she can call the doctor. I'll be right back!"

When he blasted out of the door, he saw Frank and Claire Richards, the parents-to-be of Brook's baby. The pair looked at him in alarm, rising from their chairs in the corridor. He barreled to a stop at the nurses' station. "Brook says she's got to push! I am not delivering this baby, so could I please get some help in there?"

The nurse behind the desk grabbed the phone, punching several buttons. "Dr. Fielding? We need you in Birthing Room Three." She strolled from behind the desk. "Okay, calm down. First babies are notoriously slow, especially for teen moms. I'm sure we've got plenty of time."

Sloan followed her back to the birthing room. Frank Richards reached for him as he passed. "Is everything okay? How's Brook?"

"It hurts!" Brook's shrill voice came into the hallway

as the nurse opened the door and hurried inside. "I have to push!"

"Brook, as you can hear, is in pain, and I think we're getting closer to having a birthday here."

Claire looked at him hopefully. "Has she changed her mind about letting us—or at least me—in during the delivery?"

"Not that I know of. I'm sorry. I know you're both excited about the baby, and I'm happy about that. But Brook feels like this is her only chance to have the baby to herself."

"You'll let us know when the baby's born, right?" Frank put his arm around his wife's shoulder.

"Yes. You'll be the first ones outside that room to know."

Sloan went back into the room, averting his glance from where the nurse was stationed between Brook's sheet-covered legs. His daughter extended a hand in his direction. "Daddy!"

He winced even before she clutched his fingers in the same death grip. "Hey, honey. See, I brought the nurse." He pushed her sweat-soaked hair back from her forehead with his working hand, taking care where the strands had caught on the silver eyebrow stud. "She called the doctor, and everything is going just great."

"Nooo, it's not. She won't let me push and I need to!" Brook's grip tightened as the numbers climbed on the monitor. Her face contorted and she clenched her teeth.

"Brook, honey, I said don't push until the doctor gets here!" The frantic edge to the nurse's voice had Sloan looking over at her.

"What's wrong?" Fear made a cold sweat break across the back of his neck. Oh, God, and he could look forward to a repeat of this whole process in another month. He mouthed a silent prayer for the health of the two women he loved and the babies they carried.

"Nothing's wrong, but I think we're about to have a baby."

The door to the room opened and Dr. Judy Fielding walked in with another nurse. "Without me?"

Everything after that moved at warp speed. The doctor got gowned and gloved, and Sloan counted, helped Brook rest between contractions, kept her focused. And not fifteen minutes later, the doctor announced, "It's a girl!" As a nurse carried her to a warming table to clean her up, the baby cried.

And so did Brook. "I want to see her. Please? Can I hold her?"

"Of course, honey. Just let us get her cleaned up and weighed. You want her to be pretty when you see her."

Joy and sorrow mingled deep in his chest when the nurse placed the pink-blanket-swaddled bundle in his daughter's arms.

His granddaughter.

His heart squeezed, as though it were trapped in Brook's grip.

Fresh tears streamed down Brook's face as she cradled the newborn. "Oh, look at you. You're beautiful." She edged the blanket aside near the tiny face and shifted her, holding her out so Sloan could see better. "Look, Daddy. Isn't she beautiful?"

"Yeah, honey. She sure is. Just like you."

"Get the camera, Dad. Take a picture now. While she's just mine."

Luckily the digital camera had a good-size screen and autofocus. Because there was no way in hell he'd be able to see through a little viewfinder with his blurry eyes.

ANTISEPTIC CLEANERS from the hallway clashed with the scents of burgers, fries and burnt coffee in the hospital's café. A lot of the folks at other tables and lined up at the counter had shell-shocked expressions, as though they ate without tasting. Taking another swig of coffee, Sloan grimaced, wishing his own numbness extended to his taste buds.

"That bad, huh?" Jenna asked.

"Yeah, but I need the caffeine."

"If I'd known, I'd have brought you some good stuff."

"This'll do." He pulled the camera from his shirt pocket, turned it on review mode. "You want to see my grandbaby?"

"Of course." Jenna took the camera and began scrolling through the pictures. "She's adorable. But poor Brook looks like she's been through the wringer." She sighed. "I wish I could go upstairs with you and see the baby in person. And Brook, too. I can't even imagine how she must be feeling right now." The camera chimed as it shut down. Jenna slipped one hand from the table to caress the spot on her belly where Sloan could actually see movement beneath her soft blue T-shirt. Only one more month before their child was due.

"I wish you could, too. But she's too overwrought right now to see you. Not to mention still exhausted from giving birth yesterday. I'm sorry." Sloan caught a glimpse of a tall young man through the coffee-shop window and cursed under his breath, grabbing the camera and returning it to his shirt pocket. He shoved back his chair and rose.

"What?" Jenna asked.

"Sorry, sugar, but I have to go. I think I just saw Dylan and his mother heading for the elevators. I'll call you later." He leaned over to place a quick kiss on her mouth, brushing his hand over her belly at the same time.

"Okay. Call me if you need anything! And Sloan," she called to him as he reached the doorway, "don't do or say anything hasty!"

He grunted. Hasty. Not going to be a problem at all. The elevator took forever to reach the maternity floor, giving him plenty of time to think. When the doors opened, he shot out, barreling toward Brook's room. The wooden door to the private room was still closed. He opened it and slipped through. Save for his napping daughter, no one was there. Turning on his heel, he headed for the nursery.

He found Dylan and his mom standing in front of the Plexiglas window, staring at five babies in their bassinets. "I'm not sure which one is her," Dylan said.

"Second from the right."

The kid jumped, turning. His eyes widened, and he took a step back. "M-Mr. Thompson. I—I—"

"We—" Mrs. Burch slipped her arm through her son's as she spoke "—just wanted to see the baby."

"I suppose I can understand that." Actually, it shocked the hell out of him, but Sloan kept his best poker face in place. He nodded again toward the window. "That's Emma, there."

"How's Brook?" Dylan asked. "Is she okay?"

"Physically she's all right. Well, as all right as any woman who just had a baby. Emotionally…" Sloan narrowed his eyes at the boy responsible for his child's pain.

The lanky teen's Adam's apple bobbed as he swallowed hard. "I didn't think she'd want to see me."

"You thought right."

"But I…" The boy's voice dropped as he turned his attention to the nursery, to the baby he and Brook had created. "I wanted to see *her* at least once." He leaned his forehead against the glass, raising his hand to press his fingers to it.

Maybe it was the fact that the kid's first question had been about Brook's well-being. Or maybe it was because Sloan was just getting soft in his doddering grandfatherhood. Whatever the reason, he found himself asking, "Do you want a closer look? You want to hold her?"

"Really?" Dylan pushed off the glass. "You'd let me?"

"Yes," his mother said. "Please?"

"Let me see what I can do. Wait here." He left them admiring Emma through the window and went down the hall alongside the nursery, to the back entrance. After getting the attention of one of the nurses, who were well aware of Brook's situation, he explained that the baby's birth father wanted the chance to hold his daughter.

When Dylan was settled in a chair in the empty family room across from the nursery, his mother hovering at his side, a nurse wheeled the bassinet into the room. She placed the baby in the boy's arms, instructing him in the proper handling of a newborn. Assured everything was under control, she left them alone.

Emma chose that moment to yawn and open her eyes, staring up at Dylan.

"Wow," he said. "Hi." When the baby squirmed, he looked to his mother in panic.

"It's all right. You've got her." Mrs. Burch leaned forward and ran a finger over the baby's cheek. "Hi there, sweetheart. Aren't you just precious?"

Sloan pulled his camera out, snapped a picture without even thinking about it. The flash made the baby scrunch up her face. Dylan looked up at him. "Can I get a copy of that?"

"Sure. You want me to take a few more?" These pictures would probably be the only thing the kid ever had to remind him he had a daughter out in the world. Seemed like the least Sloan could do.

After a variety of poses, including some with Mrs. Burch holding the baby, a soft knock on the door was followed by the hesitant appearance of the Richards. "Hi. The nurses said Emma was in here. Is it all right if we join you?"

Sloan looked at Dylan. "This is Frank and Claire Richards. Emma's parents."

"Oh." The boy, who'd already signed his relinquishment papers, glanced from the couple in the doorway back to the baby in his arms. "Oh. Yeah, uh, sure, come in." Cradling the infant like the fragile, valuable thing she was, he rose from the chair. "We, uh, should probably get going anyway. Dad will be looking for us before too long."

Mrs. Burch's startled expression made it plain that Mr. Burch had no idea his wife and son were visiting the baby.

Claire Richards held out her arms, but Dylan turned toward Frank. He leaned over, awkwardly kissing Emma's cheek before he transferred her into the adoptive father's embrace.

Sloan found his throat tightening. He rocked back and forth on his feet, feigning a nonchalance he didn't feel.

"Mom, do you have that thing we brought for her?"

Dylan's mother fumbled in her purse, pulled out something and passed it to her son. Dylan handed the little stuffed bear with the Georgetown University T-shirt to Claire. "I hope it's okay to give this to her. I didn't know what to get her, and this is where…I leave for Georgetown in a few days. I wanted her to have something from me. Something so she knows I—I was thinking about her. You'll save it for her, won't you?"

Claire clutched the bear to her chest, nodding. Moisture glistened in her eyes. "Yes. We'll make sure she knows this was from her birth dad."

The boy swiped the back of his hand over his eyes before leaning over for one more look at the baby. Then he turned and strode from the room. Mrs. Burch, tears spilling down her cheeks, followed him.

Sloan locked gazes with Frank Richards and cleared his throat. If it hurt this much to watch Dylan take his leave of the baby, he could hardly wait to do it again tomorrow with Brook.

"FIVE MORE MINUTES, Dad! I just need five more minutes alone with her." Brook sniffled, rocking the baby in her arms. Prepared to leave, with her packed bag sitting alongside the chair, she knew the time had come for her to surrender Emma to the Richards. She traced the tiny flowers on the soft pink dress Aunt Rae had bought for the baby at Brook's request. She wanted Emma to be irresistible when the Richards took her home.

"The longer you drag this out, the more it's going to hurt," her father said gently.

"How can it hurt any more than it already does?" She felt hollow inside. "Doing the right thing *sucks,* Dad."

"Tell me about it." He let go of the door handle and came to kneel at her side. "Honey, you still have a choice here. The Richards are good people. You've talked to the birth mothers of their two older kids, and you know they'll honor the stipulations you made for the open adoption. They'll love Emma and take good care of her. But…you don't have to do this."

"Yes, I do." Brook squeezed her eyes shut, lifting the baby higher. She inhaled, barely registering the sweet baby smell through her clogging nose. "It's the right thing for *her.* She's going to have a stay-at-home mom, a dad, an older brother, a big sister, and a dog. She'll have her own bedroom in a *two-bathroom* house. With them, she'll have everything." Tears slid out from be-tween her eyelids. *Except me,* she wanted to add. But with the open arrangements they'd made, Emma would get to have her. Sort of. If Brook could stand to see her. If the pain didn't get any easier to handle than this, she might have to rethink the amount of contact she wanted with her daughter.

"Sometimes love means letting go," she whispered.

"Yeah. I suppose sometimes it does. Most parents don't have to do it quite this soon, though."

"Could you just give me a few minutes alone with her? I'll call you when I'm ready for all of you to come back in." Brook looked down at her daughter and at her father's big hand stroking the infant's arm.

"Sure, honey." Her dad lifted Emma's tiny fist, kissed it, then reached up to cup Brook's cheek. "You take all the time you need."

His knees creaked as he climbed to his feet. "I'll be just outside the door."

Once he'd left, she let her tears flow. "Oh, Emma, I love you so much." She held the baby tighter, until Emma squirmed to let her know it was too much. "But I just can't take care of you. Not the way you deserve. But never, ever doubt for a second that I love you."

Out in the hallway, Sloan leaned against the now-closed door, dropping his head to study his shoes. A shuffling sound came from the other side of the hall-way. He looked up to find the Richards watching him. Claire bit her lip, and Frank wrapped his arm around her shoulders.

"She hasn't changed her mind, has she?" Claire asked, voice shaky.

"No. She just wants a few more minutes to say good-bye to Emma in private."

"It's not really goodbye," Claire began, then stopped when he narrowed his eyes at her.

Sloan sized up Frank. Only a couple of years younger than him, the engineer for GE seemed like an upright guy. Sloan crooked a finger at him. "I'd like a word with you. Man-to-man."

They drew just to the side of the doorway. Sloan spoke softly. "Frank, I know that you're going to love Emma. That you're going to take good care of her. But I want you to remember that not only do you have a responsibility to that baby girl who will be your daughter, but you have a responsibility to *my* daughter, too. You do right by both of them." He had to stop and clear his throat, fight the moisture in his eyes. That would blow his tough, protective dad image all to hell.

"Sloan, father to father, man-to-man, I give you my word. We'll honor the gift Brook is giving us. We'll make sure Emma knows how much Brook loved her. Loved her enough to share her with us." Frank held out his hand, and Sloan grasped it tight.

"Good."

"Dad." Brook's muffled voice called from inside the room. "I'm ready."

Maybe she was, but he didn't think he'd ever be ready for this. He straightened his spine, nodded to the Richards, then opened the door. *Tighten your boots and carry on, soldier.* If his daughter could do this, so could he.

She looked incredibly young, standing in the middle of the room in an oversize T-shirt and a pair of jeans, rocking her daughter in her arms. And yet, when she glanced up at him, he saw wisdom and maturity in her eyes—the very things he'd longed to see in her. But if he could, he'd undo them in a heartbeat, and take back the self-centered, exuberant, drive-him-crazy kid she'd been just nine short months ago.

Brook strode to Claire. She cuddled the baby to her chest for a moment, then placed her in the other woman's arms. She leaned over and kissed Emma's forehead. "I love you, Snickerdoodle. Be good for your mommy and daddy."

Sloan swallowed the huge lump in his throat, gritted his teeth and vowed not to cry. At least not where Brook would ever see. She needed his strength.

Claire threw her free arm around Brook and hugged her. "Thank you," she whispered.

Sloan picked up Brook's suitcase as she pulled from Claire's embrace. Without another word, his daughter headed for the door. He followed, pausing only long enough for one last look over his shoulder. "You take good care of her."

"We will," Frank said. "We will."

He caught up with Brook outside the elevators. Her shoulders shook and she stared straight ahead, watching the numbers on the display. He reached for her, then pulled back, unsure if she wanted his touch or not. She seemed desperately trying to keep it together and he didn't want to cause her to lose her tenuous control.

An empty car appeared, and he guided her into it, pressing the button for the lobby. As the doors slid shut, she threw herself into his arms, sobbing against his shirt, all pretenses gone. A little girl herself again. "Oh, Daddy. I miss her already. Make the pain stop."

He kissed the top of her head, holding her tight. "I would if could, Snickerdoodle. I would if I could."

CHAPTER EIGHTEEN

"IT'S A BOY!" the doctor said. The baby cried, a loud, lusty holler. "A boy with a great set of lungs."

Jenna slumped back on the bed. She reached down to touch the infant on her belly. A boy. That qualified as another surprise. She'd completely bought into Sloan's fantasy of a little girl with red hair.

Sloan stopped in the middle of planting a congratulatory kiss on her forehead. "A boy?" He looked down as a nurse rubbed the baby with a towel. "Holy moly, it *is* a boy."

The doctor laughed. "I am pretty accurate at identifying the parts once they're born."

"Did you not want a boy?" Jenna's shaky voice reflected the exhaustion of the seventeen-hour labor she'd endured. Didn't all men want a boy? Especially men who already had two daughters?

"No, no, sugar, that's not it. It's just…" He shrugged. "I just assumed it would be a girl. Kinda thought I didn't make boys. And I don't know anything about raising boys. Except, of course, for the fact that I was one. Once upon a time."

Jenna smiled at him. "I guess we'll learn together, won't we?"

"You want to count all the fingers and toes now, or can I take him to weigh him and get him all cleaned up?" the nurse asked.

Alarmed, Jenna scanned the baby. The nurse reassured her, "Everything's there, hon. I just meant did you want him for a few more minutes or is it okay for me to take him? We're just going to the other side of the room." She pointed to the warming table. Jenna nodded her approval.

Sloan leaned over the bed to nuzzle her ear. "Thank you, sugar. He's beautiful, just like his momma. I love you."

She never got tired of hearing that. "I love you, too." The rest of the time with the doctors and nurses sped by in a blur for Jenna. Eventually she dozed off, with Sloan sitting in the reclining chair by the window. She awakened to find him parked in the same spot, staring down at the infant in his arms with a rapt expression.

"My two guys," she said.

Sloan looked over at her. "Well, hey, sleepyhead. We wondered when you were going to decide to participate in this family bonding time."

"Excuse me for being exhausted after giving birth to your son." A weary smile took the sting out of her words.

He climbed from the chair and brought the baby to her, placing him in her arms. "Here you go, Mom."

"Looks like someone else is pretty tired, too." The baby slept without stirring as she tightened her grip on him.

"I guess being born is as hard work as giving birth."

Sloan rummaged in the duffel bag on the floor, pulling out the camera to take the first photos of mother and son. "If I don't have pictures to show Ashley when I get home tonight, I'm going to be in big trouble."

"Did you call everyone?"

"Not yet. I thought maybe you'd want to call your family first."

So they got on the phone and spread the word. And discovered they hadn't bothered to agree on a name for the baby—other than Lorelei, which didn't seem right anymore. When Sloan left for the evening, they still hadn't come up with anything but decided to sleep on it, and maybe get some input from the family visitors tomorrow.

SLOAN ARRIVED early the next day with a bouquet of blue daisies. Jenna was wrestling with the baby, trying to get him to latch on. Several frustrating attempts later, their son suckled at her breast. Sloan's eyes widened. "That has to be the most beautiful thing I've ever seen."

"Didn't Beth nurse the girls?" Jenna shifted the pillow she had the baby propped on, adjusting him.

"No. She had this fixation about it. Couldn't see herself, uh, well, just didn't want to do it."

Jenna chuckled at his stumbling. "Couldn't see herself as a cow, huh?"

"Now, that's not how I see it, and I didn't say that, so don't be getting me into trouble for things I didn't say." He redeemed himself by changing the baby's diaper after Jenna finished feeding him. They launched into more discussion about naming their son, the lactation consultant stopped by for a visit, and the morning turned to afternoon, bringing visiting hours.

Jenna's dad carried a bunch of balloons, which he fastened to the end of her bed. Her mother held a paper shopping bag, but she set it on the floor and went straight to the baby, lying in his bassinet. "My, what a big boy you are!" She picked him up.

Jenna leaned forward, arms outstretched. "Easy, Mother. Be careful of his head."

Her mother smiled at her. "I have handled babies before, Jenna. Why, once you were a baby yourself, and somehow you survived my mothering."

Perched on the edge of her bed, Sloan bristled. Jenna elbowed him in the ribs and just smiled as her dad enfolded her in a tight hug. "You did great, sweetheart. He's a fine-looking boy." Her father turned and extended his hand to Sloan. "And you did well, too, Sloan."

"Thank you, sir, but Jenna did all the hard work."

"Yes, I did, and I'm glad you noticed."

"What's his name? Did you decide?" her mother asked, jiggling her grandson.

She looked to Sloan for his approval, and he nodded. "Yes. We're calling him Robbie. But his full name will be Robert Steven. After you and Sloan's dad."

A huge grin lit her father's face. "Oh, Jenna. Thank you. I'm honored." He turned and went to her mom, taking Robbie from her.

"Quinn?" her mother asked.

"Yes, Quinn," Jenna said, at the exact same time Sloan shook his head.

"Thompson."

"Quinn."

"Sugar, I thought we'd agreed that he would be a Thompson?"

"Apparently the two of you still have some things to discuss before I fill out the birth certificate," said the nurse who'd just appeared in the doorway. "I'll come back later."

James and Rachel showed up next, bearing a small ivy plant in a pastel ceramic baby shoe. "Where's Molly?" Jenna asked.

"She's home with my folks. We don't bring Molly into hospitals unless we have to. Too many germs," James said.

"Oh, right." Jenna sometimes forgot their daughter had had a heart transplant. "Well, maybe you can bring her to visit us once we go home."

"I'm sure she'd like that." Rachel took possession of the baby from Jenna's dad. She peered down at him, then looked over at James. "Oh, he's adorable. Remember when Jamey was this little?"

"Uh-oh. I don't like that spark in your eyes, Mrs. McClain. You've got that baby-hunger look. Give him back to his mother and step away from the infant."

"Jamey just turned two. Don't you think that's a good space?"

"I'm too damn old for more babies."

Sloan laughed. "Yeah, that's what I thought. But now…I'm feeling younger than I have in years."

"Let me know if you still feel the same way after a week's worth of not sleeping all night."

The room grew silent, and they all stopped to stare at Jenna and Sloan.

"Oops, sorry. I forgot that you're not actually together. Boy, I put my foot in my mouth good that time." James groaned. "With my training, I'm supposed to be able to avoid that."

"It's okay," Jenna said. But it really wasn't. More and more she longed for the full relationship she'd never expected—the full dinner, not just the dessert. How could something you never knew you wanted hurt so much not to get? Somehow, she had to find a way to remember to be thankful for what she had, and to live well, love much, and laugh often, just like Gram had preached.

The hustle and bustle in the little room increased when Margo and Johnny arrived. Her parents left, promising to come again after she'd settled in at home. During a lull in the visits, Jenna made Sloan bring her the shopping bag her mother had left in the corner of the room.

She pulled out the card first. "For My Daughter As She Becomes A Mother," read the outside. And the inside made her sniffle. She'd never expected anything quite so…emotional from her mother. Sloan handed her the first package, a small box wrapped in gold paper. Underneath a layer of cotton was a folded-up note and a ring with a diamond in the middle and two pink stones on the sides. The note explained that the ring had been given to her mother when she'd given birth to her, and now she wanted to pass it on—suggesting Jenna might want to add a blue stone or two to balance out the ring. Jenna wiped at her nose as Sloan handed her the other package. She tore into the paper and started to laugh. She held up the package for Sloan to see. "Man, my mother has really changed since Dad's surgery. First the heartfelt card and ring, now finger paints. She never let me have finger paints when I was little. I always had to go to Gram's house for that."

"Yeah, well, notice that she's given the paint to you, so it's still not at her house."

"But it's a step in the right direction. Maybe there's hope for her yet."

"Ever the optimist, aren't you, Jenna?" Sloan leaned down and kissed her. "I love that about you."

"I'm here! The big sister is here!" Ashley announced, barreling through the doorway. "Where's the baby? I wanna hold him!"

Sloan got up from the bed, shaking his head. "Shh! Keep your voice down or you'll scare your brother. And I can't let you hold him unless you wash your hands first. We don't need him getting sick."

"I'm not sick, Daddy."

"I know." He pointed toward the bathroom. "Go wash anyway. Use soap."

Sloan's father came into the room. "That child has enough energy to power a platoon. Sorry. She zipped off the elevator before I could stop her."

Jenna looked behind him for another figure. "Did Brook come with you?"

Sloan's father shook his head. "No. Just slammed her door and cranked up her music when I asked."

Jenna sank back into the pillows. She slowly put the things from her mother into the bag while Sloan watched. "Sugar, did you really expect her to come?"

"Ever the optimist, right? I didn't expect, but…"

"But you hoped," he murmured.

She nodded. "Yeah. I hoped."

"It's only been a few weeks since she gave up Emma, hon. Give her time. But keep that hope, huh? Maybe one day…"

Maybe one day…

Jenna was struck by the absurdity of the situation. The one thing she'd never imagined having was a family of her own. Couldn't envision being tied down by all that responsibility. Now she had a sort-of family, and longed for the whole thing to fit. She'd even wear the apron if that's what it took.

But even at her most optimistic, she wasn't holding her breath. Somehow she'd be happy with what she had.

THE SILK BRANCH of multicolored leaves slipped from Jenna's hand. As she bent to retrieve it, a tiny gurgling sound caught her attention. She turned to find her three-week-old son awake in his infant seat on the shop floor. "Well, hey there, little man. You like the pretty leaves Mommy is putting on the tree? Look, this one is yellow. And this one is red. That means fall is here. We're a little late with it, but then, I've been pretty busy the past month, haven't I?" She continued to chatter to Robbie while fastening the seasonal changes to the display in the center of the store.

The door chimed to announce the arrival of a customer. Jenna turned, and the greeting died in her throat.

Brook gave a self-conscious wave. "Hi. I, uh, well, with the holiday shopping season coming up and all that, I thought I'd stop over and see if maybe you were going to be needing help? And maybe you'd think about giving me back my old job?"

"Really?"

Brook nodded. "I miss working here. I miss…you."

Almost afraid to breathe, Jenna just gawked at the teenager. Robbie chose that moment to start fussing.

Brook's eyes widened as she looked around Jenna to see the baby. "Oh. That must be Robbie, huh?"

"Yes."

"Can I—can I hold him?"

"Sure." Jenna knelt on the floor to lift the baby from his seat, then rose to her feet. Though hopeful, as Sloan had encouraged her to be, she'd never expected this day to come so soon. "Robbie, meet your big sister, Brook." Gingerly, she transferred the infant into Brook's arms, then stepped back to watch.

"Hey, handsome." The girl stared down at him, studying him. "I think he has Dad's nose."

"And chin, and cheeks and eyes. You know, it's just not fair. I did all the work, and he's the spitting image of your father."

Brook offered her a tentative smile. Then she

looked back at her new sibling. She closed her eyes, bending her head and inhaling. "I love that baby smell."

For a long moment, she just cuddled the baby close. When she opened her eyes, Jenna saw a shimmer of unshed tears. Her own chest tightened. "Brook—"

"It's okay. Really. I've been working with a therapist. I'm not going to have a breakdown or anything just from holding him. Even if he does smell like Emma."

Robbie squirmed in her arms, kicking his legs and waving his fists. Jenna knew what would come next. "He's working up to a good cry. He's probably hungry."

Right on cue, her son began to wail. Looking uncomfortable, Brook bounced him, moving closer to Jenna and handing him to her. "Well. That's one good thing about a brother. You can give him back when he's hungry. Or tired or dirty. Or won't stop crying."

"Yeah, there is that." Jenna strolled toward the office. "I'm going to feed him. You can stay if you want."

"No, I think this was a good start. How about I come again tomorrow? You can think about letting me work here, and we can see if I—if we—can do this."

Jenna paused in the office doorway. "Okay, Brook. You come back whenever you want."

"Just one thing—don't tell Dad."

"Brook, I don't like keeping things from your father. It's not right."

"Look, I don't want to get his hopes up. Not until we find out if I can be around Robbie. And if you and I can get along again. Because you know as soon as he finds out I'm over here at all, he's going to want us to be doing stuff together."

"All right. I don't like it, but I'll do it. I don't want your father hurt any more than he's been, either."

In the days that followed, Brook showed up often after school, returning home before Sloan got off work. Awkward at first, the relationship between Jenna and the teen slowly regained some lost ground. And Brook spent more time cuddling Robbie, only once breaking down in tears—on a day she'd received a new picture of Emma from the Richards.

Two weeks later, on a Friday afternoon, Brook followed Jenna into the office. Robbie wailed in his mother's arms. Jenna motioned toward a chair as she sank into the other herself, unbuttoning the top of her blouse. The teen chose to prop her butt on the edge of the desk.

Like a starving beast that hadn't been fed in ages, Robbie latched onto Jenna's breast with an eagerness that had Brook exclaiming, "Whoa! Now that looks like it hurts worse than the milk drying up did."

"Nah. He's just enthusiastic, that's all."

"Typical guy, huh?"

Jenna laughed. How she'd missed this kind of conversation with the young woman. "I guess. Yes, at this point, I'd say your brother is definitely a breast man."

"Be interesting to see how that pans out when he's older." Brook picked up a pair of pliers from the desk, opening and closing them. "Look, I have to talk to you about something."

Jenna readjusted her son. "Okay. So, what's on your mind?"

"The day Dad brought you and Robbie home from the hospital, after he'd come back to our house…well, late that night I went down to the kitchen for something to eat. And I saw Dad on the back steps. He was staring over here at your place. He had the strangest expression on his face. It took me a minute to realize he was crying."

"Oh." Though Jenna had held him while he wept over his grandbaby going home with another family, she'd never imagined he'd shed tears over her and Robbie. That hurt in an unexpected way. Another reminder that love wasn't all sunshine and roses, but came with a sometimes bitter, sometimes painful side.

"He's been running around like a nutcase lately. He's trying to be there for me and for Ashley, and he's doing his damnedest to be there for you and Robbie, too. He's torn between our place and your place. And he's not laughing anymore." Brook nailed her with a penetrating, no-holds-barred gaze. "Do you love my dad?"

"Yes. I do."

"And Ashley?"

Jenna nodded.

"Okay, then—"

"Brook, you didn't ask about yourself."

The hard-edged attitude in Brook's eyes softened for a second. "I'm not that self-centered anymore. I don't matter."

"Oh, Brook. That's where you're wrong. You matter

a lot. In fact, I think you matter the most, and yes, I do love you. Otherwise I wouldn't have cared what you thought or felt about me and your dad."

"Really?" Her voice cracked, and she cleared her throat and gave her hair a nonchalant toss. "Cool. Well, then, I'd like to invite you and Robbie for dinner tonight."

"Uh, sure. We'd like that." She looked down at her son drowsing at her breast. "I'll bring Robbie's dinner with me, okay?"

A half smile just like her dad's appeared on Brook's lips. "I'd like to see you try to leave Robbie's dinner behind."

"Does your father know about this?"

"Nope. Just like he doesn't know that I've been coming over here. We're going to surprise him."

SLOAN TOSSED a quick glance over his shoulder as he headed toward the house from the garage. The trees along the fence had begun to shed their leaves, making it easier to see Jenna's building.

He sent Jenna and their son a mental love note and a promise to stop by as soon as he had things settled over here.

In the kitchen, he peeled off his coat and inhaled. "Hey, something smells great. What's for dinner?"

Brook appeared in the doorway to the dining room. "Fried chicken, mashed potatoes and gravy, coleslaw."

"Biscuits?"

"Yep."

"You didn't cook all that?" He lifted a white-and-red bag from the counter, arching an eyebrow at her.

"No, it's takeout. But still, I get credit for dinner, right?"

"Absolutely." He squirted some dish soap into his hands and washed up at the kitchen sink. A beautiful pencil sketch Brook had done of Emma hung on the refrigerator. The form was well detailed and damn near perfect, at least in his eyes, but more impressive was the amount of emotion that came through in the work. Jenna had been right about Brook's talent, and he'd encouraged her to take more art classes at school this year. He found it hard to look at the drawing every day, but Brook wanted it in the middle of the family action. It seemed she was handling Emma's adoption better than he was.

Still drying his hands on the tattered towel from the stove handle, he went into the dining room to find the table set with proper plates and silverware, the steaming bucket of chicken making an appetizing centerpiece.

Then he noticed the table was set for four. "We having company?"

Brook nodded. "Yes, we are."

Ashley's giggling from the living room gave her away. "Come in here, Peach. I hear you."

Something held behind her back, she skipped into view, sliding into her seat at the table. Whatever she was hiding went under her leg. "Hi, Daddy."

"Hi, yourself." Sloan sat down. "Well, when will this mysterious guest be here? I'm starving."

"Close your eyes," Brook told him.

"What? Come on, Brook, I'm in no mood for games tonight. I need to eat dinner and get everyone settled so I can go over to Jenna's."

"Da-ad. It's Family Fun Night tonight. Did you forget?" Ashley's face drooped. "You promised we could have it again tonight. We haven't had it in forever!"

Sloan's cheeks warmed. "You're absolutely right, Peach. I'm sorry. Life's been so crazy lately. Let Family Fun Night begin." He'd make it up to Jenna later. He glanced at the extra place at the table. "So, why are we having a guest? Family Fun Night is supposed to be reserved for family, with very few exceptions."

"Exactly my point," Brook said. "Now close your eyes."

Sloan did as she asked. After all, the sooner this started, the sooner it finished, and the sooner he saw the other part of his family. He wondered if poor Jenna felt like a leper, forced to keep her distance. And how would Robbie feel once he was old enough to understand?

The chair on the other side of the table scuffed against the wooden floor as Mystery Guest settled in.

"Okay, you can open your eyes."

He did, prepared to act surprised.

But he didn't have to act. His eyebrows headed for his hairline and he tried not to gape like a goldfish out of water. Jenna, their son cradled in her arms, sat across from him.

Ashley squealed, clapping her hands and bouncing in her seat. "Surprise, Daddy! Look who's coming to Family Fun Night! And I didn't give away the secret!"

"No, Peach, you sure didn't."

Jenna smiled at him, then looked toward Brook. He followed her lead. "Brook? Did you set this up?"

She nodded.

"Thank you. This is a wonderful surprise." He held out his hand to her, and she came forward, taking it. "What brought this on?"

"You deserve it. Both of you. Actually, all three of you. Ashley deserves it, too. I've been acting like a selfish brat." Letting go of his hand, she walked over to Jenna. "Can I have him?"

Sloan watched in awe as his oldest child held his infant son in her arms.

"My therapist says sometimes facing the things that you think will hurt the most can be healing. Aunt Rae told me the same thing. She also said Thompsons are tough. That we suck it up and carry on. She told me a war story about Grandpa, and lacing boots tighter. Anyway, I know I'm always going to hurt over Emma. But it's not fair for my hurt to get in the way of all of you being happy. *Us* being happy," she clarified after a sharp, pained look from Jenna. Brook rocked the baby, who stared up at his big sister, waving his hands in the air. "So, I figured it was time to fix this. Ashley?"

Ashley climbed from her chair, retrieving the hidden item from under her leg. She placed a sheet of red construction paper in front of Jenna. Then she scrambled to the sideboard, opening a drawer. She clasped something in her hands, something he couldn't see until she added that to the plate.

A familiar green velvet box.

His stomach jumped.

Jenna's eyes widened as she scanned the card, then opened it and read the inside. "Brook? Are you sure about this?"

Brook nodded. "Yeah."

Jenna passed the card to Sloan, then picked up the box. Torn between watching her with a gift he'd never truly expected to give her—how the hell had the girls known about that, anyway?—and finding out what was going on, he peeked at the card front. In Ashley's slanted print, in purple crayon, it read, "Plese mary are Dad."

"Wh-what's this?" Jenna asked, holding out the box like it smelled funny.

"That's something Dad bought for you a few days after he found out you were pregnant."

The box creaked as she opened it. She gasped, and a pink flush tinted her cheeks.

"Brook?" Jenna said. "Are you *sure* about this?"

She nodded, drawing the baby closer. "I'm not going to call you Mom, but—"

"I want to!" Ashley interjected. "I'm going to call her Mom if she marries us! Molly calls Aunt Rae Mom now."

Looking befuddled, Jenna turned her attention back to Sloan. Heart beating fast, he rose from his chair, waving his hands over his head and shaking his butt from side to side. Not exactly the most original mating dance, but hopefully one that would win him the girl. Ashley giggled behind him, and Brook rolled her eyes. "Dad, *what* are you *doing?*"

He maneuvered around the table, coming to a stop in front of Jenna. "I'm dancing, Brook. Don't you know happy dancing when you see it? I realize we're not at the bowling alley…" He knelt down, taking Jenna's hand in his. "Well, sugar. Looks like the tribe has offered their opinions on the subject. So, will you marry me? Make us all one big family? What do you say?"

Like dawn breaking after a long stormy night, a smile slid into place on her face. "Yes. I say yes, Tex."

Sloan jumped up, pulling her out of the chair and into his tight embrace. "Great. Now we can have our cake and eat it, too."

"I think you mean we can have our steak and potatoes, *and* our dessert, don't you?"

"I thought we were having fried chicken," Ashley said.

He laughed, deep and hard, sending warmth straight to the center of his chest. When Jenna joined in, he knew he'd managed to not only survive this life test, but ace it.

And his life—their lives—were going to be so much richer for it.

IF DOING THE RIGHT THING PUTS YOUR LIFE AT RISK... SHOULD YOU STILL DO IT?

TARA TAYLOR QUINN

Once a woman of wealth and privilege, Kate Whitehead now lives an ordinary life in an ordinary San Diego neighborhood as Tricia Campbell. Two years ago she escaped her powerful and abusive husband and became a different person. She disappeared for her own safety— and that of her unborn child. Then a newspaper article threatens her newfound life: her husband, Thomas, has been charged with her "murder." Tricia must make a difficult choice: protect herself and let an innocent man go to jail, or do the right thing and save a man who could destroy everything.

HIDDEN

"Quinn smoothly blends women's fiction with suspense and then adds a dash of romance to construct an emotionally intense, captivatingly compelling story."
—*Booklist* on *Where the Road Ends*

Available the first week of July 2005 wherever paperbacks are sold!

MIRA®

www.MIRABooks.com

MTTQ2194

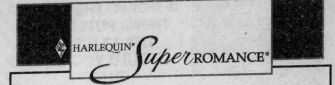

SUDDENLY A PARENT

FAMILY AT LAST
by K.N. Casper

Harlequin Superromance #1292

Adoption is a life-altering commitment.
Especially when you're single. And your new
son doesn't speak your language. But when
Jarrod hires Soviet-born linguist Nina Lockhart
to teach Sasha English, he has no idea
how complicated his life is about to become.

Available in August 2005
wherever Harlequin books are sold.

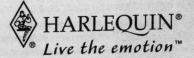

Live the emotion™

If you enjoyed what you just read,
then we've got an offer you can't resist!

Take 2 bestselling love stories FREE!

Plus get a FREE surprise gift!

Clip this page and mail it to Harlequin Reader Service®

IN U.S.A.
3010 Walden Ave.
P.O. Box 1867
Buffalo, N.Y. 14240-1867

IN CANADA
P.O. Box 609
Fort Erie, Ontario
L2A 5X3

YES! Please send me 2 free Harlequin Superromance® novels and my free surprise gift. After receiving them, if I don't wish to receive anymore, I can return the shipping statement marked cancel. If I don't cancel, I will receive 6 brand-new novels every month, before they're available in stores. In the U.S.A., bill me at the bargain price of $4.69 plus 25¢ shipping and handling per book and applicable sales tax, if any*. In Canada, bill me at the bargain price of $5.24 plus 25¢ shipping and handling per book and applicable taxes**. That's the complete price, and a savings of at least 10% off the cover prices—what a great deal! I understand that accepting the 2 free books and gift places me under no obligation ever to buy any books. I can always return a shipment and cancel at any time. Even if I never buy another book from Harlequin, the 2 free books and gift are mine to keep forever.

135 HDN DZ7W
336 HDN DZ7X

Name	(PLEASE PRINT)	
Address	Apt.#	
City	State/Prov.	Zip/Postal Code

Not valid to current Harlequin Superromance® subscribers.

Want to try two free books from another series?
Call 1-800-873-8635 or visit www.morefreebooks.com.

* Terms and prices subject to change without notice. Sales tax applicable in N.Y.
** Canadian residents will be charged applicable provincial taxes and GST.
All orders subject to approval. Offer limited to one per household.
® are registered trademarks owned and used by the trademark owner and or its licensee.

SUP04R   ©2004 Harlequin Enterprises Limited

eHARLEQUIN.com

The Ultimate Destination for Women's Fiction

For **FREE online reading,** visit
www.eHarlequin.com now and enjoy:

Online Reads
Read **Daily** and **Weekly** chapters from
our Internet-exclusive stories by your
favorite authors.

Interactive Novels
Cast your vote to help decide how these
stories unfold…then stay tuned!

Quick Reads
For shorter romantic reads, try our
collection of Poems, Toasts, & More!

Online Read Library
Miss one of our online reads?
Come here to catch up!

Reading Groups
Discuss, share and rave with other
community members!

For great reading online,
visit www.eHarlequin.com today!

INTONL04R

HARLEQUIN®

AMERICAN *Romance*®

The McCabes of Texas are back!

Watch for three new books
by bestselling author

Cathy Gillen Thacker

The McCabes:
Next Generation

THE ULTIMATE TEXAS BACHELOR

(HAR# 1080)
On sale August 2005

After his made-for-TV romance goes bust, Brad McCabe
hightails it back home to Laramie, Texas, and the Lazy M
Ranch. He's sworn off women—and the press. What he
doesn't know is that Lainey Carrington, a reporter posing
as a housekeeper, is waiting for him—and she's looking
for the "real" story on Brad!

And watch for:

SANTA'S TEXAS LULLABY (HAR# 1096)
On sale December 2005

A TEXAS WEDDING VOW (HAR# 1112)
On sale April 2006

www.eHarlequin.com   HARTMC0705

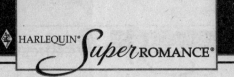

HARLEQUIN *Super*ROMANCE

ANOTHER WOMAN'S SON

by Anna Adams

Harlequin Superromance #1294

**The truth should set you free.
Sometimes it just tightens the trap.**

Three months ago Isabel Barker's life came crashing down after her husband confessed he loved another woman–Isabel's sister–and that they'd had a son together. No one else, including her sister's husband, Ben, knows the truth about the baby. When her sister and her husband are killed, Tony is left with Ben, and Isabel wonders whether she should tell the truth. She knows Ben will never forgive her if her honesty costs him his son.

*Available in August 2005
wherever Harlequin books are sold.*

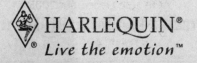

HARLEQUIN®
Live the emotion™

www.eHarlequin.com   HSRAWS0705

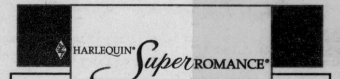

DEAR CORDELIA

by Pamela Ford

Harlequin Superromance #1291

"Dear Cordelia" is Liza Dunnigan's ticket out
of the food section. If she can score an interview
with the reclusive columnist, she'll land an
investigative reporter job and change her boring,
predictable life. She just has to get past
Cordelia's publicist, Jack Graham, hiding
her true intentions to get what she needs.
But Jack is hiding something, too....

Available in August 2005
wherever Harlequin books are sold.

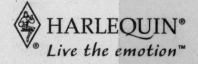